something like *Sugar*

something like *Sugar*

Elsie Bea

ISBN (paperback): 979-8-9906366-2-0
ISBN (e-book): 979-8-9906366-3-7
Library of Congress Control Number: 2025914920

Developmental Editor: Kimberly Hunt
Copy & Line Editor: Ramona Mihai
Cover Design: Molly Donahue
Proofreader: Ramona Mihai

CONTENT WARNING

While lighthearted with a happy ending,
This work is intended for a mature, adult audience.

This work contains on page intimacy with explicit descriptions and situations that may be unsuitable for readers sensitive to certain topics or themes. Please note that reading content tips may lead to plot or character spoilers. Read at your own discretion.

Content Warnings: trauma, loss, depictions of PTSD, grief, parental death, verbal abuse, sexual assault, fighting, depictions of court, stalking, abduction, drugging by needle, violence, underage drinking, reference to underage sexual activity, rape, sexual assault, and/or violence, explicit language and graphic sexual content.

For the good girls.

And for my husband, who puts up with me publishing sentences like that.

Chapter One

SHANA

I kid you not, it was *ten* inches long." Lemon holds up her forearm for reference. "Tell me how I was supposed to say no to the tour bus after that."

Devyn fans herself, eyes hinting at approval as she sips a caramel macchiato in my usual booth at Sugar Stable, the local milkshake bar and only coffee spot in Pine Forest.

I sip my drink too, a root beer float, because coffee is the nastiest thing I've ever tasted next to tea and alcohol. I don't get how my friends can enjoy this stuff. Then again, I don't really understand most of their choices.

My long curls hang in front of my face like a shield, my cloak of darkness to hide the crimson blush spreading across my cheeks as my friends contemplate which other items might be longer than this rockstar's...*penis*.

Devyn nudges me. "You okay, Shay?"

We've been coming to Sugar Stable weekly since she moved back to Pine Forest and started her pageant program. My best friend is a former Miss American Rodeo Queen. Naturally, the news of her very own program starting in our little rodeo town spread like wildfire over the past month. So many dancers from my studio wanted to participate that I somehow got roped into board membership. And I get it, pageantry and dance go hand in hand, but the glitter, the glitz, the sheer amount of *pink*.

Those are not my vibes.

I'm an athlete. I teach competitive gymnasts how to soar through the air and stick their landings, not how to strut down a runway or talk in front of a crowd.

I don't even want to speak in private. That's the beauty of dance. Nobody expects you to be verbal.

It's not that I don't like being a part of the pageant board. *I do.* I love spending time with my friends. But we all know the real reason I'm here is so I won't be *there.*

Only, it's not great escapism today. While we're supposed to be discussing costumes and fundraising, somehow we've diverted to the male anatomy and its relation to our friend Lemon's latest one-and-done.

I sigh, blowing hair strands in front of my face as I contemplate why it bothers me that she's so vocal about her sexuality.

It's not like Lemon isn't a grown woman. She's allowed to have *trysts.*

But how is everyone so open to all of this?

One minute you're a teenager, and it's taboo to show your bra strap, and the next thing you know, you're twenty-eight and everyone is a closet porn star.

"Am I the only one who doesn't want forearm sex?"

"You said that out loud."

Devyn shares a quick look with Lemon that says maybe they should finish their big girl conversation another time, and I can't stand to meet their eyes.

They're looking at me like…

"You feel sorry for me."

Lemon's brow pinches, but she doesn't deny it.

"I'm the weirdo. Aren't I?"

I push my drink away and pull my knees against my chest. My free hand, seemingly sentient, whips up and tightens the hoodie strings around my face until only my nose and mouth are visible.

"*Shana.*" Dev pries my hands away and loosens the fabric. "There, that's better."

"Shana's not here," I mumble. "She's joined the convent with her erogenous equals."

Her green eyes meet mine, familiar in ways I can't explain…*safe.* And she can see from that one look alone, the unsettling effect intimacy still has on me.

Sheltered Shana, her eyes seem to say. Not mocking, simply remembering alongside me.

She squeezes my hand. "I haven't been around, and I'm sorry. I was so focused on my own problems I didn't know what you were dealing with. I didn't even ask, I—"

"Stop." I pull my hand back to my lap, noting the way her features pinch as I do. It hurts me to hurt her, but these thoughts in my head are too much to explain in two or three coffee sessions. "We don't have to do this now. I'm just glad you're back."

She exhales, offering a smile instead. I missed that smile so much when she left, and it's hard to ignore the way it feels letting her back in, pulling out a dull knife from a hardened wound.

"I know we have a lot to catch up on," she says with her signature eye roll, "but not *that* much has changed. I don't want to have sex with a forearm, either, just so we're clear."

"Well, neither did I!" Lemon slaps down her menu. "I simply wanted his *junk* to be the size of one. Much more sanitary than an arm any day." She winks.

A giggle slips from my lips, and I lower my hood, grateful for friends so understanding of my…*innocence.*

"Do you feel better knowing Lemon is the only ho of the group? *I'm* a married woman, remember?" Devyn plucks the cherry from Lemon's sundae and pops it into her mouth.

"You cherry taker!" Lem folds her arms over her chest.

Laughter surrounds me, friends and bodies and sounds…but suddenly, the only thing I can focus on is who I see when I turn my head.

The heat my body creates with that single connection could melt every dessert on this table in an instant.

Green eyes familiar in ways I can't explain.

"I didn't mean to make you feel uncomfortable." Lemon nudges me out of the spell. "We all experience things at different times and levels." She drones on, assuring me I'm *not* the odd woman out, while I'm fairly certain I am the only twenty-eight-year-old virgin ever.

When I moved back in with Dad, he needed me.

I squeeze Lemon's hand so she knows we're okay. We may be on completely opposite ends of the spectrum in terms of intimacy experience, but she's one hell of a friend, working with Dad for over a year now. The home health team she's employed with takes care of him around the clock.

The retirement he won't live to take is paying for it.

And truthfully, I'm not needed at home when they're around to care for him. His needs have gone beyond that of a family caretaker. They're clinical.

Terminal. Terminal. Terminal.

I'm just watching him wilt and crumble in a forgotten corner, empty promises of get-well bouquets, shoved to the side and left to die.

It's become second nature to pray, *plead* that he'll have a good enough day to sit up and talk, silently bargaining with God for just a little more time with the only family I have. Another day to see him crinkle the edges of his eyes when he rattles lines of Shakespeare.

Another day he's alive inside and out.

Lately, there have been fewer good days.

"You can't be alone forever, Shaker. Promise me you will seek connection outside of dance."

"What's the point?" I say. *"Look at you...And Mom? People die. And the ones who don't just walk away. Devyn left for a decade because of love!"* I shake my head. *"I'd rather be alone than set myself up to be broken."*

"Cowards die many times before their deaths." He places Mom's ring in my palm and closes my fist. *"The valiant only taste of death but once."*

That was over three weeks ago.

The last good day.

So, what's my excuse? Even Dad's telling me to put

myself out there and meet someone, in more or less Victorian words.

I don't *mean* to be a virgin, I just am. How do you explain that to other adults?

I was a very focused teenager and an even more determined college student. I was worried about one thing and one thing only: perfecting my craft.

I didn't have time for *sex*.

And now I'm so far behind that anyone I meet is going to expect I have at least *some* idea how to do things that I have exactly no idea, what-so-ever, how to do.

Do you *do* sex? Or *have* it?

I don't even know.

It doesn't help that Lemon is going further into this the longer we sit. I appreciate it, but it's not exactly helping to hear about her perceived lesser sexual experiences. It's just revealing how very few things I know.

What even is a cock ring?

"It's fine!" I say as she starts on about her first time giving oral. I do not need to hear that.

Or maybe I do.

My friends look at me expectantly, like they want me to tell them more of my feelings, but I don't share those. Assigning words to the way my heart beats, or brain fixates, or my chest rises and falls—it's never made sense to me.

So I dance, and my body filters emotions to something tangible. The music shapes them to meaning.

Perhaps it's why dance is all I've ever wanted.

In my darkest childhood hours, I used to think it's all I'd ever need.

But children grow. They dance and they learn and they leave. And when the studio closes and they take their sparkling tulle and giggles home with them, I go home too. And there aren't friends or fun, and certainly no *forearms* waiting for me there.

There's the only family I have left.

Dying.

Lemon smiles up from her phone. "I'm gonna bug Jeremy at Cowboy's Paradise while it's still happy hour. Wanna come?"

"Sounds fun!" Dev stacks our used cups in a pile for the man bussing tables. The man my eyes can't stop searching any time I step foot in this milkshake bar.

Lemon follows my focus. "You're totally staring at Dustin."

"What?!" I flick my eyes to Dev and mime a *zip-it* to Lem.

Devyn cannot know.

She's *just* returned home.

Ten years without my best friend, and she's finally back. I can't risk ruining the rebuild of our friendship when I'm already on the verge of losing Dad.

"I am not *staring*," I whisper.

Was I?

Shoot!

"You guys have fun," I say. "I'm gonna stay here and put together a recital schedule. Same time Sunday?"

"It's October," Devyn deadpans. "And recital isn't 'till Christmas, Shay. Come with us! You might meet the perfect forearm for all you know."

"You did not just say that." I shake my head. "There are no *forearms* in this town that I haven't known since kindergarten. You should understand that better than anyone."

Lemon snorts at my jab, Devyn having become mighty comfortable with her high school sweetheart since moving back home. She doesn't try to hide the smile emerging at the mention of her childhood crush.

It must be nice.

"Come with us, Shay! Jeremy's gonna be mad you didn't want to see him."

"Well, good thing I'll see *Jeremy* at barre class in the morning. Unlike you divas, he wakes up at a normal hour and makes it on time."

Dev studies my face. "I know you have a lot going on, but that's exactly why you need to let loose. Meet someone who makes you smile. You don't have to hide in your hoodie all alone, Shay."

I bristle at the topic. I hate when people bring it up, even if I appreciate that they do.

It's complicated.

Everyone knows my dad is in his last few months, just living at home. *Waiting to die*—that single thought, a leech always feeding off my mind.

And they all feel sorry for me.

I don't even blame them. *I* feel sorry for me.

Shana Holiday, the last of her kind.

Like a young adult, dystopian novel where I find out I have hidden powers, or a fated mate, or some duty and calling to save all of mankind how my ancestors always planned.

Then at least there would be a reason for my fate.

For the solitude I face.

But there's not.

It's just *Shana Holiday, the last of her kind.*

Even my friends can sense my impending doom. So, meeting someone right now? A relationship? Someone that *makes me smile*, as Devyn put it…that's just not in my cards.

This is reality. My dad is dying, I am a strange, emotionally stunted ballerina who only feels in song and loves in movement, and things like *smiling someones* and *love…* that's another person's story. Not mine.

"I'll see you tomorrow," I tell her, noting the feeling of disappointment with the downward turn of her frown, and the guilt that indicates *I* put it there.

She stops by the door, hugging her brother before turning away.

Something *I* should have done before he saw me.

And when his eyes meet mine from across the room, I feel something that has me scooping my laptop into my bag and darting from the Sugar Stable to my studio, as fast as my legs will allow.

Because I can't un-feel it any more than I could all those years ago.

Dustin Campbell makes my heart dance.

Chapter Two

DUSTIN

A ballerina dances in the floor-to-ceiling window across from mine, her body calling me, night after night. Not for its grace, but for its *strength*. The unrelenting power that propels her through leaps and spins, with a humble smile.

She could out-press every grown man at the gym with thighs I shouldn't think about.

She doesn't see the beauty within that strength.

And I want her for that even more.

The way she hides beneath dark hoods and a mess of curls, tucked in the corner of my bar, headphones snug as her eyes drift closed and her toes tap to the beat of a song nobody can hear but her.

I could tell her how beautiful she is.

But she's got something I can't bring myself to touch. Something real and honest. Something pure.

And even if I'll never be half the man she's worthy of, the shared streetlamps of our courtyard grant me a spotlit view of my secret ballerina.

Every night, my own private show.

Just me, the lights of the town-square, and my *muse.* A song with a body. An invisible girl in a corner booth, transformed like phoenix, blazing in a fire so bright you'd only miss it if you fought the moon for residence.

My sister's best friend is the most stunning woman to walk this earth.

But while I allow myself a peek through her open window, I can't allow myself to pass through that glass.

Shana Holiday is far too sweet for someone like me.

"You comin', Hott Stuff?" Mandy…*or was it Mindy,* pokes my arm from where she's leaning against my register. It annoys me she's on this side of the bar at all, knowing me for all of two weeks.

We matched on Flinger. It's not like this is a relationship.

I take in her bubble gum eighties vibes, complete with dangling earrings and neon leg warmers. "Is this a costume thing, or do you always dress like Footloose?"

I'm being a dick, and fuck if it isn't because she ruined my view of Shana from across the courtyard.

I sift my fingers through my hair and pull it into a tight bun at the back of my head, wishing emotions were so easily tidied. Thinking about Shana any more than I do is spiraling. She's not mine.

Devyn's best friend, I remind myself.

And I'm not hers.

But I'm certainly not Mindy's either. I made it clear in my bio I'm only on this app for physical reasons, but does *she* know that?

I'm not that confident she does.

"I texted you the info, silly. It's Barbie or Barbells themed. I mean, you could like, take your shirt off and be fine," Mandy says, batting her twice-fluffed eyelashes my way. I realize she wants me. I'm not an idiot. She's the kind of woman I *should* be with, a butterfly tattoo on the middle of her lower back, lip filler and concealer over the worry of her eyes. She's rough, hardened to the world, like me.

Even if I don't know her name, I know that much with one glance.

"Are you Mindy or Mandy?" I cringe, but she just waves it off, unwilling to make me the bad guy.

I don't like that.

I *am* the bad guy who doesn't remember her name.

Do I even want to fuck this woman?

"It's Miranda, but that's all right, everyone calls me some variation of Mandy, or Mindy, or even Manda. It's okay, really." She tucks bleach blonde hair behind her ear, and then I just feel like a shithead, because she's cute and trying, and I'm fucking weak for someone I'll never be with.

It's not Miranda's fault I'm like this.

And it's clear from the way she's texted this week, inviting me to meet her close circle of friends at this party tonight, that she wants what I can't give.

"Miranda, can I be honest with you? I'm—"

"Emotionally unavailable?" She throws me a sideways grin.

"Yeah."

"I could tell." Her smile softens. "I get it." She ties back her ponytail, exposing her midriff to the October air with a shiver.

"Here." I offer a jacket.

"Thanks." Miranda slips into the oversized zip-up. "She's a lucky girl."

"It's not like that."

"Lie to yourself if you wish." She blows a bubble and lets it pop. "You look like a wounded puppy."

"A what?"

"You gain nothing lying to yourself, trust me, now can we can move on to *my* personal crisis."

"Your…what?" I scratch my beard. "Lying to myself? I'm not lying to anyone. So let's say I love her, whatever, but just because you love someone, doesn't mean you're worthy of that person. What if they can do better?"

"You're absolutely right!" Miranda's eyes shine with realization. "I do deserve better than him. No matter how many times he claims to love me."

"What?" I'm so confused. "Were we talking about me or you?

"Look," She types a text and then shoves her phone back in her purse with a frustrated sigh. "I don't know what your reasons for not being with this person are, but my reasons for being on Flinger were specific, and I'm sorry I used you, but you kinda used me too, it sounds like. Emotional placeholder and all. Anywho, I have an ex I need to make aware it's over. Can you just stand beside me looking hot and angry for the next hour with your shirt off?"

Surprise and relief wash over me, and we both laugh, but hers is replaced by a tight-lipped seething when her phone buzzes again with a middle finger emoji.

"God, he's such an ass." She types back furiously.

I get the impression from her tense shoulders and shredded bottom lip that this man has been a constant source of worry, and everything I thought tonight was about dissolves to dust.

I'm not going to fuck Miranda. She reminds me of my sister, vulnerably brave, and I feel the instant need to keep watch around this ex of hers tonight, despite her hard exterior.

"C'mon," I wink, "let's show this idiot how stupid he was for messing it up with you."

We lock up and walk through the courtyard. The streetlamps light the shop windows we pass while Miranda fills me in on the shithead who proposed to her after three months and got mad when she needed space, calling her place of work and telling them she would no longer need employment as *his wife.*

"The worst part is I actually fell for him. I thought I loved him. So stupid, because he said everything I wanted and I hardly took a breath before I said yes. Before I knew it, my lease had been terminated and all my stuff was moved into his apartment. When I told him it was too much, too fast, he started texted me these." She shows me her phone.

I don't need to read more than a few exchanges to see what's going on. I memorize his number and whip my own phone out, sending the douche bag's information to an old law enforcement buddy, satisfied with his reply of a simple check mark emoji. This asshole won't be bothering Miranda any longer.

It's infuriating that entitled men take advantage of women like Miranda, texting her degrading remarks and refusing to take a no. I'm suddenly glad I'll be at this party to protect her.

Protect her.

A memory flashes in my mind, and I steal a glance at one window I can't ignore.

Only this time I wish I hadn't.

Because the same moment Miranda leans in with a thank you kiss to my cheek, draped in my hoodie and linked to my arm, my eyes meet Shana's.

And all I see are tears.

Chapter Three

SHANA

I choke on the powder from the force of my slippers in the rosin box.

Tears fall in droplets, but that doesn't stop me from leaping full force and twirling around in a series of moves that has me beholden to the earth beneath my dance floor. It's just me and the space I create.

Grand Jeté!

Her lips on his skin.

Chaîné!

His hand in hers.

Fouetté, fouetté! Leap!

Not yours.

I fall forward into a deep lunge, pulling my body around in a frenzy of pain, jealousy, and absolute sacrifice. Before I know it, I'm flush with the floor, in a straight split that could cut the earth in two so precisely, it mimics how I feel in my heart.

Torn.

Half of me a sad, lonely child, and the other a fierce

warrior of tomorrow…even if I don't know what it may bring.

But I'm on my feet before the tears even dry on my skin, wiping them away as I storm to the dressing rooms. There, I unlace my pointe slippers and carefully cradle each swollen foot in my hands.

I'm rough on my feet. But they've always carried me through anything. Dance got me through my mom's death when I was just a little girl with a pair of pompoms and no clue what terminal illnesses were.

But it seems those illnesses like knowing *me*, because they didn't stop at one parent.

It's dance that will get me through this again.

When I'm *the last of my kind*, dance will be here like it always is.

But I do need to live a little.

Maybe I *should* get out with the girls to Cowboys Paradise and take shots of colorful liquids and fire… or maybe just a beer to start, because that sounds super intimidating.

But I should be there.

Trying things. Meeting people.

Getting over this carnal deficit.

I shouldn't be a twenty-eight-year-old virgin waiting for a fairytale someone to show up and make life better. It doesn't work that way, and I don't know why I've let myself hide in my hoodie, as Devyn puts it, for so long that I've blinded myself to an entire world of dating and relationships. Or heck, even just a fling like Lemon.

I can already feel my cheeks heating at the thought

of meeting a total stranger for physical reasons, and then what? Just never talking again?

That's a thing normal people my age do.

Doesn't make it any less weird.

But what's the alternative?

What if Devyn's right, and I find the perfect *forearm*, for lack of better terminology, and I blow it because I know absolutely nothing about sex?

Will people even want to date me if they know I'm a virgin?

What if I'm horrible at it? Is there an expiration date on when you can become decent at something like that?

Finishing up my massage and lotion routine, I shove my feet into a pair of cozy socks, and my favorite purple converse.

I flex and point, appreciating how the shoes form to my feet and allow for movement—even when bound, and it hits me then, why these shoes are so dependable.

But I can't bring myself to put a voice to the words floating through my head. The ones somehow finding a common link between my trusty shoes and my...*virgin problem*.

The reason they're so great at what they do is because they're broken in.

I cringe, because it *is* cringe, and I open the door to the courtyard as I let that thought sink in. Goosebumps scatter over my arms and legs, the lace skirt and shawl barely providing me coverage from the chill of fall, but I like it this way.

The cold feels sharp and real.

Sometimes, I need the reminder that it's all real.

That I'm not just floating in a time warp, plastic-wrapped bubble, immune to all there is and ever was. That I'm not just a girl in the mirror, spinning days into months and months into years, never making eye contact with the person staring back at her.

I think about it all the way through the courtyard, my heartbeat quickening when we pass Sugar Stable. I commend myself for not searching the window to see if he and his blonde pair of lips and legs are still there.

I hardly even think about her at all.

Not about the way she tugged onto his arm with both hands, nestling her perfect face into the crook of his neck, probably smelling his cologne, which I only know from years of friendship with his younger sister, and not because I checked his bathroom or anything, is *Nautica*, and it smells *amazing*.

But *she* was there to sniff it, whoever she is.

And she's so pretty, I can't stand thinking about the way she kissed his cheek or put her lips on his skin.

Skin that I don't care about.

Skin that I've caught dozens of other preppy looking fling-a-dings pressing their lips against before her.

She won't be his last.

For the same reason he can't be my first.

Because people like him like people like her. And people like her know how to *fuck*.

Plain and simple.

That's what I've got to learn how to do.

I contemplate ways one learns this sort of thing at

twenty-eight, but I come short of nothing when I start considering there might be an app service.

A 'ride' share, perhaps?

I kick the ground with my sneakers, doing a double take when some of the rubber scrapes off the toe, but they're sturdy enough they can take it.

Just like me.

I pull my spirits back up, where I tell my dance team girls they should always be, and remind myself that if I can deal with losing my mom before puberty and growing up learning things like tampon hygiene and bra cup sizes from the pages of magazines, then I can handle sex.

I mean, I have the parts. I understand the basic mechanics.

Is it that hard?

I scrunch my nose, embarrassed at my own sordid thoughts and thankful as ever that other people can't hear them.

But when I finally reach the front door, the same yellow trim with white siding that's been there since Mom was here to greet me, flakes off beneath my fingers.

Nothing lasts forever.

My energy shifts as I push open the door, sloshing off the fantasy of being out here and trading it for the harsh reality of what's in there.

Because even in my current state of torment, and apparent sexual frustration, the weight I feel when I walk into my house and smell the threat of loss in the air, when I hear the beeps of monitors, sense the emptiness—it never disappears. I guess it's not always a bad thing.

It gives me no choice but to face my fate.

I click the front door shut as quietly as I can and pad to the kitchen. The fridge reveals three Honeycrisp apples and some frozen waffles. I'm not much of a cook, my whole life being spent in and out of cars on my way to dance rehearsals or competitions. It was just me and Dad for so long that my diet is not what most would imagine for an athlete.

Tonight, I poke at the cinnamon flakes on my plate and find them less tolerable than usual. It's just me I'm cooking for at this point. That's why.

"Shaker, that you?" The raspy voice calls me from across the house, and I'm up in an instant, running and sliding on socked feet into Dad's room.

"You're awake!" I hold myself back from tackling him in a hug. He's not awake much these days. My cheeks pull into a wide grin, and I settle for a nuzzle and a seat next to his bed instead, minding the heart monitor. He's in end-stage care, and they have a sort of protocol for these home health situations.

The beeping is constant, the wires nothing more than reminders of doom. Those monitors aren't going to save him. They're just going to be the last thing we hear before he's gone.

"I'm awake," he replies, the edges of his eyes crinkling as he attempts a weak smile. "I have to tell you, before I get all gobby mouth again."

"What is it?" I say, when he clears his throat and reaches for the water at his bedside. I position the straw into his mouth.

"A man came to see you. Didn't say who he was. Looked familiar. You know how I am with faces."

"Someone came by for me?" I set the water down.

I didn't ask anyone to come by, and the only man I hang out with is *Jeremy*. He'd have simply texted me. "Good lookin' fella." He grins. "Left you that beautifully strange plant. Think he's sweet on you."

I scan the room before I see it. It is just how Dad describes it, beautiful and strange.

I cross the room, fingering the purple, bell-shaped leaves, hanging in symmetrical rows over a large potted plant. *Digitalis Purpurea*, a card at the base of the plant reads.

A familiar chill races down my spine.

Sugar Plums.
Like you, a vision, dancing through my head.
Dry your tears, sweet vision.
I'll be watching.

"Who did you say left these?" I croak, my throat suddenly a thick knot of emotions I can't dance away.

My hands clench the paper so tightly my knuckles turn white, until Dad finally notices, grunting as he repositions.

"Hold on," I say, rearranging the pillows and angling his bed. "Is that better?"

He smiles, chuckling softly, but it's a laugh, and I'll take it.

I smile too, and sit back on the chair, this time on one leg like a child. Dad takes a look at me perched there and laughs again. We stay like that for a minute, eyes locked, *smiling*.

I'm not ready to say goodbye to the man who looks like an older version of myself staring back at me. Someone who taught me to ride a bike and lie about stupid things that don't really matter, to decide what's right and wrong, and to let music and feelings tumble out so they won't be locked up forever. He taught me to be the person I am today, and here he is, *smiling*, like he's happy he's almost gone.

Like he's not any day away from his last breath.

"I can't do it, Dad," I tell him, a tear tracing down my cheek, even though I should have no tears left to cry. Crying doesn't care what you think, though. It takes hold of you when you feel the most depleted. Even when you've got nothing left to give, the tears find a way to pull that last bit of salt out of you. I'm never sure if they're reminding us that we're still alive, despite how surreal pain may be, or if it's God's way of telling us that we're of salt and water just like the rest of it. We're of *Earth* and we're whole, even when we're falling apart.

"If there's one thing I'm most proud of, dear girl, it's the way your eyes fill with curiosity, even in the quietest moments. One could get lost for lifetimes wondering what you've been imagining up there."

"I can't be without you." I sob.

Not gracefully, not like a dancer. Like the child I am when I think of losing my daddy.

"You can, Shaker, and very soon, you will. You need to be okay with that," he tells me softly, squeezing my hand from his deathbed. The only one he'll ever lie in again before it's just velvet insides and wooden slabs holding his body.

"I can't." I look down at my hands and see I'm still clutching onto the card from the flowers.

I hold it out to Dad, shifting gears because I can't face this.

The morbid thought creeps over me again.

How am I supposed to face life when he's gone, if I can't face the mere *thought* of it now?

"It sounds like this man is in love with you, Shana." Dad scans the card.

"But it's creepy, right? He's *watching*? And the tears thing? It's strange."

"Oh, come now. What is strange? *'I do love nothing in the world so well as you—Is that not strange?'* Much 'Ado About Nothing."

"Dad! Seriously, I love a good Billy quote, but that doesn't excuse the stalker vibes and depressing plant that looks like it was grown in the literal ashes of Edgar Allan Poe. It's so droopy."

"It's also your favorite color." He points to my purple converse, and I scoff at his omnipotence.

Self-assured old fart always knows everything.

"You're just like your mother." He smiles again, sighing heavily. "She didn't know how special she was, and I mean inside and out. Boy, when she volunteered at the aquarium, and those creatures seemed to communicate with her… I'd stop and stare all day long. Give this man a bit of grace, Shaker. Love makes people do crazy things.

He likely sees it too, what I did."

"What was that?" This might be the only chance I get to ask him again.

About my mother.

About love.

Dad tucks the card into my hand and pats it closed.

I should have known he wouldn't give me an easy answer. Always a riddle. Still, I can't help but smile. It's *so very Dad*, and I love him for it. I rub away more tears as he closes his eyes, scanning his brain for a perfectly scripted response like always.

Before long, his lips turn up, and he opens his eyes to meet mine. "*Beauty within itself should not be wasted: fair flowers that are not gathered in their prime, rot and consume themselves in little time.* Venus and Adonis."

"And that means?" I say, frustrated. I mean, it's not like I even know who this guy is. He could be *anyone.* "Even if I didn't want to '*rot and consume myself*' as you so graciously put it, this isn't the sixties. You can't just meet a guy at the sock hop and assume he's not a dateline serial killer with a human skin fetish these days."

There's also no sock hop.

Dad drifts back to sleep, so I lower his bed and tuck the covers snugly around his body. When I feel like he's got everything he needs in arm's reach, and his call bell is available, I switch off the lamp and make my way to the door.

I stop by the Sugar Plum plant on my way out and take a moment to really think about it.

Who the hell sent this? Who was watching me dance?

Only one answer makes sense.

Letters, words, heartbreak.
Only one man saw me cry.

There's only one man in my life with a history of secret note sending, and while he never admitted it outright, I know.

I had an inkling the gifts appearing through the years were from him, my secret admirer.

My best friend's older brother.

It was sweet.

Until it stopped.

The last one came the eve of my college move-in, a shattered bedroom window and a letter taped to a rock. I supposed my silent watcher was angry I'd be leaving, but rather than reveal himself—or his feelings for me—he gave up.

Broken promises have been folded in my music box for a decade.

Dustin Campbell will never act on how he feels. Maybe in every other part of his life, sure.

I'm just not worth fighting for.

So what? Now *he* feels sorry for me, too?

In my room, I peel the spandex leo from my body and stand in front of the fan to cool from the range of emotions that plague me.

I slip into an oversized shirt and flop onto my bed. I open my phone to a few texts from Dev with pictures from Cowboys Paradise.

I roll my eyes at the man whose number she got for me.

I can practically hear: "I met your future hubby!"

Nope. Not for me.

Not that the guy she met wasn't good looking, it's just that husbands…*boyfriends*…aren't what I need right now. I'm looking for something specific.

The step *before* the special someone.

A sex coach.

And I'm not going to find one in Pine Forest where I can't even go to the grocery store without running into the same obstetrician who birthed half my graduating class.

That droopy stalker plant is living proof I understand nothing about the male species.

I'm certain, now more than ever, that my best friend's brother, the very same one with a Flinger model down his throat only yesterday, is the person who sent me those flowers today.

The card still burns a hole in my hoodie pocket.

"Dry your tears, sweet vision."

An old corkboard picture of me and Devyn at the lake flutters beneath the air conditioning vent.

"You look good in board shorts. A vision."

Irony stings.

Notes. Secrets.

I've lost too many pieces of my heart for one lifetime, and I won't lose more because he feels sorry for me.

Not when he'll never give me the whole of his.

I've tried.

I thumb the folds of the note, muscle memories of paper footballs from my past taunting me more than the blonde's kiss.

I don't need his plants or his pity.

I pull up the app store, and I download Flinger.

Chapter Four

DUSTIN

So, I should just throw decades of hard work down the drain and buy real estate because you told me to? That's bullshit!" I slam my fist against the freezer, trying not to chuck my phone across the room.

Every fuckin' time.

"You call it bullshit; I call it keeping your investors happy," Dad starts, but this is one conversation I've had enough of.

"If I'd have known you were gonna throw that *investment* of yours in my face every time you wanted control of my business decisions, I'd have declined the offer altogether. It's not worth the trouble of dealing with you in my ear every time I turn around."

"Then pay it back."

His end of the line goes quiet, except for the creak of his desk drawer. I know the sound by heart. It's the way he's communicated since I was a child.

With money.

"Tell you what," he says, "you come to the city for

"

Business Week, talk with some of the investors about your bar—"

"Café. I keep telling you it's a milkshake bar. A social hub for families, not a nightclub like you keep—"

"Potato, Pot-ah-to, Son. Point is, come see what there is to offer out here, get some parties interested in putting real money into your ventures so you can offer more than strawberry shakes after little league, alright? You do this, and I'll give you the downpayment for that property on Mullins and Main you keep looking into."

"How do you know that?"

The self-assured asshole chuckles in way that brings me back to my teenage years, broken and belittled, doing anything I could to prove to the mightiest man I'd met that I was still worthy.

That I wasn't just the fuckup that deafened one of my classmates when my fists became my fate.

"It doesn't matter why! *You have tainted the Campbell name."*

I still hear him scream it.

I wish I'd known that no amount of transformation would make him happy. Nothing less than being a carbon copy of him will do.

He thinks he's so much better than Mom, but Devyn and I are his little shelf trophies all the same. He's just waiting for another feather to place in his cap, even if he has to pluck them from his own children.

"You think you can investigate a property anywhere on the East coast and I won't know? Come on, Son, you know better. I *own* this trade. And as I've tried to tell you and your sister for years, if you'll only listen, land is power. With that power, you can have whatever you want."

I scoff, loud enough I hope he hears it across the line. "What I want isn't for sale."

It grows quiet again. But this time there's no drawer opening or pen scribbling to fill the void.

"Where do you see yourself in five years, Dustin?"

In the business sense? In life? Since it's Dad, I assume everything's about money. And his argument—as fucked as it is—is sound.

I wouldn't be able to afford this life had he not stepped in where I failed and helped me get the Sugar Stable up to standards. Now it's the talk of the town, and the revenue I've put away is steadily padding my next business venture.

One it seems he'll never accept.

"You know the answer to that." I bang the phone against my forehead, tired of him turning every damn call into a meeting for the Future CEOs of America or some shit. "My *workshop*. For the fiftieth time, my plan is to manufacture customized, handcrafted furniture to independent wholesalers. It's niche, but there's a market for it."

"Making tables and chairs isn't a career, Dustin. How will you earn a living making furniture? There's no guarantee of profit in this economy for artistry! How will you provide for a family if you—"

"A family? You want to talk to me about raising a family? You flat out left yours in the fuckin' boondocks for a twenty-something year old pair of tits on legs, and you're gonna talk to me about how I'll handle a family? Fuck off, Dad. Right the fuck off."

"I can fuck off, huh?" Dad chuckles. Even at thirty years old, my spine straightens when he laughs like that. "How about this, *Son*, I'll fuck right off to Cabo for the next two weeks while you spatter yourself in chocolate sauce and fry batter like a damn teenager."

"Fuck you," I breathe.

I hope he heard it.

I also hope he didn't.

And I fucking hate that.

"I *will* see you at Business Elite Week, where you will present your quarterly reports for Sugar Stable to my friends on the restaurant board. If you're lucky, one of them will buy you out of that dump so you can make real money, with or without the cherry on top."

"Fine."

What other choice do I have? I go to the conference and schmooze these rich assholes or he pulls the plug on my Sugar Stable loan. I can't pay it all back yet, and he knows it.

He knows everything.

Right off the interstate, not too far from the city…I want that property on Mullins and Main like I want my last breath.

It's craftsmanship the way I dreamed since I was a kid in a cell, stuck in my head and whittling my worries into scraps of wood, turning jagged nothings into something new.

I slide a five-gallon bucket beneath the ice-cream machine and add the ingredients for mint chip so routinely it's like brushing my teeth. Dad's words invade my thoughts, *spatter yourself in chocolate sauce like a damn teenager.*

Shana Holiday could never love me.

When it all boils down, I'm just a fuckup, and no matter what I do to prove myself, I'll always be that same delinquent blinking at the crack of the judge's gavel, terrified I'll never be more than the record states.

Guilty.

"I'll be there."

"Great, I'll send your tickets and itinerary out this week," he says cordially, like I didn't just tell him where to go fuck himself.

But that's Dad. Fake.

Just like my relationships these days.

But at least it's for a good cause. I don't have to sell the Sugar Stable to anyone. I can always decline, so long as I continue to make my payments and grow profitably.

It will lock in that property for me, either way.

I might have to suffer in the presence of my father, but I can handle it.

I load the last tub of French Silk ice cream onto the freezer and reposition the phone on my ear, prepping to hang up without so much as an I love you or a goodbye for that asshole, but he stops me with a detail that could derail my plan altogether.

"And Dustin? Bring a plus one. There's dancing."

Chapter Five

S ingle, twenty-eight-year-old female, active build, searching for…an experimental study-buddy with benefits?"

Ugh, No!

I scrub my hand down my face and scrunch my nose at my laptop screen, deleting basically my entire profile.

For the fifth time this morning.

I huff out a frustrated breath and tap my fingers to the keys once more, determined to get it right. If I can't even come up with a single selling point for my dating profile, then what chance do I have actually dating someone? Especially when I'll have to do things like talk to them.

My throat gets dry even thinking about it. Opening my mind to a stranger? And if just *that* makes me uneasy, how the heck am I gonna open my legs to one?

"No one will ever have the right forearm."

"That's random," the voice from my fantasies says. My head whips up, cheeks so red I can feel them without even seeing my face.

"I didn't—well, I…um," I mumble, my breath quickening with each second that falls upon us in the land of Dustin's Irises, the only thing I can concentrate on. Because it certainly isn't on making words flow from my mouth.

"Are you all right, Shay?"

My heart does a jig as his tongue brushes along his lips, taunting me with the heat he exudes merely forming sentences.

Saying my nickname.

"Shay?" He touches my arm, and it's everything.

Everything I remember, and so much more.

In all the years that I've known Dustin Campbell, all the moments I've stood feet away from him, sharing oxygen, space, time…I've never felt something like the zap of energy I feel when his hand cups my cheek, and eyes that shine like jade bore into mine.

Something wild takes over inside of me, and even though I hate myself for it after what I proclaimed, alone in my room with that stupid plant, I press my lips to his.

For the second time in my life.

FOURTEEN YEARS AGO

My lips are dry. I mush them together as I read the instructions on the back of the cardboard box.

The outhouse at Pine Lake is situated at the end of the long gravel road, about a mile from the campsites, nestled in an alcove of evergreens and willows.

Today, I'm happy about the seclusion. It usually creeps me out being here by myself, especially if it's for a night-time trip to pee. The sounds that happen out here when the sun goes down don't necessarily feel friendly.

Me and camping in general aren't friendly with each other, but here I am, like everyone else's family for the summer.

Only, this is the first year it's just me and Dad.

And isn't it fitting that my body decides to choose this year, three years later than all my friends, to finally shed the linings of my uterus?

"Yep, that's right, Mom, I finally got my period." I kick at the gravel beneath me, scanning my eyes up to instruction number two on the tampons I found in Devyn's cabin.

My eyes widen.

This box contains a variety, including—but not limited to—light, super plus, and ultra. My brows pinch together as I hold up the largest one and read the chart. "Eighteen grams!? Am I going to bleed eighteen grams today?"

Oh, God.

I slide down the outhouse wall and land on the gravel beneath me with a thump. It doesn't help my bleeding situation, and as I stand and twist, a bright red stain blooms against my white shorts.

"That's a bit extreme."

I jump at the voice, my heart shattering into tiny, embarrassing pieces and digging into every existing crevice of my being, when I recognize it as Dustin's.

"Saw you sneaking from Dev's room this morning. Have you been crying?" His eyes shift to the instruction pamphlet dangling from my other hand, and he rubs the back of his neck. We stand in awkward silence for what feels like an eternity before he takes pity on me and nods to the box.

"I-If it's your first time," he avoids my eyes. "You could try the smallest size and check it after your swim… assuming that's where you were headed."

I literally cannot move. I've read about momentary traumatic paralysis that can lead to one entering a catatonic state, trapped inside their minds forever.

"If not, uh…I think my sister has *pads*. Shana?"

Yep. This could be that.

"But you can't talk if you're catatonic."

That's all I manage to say, because my stupid brain doesn't know how to behave when it's not making me plié and just lets random thoughts slip out of my mouth as it pleases.

To the boy I'm in love with.

The boy I didn't think knew I existed apart from his sister.

The boy who just explained *tampon sizes* to me.

He bites his bottom lip, toying with a piercing he placed there against his mother's wishes, and a frenzied energy kicks up in my belly.

A wild, wisp of a thrill dances in my soul.

I watch him watch me, too in my head to move, but also unwilling, if that means his eyes remain on me a fraction longer.

"You're funny, Shana Holiday."

"Funny? What's funny about your best friend's brother explaining tampon sizes to you in the middle of the forest while you bleed all over the pine needles and probably ants and things I crunched beneath my butt just now?" I gesture to my backside before I can take in what I'm doing, but as soon as it hits me, my face goes as red as my shorts have become.

I dash into the rickety wooden stall and slam the door behind me.

It swings and hits me. *So, there's that.* And as my forehead pulses in pain, I shove the stupid hook lock into the metal loopy thing—*that barely seems close enough to reach,* and even though I can hear him snickering, I can also hear him holding back.

Which is sweet, even if it is the most mortifying moment of my life

"Hey." He knocks.

I say nothing, because I've reverted to a deceptive animalistic state and pretending I'm dead or invisible is preferable to whatever this is.

"I didn't mean to make it weird. You just seemed like you needed help, and I'm not gonna let you hide in the bathhouse all day, Shana."

I do not answer. I'm still dead.

The gravel shuffles outside the door, and I think my best friend's brother has finally left me alone to die in solitude, but bright blue swim trunks come sailing over the outhouse door.

"Did you take off your shorts?" My throat goes dry at the thought of Dustin Campbell's naked body outside of this very thin slab of wood they call a door.

He laughs. "I had basketball shorts underneath."

I frown at the blue trunks, not at all because he's not truly naked. Probably more because these are going to be huge on me, him being a muscly high school rodeo god that I'm not *at all* upset I won't see a less-clothed version of when this door opens.

Birthday suit or not, my heart sashays at his kindness, grateful I won't have to trek back up the hill with Aunt Flo stealing the spotlight.

I place the shorts on the sink as I lower myself down and go back to guesstimating how many grams of blood loss I'll have today.

More than ever, I miss my mother.

I could have asked Devyn about tampons and such if she hadn't run off with Hunter at the crack of dawn, panting like an obsessed puppy. It's gross, honestly. Even if you do like someone, do you have to like them *that* much?

I think about what Dustin said, trying the light size first. It's smart, all things considered. And after looking at that horrifying picture of the tampon expansion capabilities on the instruction pamphlet, I'm starting to think that *light* is the least scary option.

It's awkward inserting it, but I think I have it where it's supposed to go, so I stand and tug on the shorts my all-time crush just lent me, tightening the draw strings as far as I can. They hang low on my hips, exposing the ties of my purple tankini. Dad won't let me wear a two-piece like everyone else my age. *God forbid someone see my belly button.*

He's worried he'll be alone when I grow up.

I share the sentiment.

Mortification minimally lessened in my new suit, I swing the door open to find Dustin lazing under a willow, head propped on his arms with one knee up, staring at the tendrils of branches that sway beneath the canopy.

He's so beautiful you'd think he was part of the landscape, lost in the movement around him. I'm staring before I remember the door swings…loudly, and the creak brings his attention back to present.

The wind picks up, kissing my bare hipbones, and I shiver as Dustin's eyes drop from my face to the purple bows at my hips.

"You look good in board shorts. A vision."

He winks, a second of a moment, but it's all it takes for me to liquify.

"I, uh, thank you."

I can't seem to get words right when I'm around a guy I like. But it's silly. It's not like I have a serious shot with this one, anyhow. He may be flirting, but he's two years older than me, hates his sister, and by the rules of science, also hates me.

Right?

But he helped me in a way my best friend wasn't even aware I needed.

"How do you know all that about…"

"Periods?" His lips twist, and *that* riles me up.

"Dustin Campbell, are you smiling about this?"

His grin widens, shoulders shaking as he flicks his

tongue over his lip ring.

He leaves it there.

To play with.

My brain can't stop thinking about his tongue to send breathing signals to my lungs, and I take in a sudden gust of air that I release on an outraged exhale.

"Am I missing something? What part of leaking gross bodily fluids on your favorite pair of dance shorts, having to practically burglarize your best friend's cabin for feminine hygiene products you don't even know how to use, then having one of the cutest guys you know encouraging you to shove a tiny cotton umbrella inside of you, is funny?"

I take a breath.

And then I die internally.

Dustin Campbell grins at me.

Just grins.

"Please take pity on me and forget this ever happened?" I cross my arms over my chest and pout down at the Dustin-shorts that cover up my blood-stained bathing suit bottoms, but his fingers find my chin and lift until our eyes meet.

My entire body stills as I hold my breath, unwilling to let the air we're sharing escape my lungs.

It's the closest we might ever be.

"Don't worry, Shana. It's fine."

Relief floods me.

"Thanks, Dustin. You have no idea how—"

"As long as you give me intel on my sister."

My cheeks heat again as he drops his hand.

"Is she into Hunter?"

Most everyone knows she likes Hunter. Even Hunter knows she likes Hunter.

I nod.

"That's why they keep ditching me. Well, you *and* me, I guess." He shakes his head. "They're just too chicken-shit to tell me. I don't even care, ya know? He's my best friend. Better him than the other creeps in town. I just want the truth. We've never had secrets, until now."

"You know, you're a good brother. She likes Hunter because of you. You showed her what good men look like, even…" I swallow, apprehensive at first, but I've known this family my whole life, so I say what my best friend's brother needs to hear, "even when your dad makes that hard."

"Thanks, Shay." He says my nickname for the second time in a few minutes, and this time around I can't ignore how good it sounds falling from his silver-ringed lips. "So," he nudges me with his shoulder, "tell me more about this 'cutest guy you know' thing?"

"You said you weren't going to bring it up!" I hide my face in my hands, but he lowers them to my lap, brushing back my hair.

"I never said that. I said it was fine."

And when his lips touch mine, I agree.

It's fine.

Chapter Six

DUSTIN

PRESENT DAY

She kisses me. For the second time in our lives.

The difference now?

We're not awkward teens behind a rickety stall. Shana Holiday is all *woman* wrapped around my tongue.

"I'm sorry!" She peels away, clearing a mess of dark waves from her face to reveal panicked eyes that veer from mine. "Just forget it happened, okay?"

She gives me no choice before she's scooping up her bag and shoving past me, the door to Sugar Stable slamming behind her.

I tell myself not to follow. Ignoring her advances has always been what's right, even if they do match my desires identically.

I shouldn't have sent the plant.

But the tears that streaked her cheeks were unbearable. I needed to see her smile, if only from a window.

I tug at my hair as I pace the closed café, tossing rogue ice-cream scoops into the dish sanitizer for *some* semblance of mental organization.

But I'm thrown so-the-fuck off.

Her presence lingers, even after she's gone.

In her booth.

On my skin.

In the cherry gloss I still taste on my lips.

"Shana!" I storm through the courtyard, with nothing but glowing lamps and the erratic thumping in my chest to keep me company. "Shay, wait up!"

I'm not sure what I'll do as I push through her studio door, but nothing in the world could compel me to be elsewhere.

"I never said I'd forget it happened," I belt, catching my breath in the studio. "Remember?"

Her chest rises and falls, as the moon spills through the blinds of my favorite window, casting slashes of light across her body. She slips off her oversized hoodie, nothing but scraps of a leotard beneath, and it's all I can do to keep my focus from wandering everywhere it rightfully shouldn't.

"Shay, would you talk to me?"

No, her backside screams.

I follow her to the adjacent dance hall. Bright pink walls shelve dozens of framed awards and collections of trophies. She floats across the polished floor, making work of both ignoring me and checking whether I'm still present.

Like *she* isn't the one who just kissed *me.*

"Shana, please. Can we talk about it?"

She ignores me, connecting her phone to the speaker.

"Pretending I'm not here isn't going to convince me you're invisible."

A song starts, and I can't stop the smirk that forms when she gets on with her warmup like I've already gone.

"Since I haven't been instructed to leave," I say to her reflection, *"I'll watch."*

Her eyes pin to mine in the mirror.

Even if we can't be together—*and I know that inherently*—I will always protect her.

Drops of tears I'll turn to sparks of fire.

"Shana, please. It's not even about the kiss. It's important." I backpedal when I hear how that sounds, "Not that our kiss wasn't *important,* I mean…"

Fuck.

"What is it, then?" She spins around. "The important thing." Arms fold across her chest.

"I need a coach."

Her eyes flare.

"For dance," I finish. "My dad has this function—"

She shakes herself from what seems to be a daydream. "Not a good idea, Dustin. Look, I'm sorry I kissed you, but I can't teach you to dance. And I don't want to talk about it, either."

Her lips say one thing, but I can't ignore the pull between her eyes that says another.

"So, just forget it happened?"

"Worked the first time," she mutters,

"One dance lesson, that's all I'm asking. We say

whatever we need to say. No walking away, no masking. That kiss—"

"I don't want to talk about the kiss," she sighs. "You don't have to feel sorry for me, either." Her eyes narrow at that last part.

"Me feel sorry for you? Shay, I have a black-tie event, and I only know the *Cha Cha Slide.* I plead with her through the mirror, every cell I possess working overtime to ignore the closeness of our bodies. "You saw me in the Mr. Pine Forest Pageant."

"Unfortunately, the whole town did." She cracks a smile.

Finally.

"Yeah." I laugh. "Well, you know how my dad is." I shake my head. "Naturally, I'll be a disappointment either way. I just thought maybe I could embarrass him in style this time. That *and* my future investments depend on it."

"It's that important?" She raises a brow.

"The most."

Her eyes are on me, for once.

Watching.

I almost forget why they *are* watching, as I lose myself in the way they blend from black to brown to mahogany, and I choose the stains necessary to recreate the hue in my mind.

"No street shoes on the dance floor."

My lip quirks.

"Yes, coach." I remove my boots.

"*Wait!* Where are you putting those?" She scrambles in front of me.

"The closet." I retort, sod-covered boots held at my side. "I was at Hunter's earlier. They smell like horse shit, literally."

"Here, I'll set them against the wall." She tries to take the boots, but I don't release my grip.

"They'll stink up your dance room." I tug.

"Studio." She tugs back. "But that's not the point. Everyone puts their shoes and coats against the wall. It's a perfectly normal system,"

"Everyone puts their *coats* somewhere other than the *coat* closet?" I narrow my eyes when she blocks my path to the one in question. "What are you hiding, Shay?"

"Nothing!" Her voice lilts. "What would I be hiding? It's not like the closet leads to the pipes and has a huge leak or anything that I'm *very* capable of handling with Dad's tools, I'm sure. I just haven't had the time to dig them out of the shed, which is blocked by the broken-down lawn mower, and—" She stops talking, her eyes dropping to her feet. "I hate how you make me ramble."

"I don't." I lift her chin until our eyes meet. "It's my second favorite thing about you."

"Sure, it is." She rolls her eyes. "And I'll bet the first is my world-renowned set of A cups."

"Your mind, Shay. The only thing I think about more than these lips."

Lips I capture, before either of us can say more, and it's everything I remember.

But guilt is never scarce.

Just like thirteen years ago.

Chapter Seven

DUSTIN

FOURTEEN YEARS AGO

I peel my body away even as it feels wrong, and I exhale to ground myself.

It doesn't matter what we want.

I permanently blinded someone, and I've given two others irreparable brain damage, a shoulder injury... I stopped listening to the list after the page flipped, the complete statement of *damages* needing a staple for its length. And it's not my defense that's the problem; the fuckers deserved every swing.

I can't stop myself; that's the problem.

When I see someone harming an innocent, something in me snaps. Punches become hammers and kicks become stomps. Their face is my face. And my hand is my father's.

She sucks in a breath, and my heart breaks in two as tears roll down her cheeks.

"Shay, I didn't mean it like that. It's just…you and I—"

"You and I, what?" She wipes her face with the back of her hand.

"L-look, I got caught up. I never should have kissed you."

"What?" Her voice breaks, the shards slicing through me.

"I didn't mean to hurt you. You're *perfect,* but—"

"But what?" She grinds out, forcing back tears I wish weren't put there by me.

"But you're you," I say.

"What does that even mean, Dustin? *I'm me?* I'm what? I'm too young? I'm your sister's best friend? I'm not a blonde haired, blue eyed, honeycomb like your usual girlfriends? Or am I just ugly, Dustin? Is that why you weren't at the formal? You looked me in the eyes by my mother's grave and asked me to save you a dance!"

'Walking liability!

Sorry excuse for a son!

"If you don't want to go out with me, just say it, Dustin."

Nothing could be further from the truth.

I take her hand and hold it against my heart, because if she won't hear me, I need her to feel what she does.

Even if I can't be with her.

Even if she'll never understand.

"Shana Holiday, you light my entire world. You're the moon in an eclipse. When you stand in my path, you are the only thing I see. Always."

Chapter Eight

One sound from her mouth is all it takes to be consumed by this moment, and I kiss her. Wholly.

I draw her closer, her breath catching when my hands find her hips and our bodies become one. Soft moans pass her lips as our tongues dance, and my cock twitches to meet her cries.

But we can't. *I can't.*

I turn her to the mirror, decidedly away from my raging cock, and my front is flush with her backside. I press her wrists to the glass above her head, *and she fucking lets me.*

Lord have mercy.

"We shouldn't be doing this." I say, even as my tongue explores her skin.

"You shouldn't watch through windows, either," she all but whispers, "yet I still open my blinds."

And that's all the invitation I need before her breasts and face are flat against the mirror, and the sexiest moan

I've ever heard soars from her lips when I finger the tease of fabric between her thighs.

It's soaked.

I work my tongue down the back of her neck. "Rock against me, baby. You're so wet."

Our reflection is sin.

Pure heat streaks her cheeks, nipples pebble through her leotard, and a large, ravenous *me* grinds against her backside, sampling her skin. She presses her neck decidedly against my tongue, and I'm damned the very instant she bends her body to meet my kisses and her pert little ass arches up, too.

Despite everything I know I shouldn't do, I keep kissing, yearning for the satisfied sounds she makes when I taste places I've only had in my dreams.

But my father's face slams across my vision, warring with the present.

"You're a walking bomb. Goddamned liability excuse for a fucking son."

It doesn't matter how many therapists assure me my traumas are managed, if someone were to hurt the woman I love?

I would kill them.

They can't fix that.

Despite every part of me screaming it's wrong to let her close, that I should *look not touch*, I ask her anyway.

"Will you teach me to dance?"

She stills in my hold, her eyes bright and calculating as they meet mine through the glass, and it might have been a *yes* until this moment. But before she can speak, a notification hits her phone that stirs my insides.

"Congrats @DancerBaby69. Your Fling has accepted. Be Ready tonight at 8!"

My heart slams against my chest.

"Flinger? *You* joined Flinger?"

The energy shifts as she turns from my hold.

Power flits over her eyes, the same ones that inspired a collection of stained oak furniture I've scattered through the town—eyes I have memorized, look relieved.

Relief she has a match? On *that* app?

"You shouldn't be on there." I grind out, unable to ignore the cherry zing across my tongue. I want to hold her and taste it there for as long as time will allow, not just this once.

I step closer, but she flinches.

"*I* shouldn't be on there? What about you? You're on there with a new pair of rhinestone boots and acrylic nails every weekend."

"That's not the same thing," I argue. It's insane to think that's comparable. "I'm *me*. And you're *you*."

My breath catches as her eyes drop to the floor.

But this isn't the little girl down the hall dancing to boybands in my sister's room. This is the grown woman I fell in love with. Her jaw tightens and chin lifts, transforming her into the ballerina I watch in the window every night.

Strong.

Elegant.

Out of my league.

"I'm *me*, Dustin? How fitting that we find ourselves right back at this place. It doesn't matter how much life we've lived together, or the length that time steals, you will always see me as *me*." She turns away, dismissing my reflection through another wall of glass. "Please go."

Shit.

"Shay, don't… You know how I feel about you. How I've always felt."

"Do I?" she asks through the mirror, head cocked to the side. "Oh, yeah." She spins to face me, a sad smile ghosting her lips. "I'm the eclipse, right? I'm *all* you can see? So you didn't see that leggy blonde when her tongue was down your throat last night? Because I *did* see."

"You saw Miranda kiss me?"

"Glad she has a name," she huffs.

I press my lips together. "Shana Holiday, are you jealous of my Flinger date?"

"Are you jealous of mine?"

Fuck.

"Yes, Dustin. I saw you with *Samantha* or whatever her name is. We have floor-to-ceiling windows across from each other, remember?

I press my tongue to my cheek at the intentional misnomer, but my chest tightens all the same. Jealousy might look cute as fuck on poised and polite Shana Holiday, but I would never dream of hurting her. "Is that why you cried?" I lower my voice. "She was just a *fling*, Shay. People on that app are fake, which is exactly why you shouldn't be on there. It's not worth it for someone like you."

"*Someone like me?* What about you?" She shakes her head. "Look, you don't have to defend it, Dustin, so just don't. Like you said, *we* can't be anything. So, you do you, and I'll do me. Better yet, my fling can do me. That's how it works right, or do I have to give him my hoodie first?"

"Shay, come on—"

"No, *you* come on. Come on and say you want me. Right here, right now. No more hot, cold, kiss then can't! Because quite frankly, I've saved *everything* for you. Every kiss, every dream, every wish on a shooting star or four-leaf clover plucked from forget-me-not gardens has been for you, Dustin Campbell. Since I was thirteen years old. But according to you, I'm just *me.*"

She steps closer, leaving no space between us as she shoves my back against the wall, so close I can feel her breath across my own. Then she swipes my boots from the floor and thrusts them against my beating chest.

"I'm tired of saving every first for someone who sees me last."

Chapter Nine

SHANA

"Oh hell to the no." Jeremy's arm shoots out as I exit the stoop, giving me an almost heart-attack. He appraises my outfit, ripped skinny jeans and an oversized black cardigan, paired with a light pink camisole and flats.

He clicks his tongue and snaps at Lemon who pops out the hydrangeas with a makeup caboodle, scaring the absolute crap out of me. "We cannot consciously let you go on a date like that."

"You guys are certifiable! You scared me."

"You're easy to stalk." Lemon shrugs.

"How do you know I have a date?" I shift to Lemon, in a conspiratory whisper. "Did you talk to Dustin?"

"I didn't say anything about Dustin." Her eyes sparkle as Jeremy's widen in shock. "But *you* did."

Jeremy yanks me into the house with Lemon on my heels, squealing in delight.

Within seconds, I'm seated in the recliner watching my boundary-deficient friends make home on the sofa.

Lemon crosses her legs to one side and Jeremy promptly follows suit toward the other, as if it's been choreographed.

With these two, it probably has.

"Spill it." Jeremy pouts. "I wanna know what Lemon knows."

"Not so fast, *Sherlock* and *Watson*."

Lem snorts, so I cut her my best teacher look while Jeremy just snickers.

These two.

"The only person who knew about my date was Dustin, and only because he wouldn't get his smelly boots out of my studio while I was trying to choreograph."

I stand and pace the floor, uprooted over dumb, muscly, unattainable, grumble of man who has the nerve to come waltzing…no, not even waltzing. I bet he doesn't know how to waltz…*traipsing*. That's what he did.

"He traipsed in there with that over-the-top nonsense of his, 'oh you're the moon, you're the eclipse, Shana, I'm not bright enough for your shadowy light,' and then he kisses me like *that's* gonna help!"

I stop in an instant, realizing what I've let slip.

Jeremy and Lemon have unanimously scootched off the couch and are crisscross applesauce on the ground, both sets of jaws practically touching the floor as they gape at me.

My phone pings the signature Flinger sound, and all three of our heads whip to the saddle bag slung across my midsection.

"He kissed you!?" Lemon squeals. "Is he pinging you now? What does it say?!"

"Calm down, it's not like that." I fish my phone from the bag. "I'm *just me*, after all. Typical Dustin."

Lemon grabs my arm. "What do you mean 'typical Dustin?' *You're the moon*? Shay, I have known Dustin Campbell almost as long as you, basically my whole life, and I wasn't sure 'typical' for him was more than two words a day out loud…which is a lot like *you* now that I'm thinking about it. Oh my God! Jeremy, they're soulmates!"

"I see it!" he agrees, framing my face. "The Ballerina and the Barista. A love so sweet you'll dance." He fans himself while Lemon claps excitedly.

I shake my head, focusing on what's important here. Not on fairytale romance ideals. Not on a man who says he wants one thing but does another.

A creepy plant and then dance lesson requests? But *oh wait*…we can't.

You're just…you.

I don't need more uncertainty in my life than I already have. I need someone who knows what he wants and goes for it. Who wants me for me.

Someone who feels like *me* is enough.

"It doesn't matter," I tell them on a quick exhale. "Dustin's not my date. It's a true Flinger match. Someone I don't know."

I smooth the goosebumps that scatter my arms with that thought, hoping my friends don't notice how terrified I am.

Lemon slinks to the couch, deflated. "I was hoping it wasn't that. Your dad told me earlier when I checked his vitals. Said he didn't want you falling victim to a skin fetish…or something."

I meet her scrunched face and my lip quirks before we both laugh.

"He wants you to be happy." She reaches for my hand, and even though it feels emotional, I let her grab it.

It's real. It's friendship I can count on, even after Dad is gone. That's who I need to fill my life with, now more than ever. People who do what they say and are there when you need them. People like Lemon and Jeremy.

And maybe someone on Flinger.

What I won't do is wait around for someone who won't come through when it matters.

The app pings again. I never checked the first notification, so I drop Lemon's hand and swipe up, reading both messages.

LawsonLaw69: Looking forward to looking at you. Still smirking at the 69 in our screen names. Glad to know a woman with a sense of humor. See you when I see you.

LawsonLaw69: Sending you the location of a milkshake bar. Meet before the show? Just across the river.

Across the river. Strategically, or so I presumed, I set my location to the college town up north; to attract people I *haven't* known since birth, small-town problems. But across the river from there, is here.

And the only milkshake bar in town is…

"You guys…he wants to go to Sugar Stable, what do I do? Lemon! What do I do?" My throat tightens thinking about the way Dustin's tongue explored the insides of my mouth when we kissed. How my lady parts responded. "We can't go to Dustin's!"

"Are you sure you shouldn't just cancel with this Flinger rando and talk to Dustin? It seems like a lot has happened between you two in the last few hours—"

"Decades," I breathe.

"Right." She presses her hands to my shoulders. "And I really think you should—"

"No!" I grab her wrist before she can take my phone again. "First of all, nobody, and I mean, *nobody* breathes a word of this to Devyn. No Dustin and Shana. No Shana and Dustin, got it?"

They nod.

"Now, I'm going out with this random lawyer guy tonight, and you know what? I'm going to kiss him!"

Jeremy gasps dramatically.

"I'm not kidding! I'm going to kiss him. And I might do more than that. Second base even!"

I don't care what they think. And Lemon has no right to judge me when she got down with an *entire band* last weekend. Don't even get me started on Jeremy's extra-curriculars.

"I appreciate your advice and all, but this thing with Dustin has gone too long."

"Too long?" Her eyes widen. "How long?" She exchanges a look with Jeremy.

"Never mind." I hand Lemon the makeup kit. "I'm going to do whatever I need to get him out of my head and off my lips. Then I can get back to usual. Everything that happened today is totally normal. And tonight, I'll have a totally normal date like a completely normal person. That's all."

Lemon cocks her head to the side. "*What's* normal?"

I stare at her reflection. Maybe I do need to confide in someone who has experience with these feelings.

"The fireworks," I finally say. "It's nothing, right?" I touch my lips. "That's normal when you kiss someone?"

"Oh." Jeremy's brows pull in. "Was…this your *first* kiss, Shay?" He looks at Lemon.

"Not exactly," I mumble.

"So, compare this with the others," Jeremy suggests. "Were there any fireworks then?"

My eyes flick to the sugar plum plant. "I don't think it works that way when they're with the same person."

"Oh, fuck." Lemon rubs her temples. She grabs my phone a second later, raising an eyebrow for permission.

I let her. I'm not equipped for this. But her fingers tap left and right, and I'm suddenly nervous.

She smiles, sliding the phone in my hand. "I told him you'll meet at Cowboy's Paradise instead. No Dustin. Not tonight at least, okay? But I still think—"

"Lemmm," I groan, "Can we focus on the man I *don't* want to pummel tonight?"

"Fine," she concedes. "But second base can also involve pummeling, just so you know." She smiles at me until my nerves slink off, and I smile back.

"Now…" She holds up a bright red dress that hardly looks longer than a t-shirt, with a low-cut V-neck slashing down the front. "I vote for this dress."

"Yeah, right. I am not going out in that." I gesture to the oversized tube top and beg Jeremy for help.

Surely, I'm not the only one who sees there is no way *that* belongs on me.

"Why not?" Jeremy presses his lips together.

"Do you see that thing? I can't wear something *sexy* like that. Everyone would see—"

"You?" Jeremy tucks my hair behind my ear and smiles. "It's okay for them to see you the way you feel inside."

"I have no idea what you're talking about." I take the fabric scraps from Lemon. "Fine. I'll put the dumb dress on, but not because I want people to think I'm—"

"Sexy?" Lemon smirks.

"I hate you both, you know that?" I shove into the hallway half-bath and yank my original outfit off. I don't see what was wrong with the jeans and cardigan combo. It's not like I want a guy to like me for being half naked.

On the other hand, I *am* there for de-virginity purposes and all.

"Whoa." My breath leaves my lungs as I look down at the red velvet hugging my body, accentuating my curves. The ribbon ties around my waist, just above my hips, falling elegantly down my side. The air kisses my right thigh, bare from the height of the slit. Skin exposed or not, I must admit, this dress feels made for me.

When I step into the hallway, my friends gasp in unison.

"Shay Bae, you look…" Jeremy shakes his head.

"Like the eclipse." Lemon beams, crossing her arms over her chest proudly.

Before I can respond, my phone pings. I frown, wishing I could say the messages from LawsonLaw69 bring me butterflies or fireworks, but they don't.

Maybe that's normal. We don't know each other after all, like Dustin and I have for years.

Still, I wish there was more of a spark when I swipe into the message.

Until there is.

I expect to see my date's response to the venue switch-up. Instead, it's a message from someone I'm not matched with.

No picture available.

I know I shouldn't open an unmatched message, but my eyes scan the screen before my brain grants them permission, and the words travel straight between my legs, a building pressure amounting to…I don't know what.

A collision?

Explosion?

Watcher: You're letting a forty-dollar plant die. Shame. It's not the plant's fault you hate attention.

Fireworks.

My heartbeat quickens, with a zip of a thrill up my spine, a rollercoaster, just before the drop, and my fingers zoom across the screen to chase it.

DancerBaby69: You left the flowers? Were you watching me?

DancerBaby69: Are you watching now?

Watcher: Yes.

I shiver, letting that one-word drip down the front of my body like molten lava. Never mind the meaning behind his words. The one where he *did* send me flowers. He *did* watch me.
And he still is now.
I like the way my body feels each time I re-read it.
Yes.
Yes.
Yes. Yes. Yes.
Wait, this is insane.
I am not turned on by this. I know who the plant sender is! *Don't I?*
My eyes shift to the yearbooks lining the bottom row of my shelf. To the ballerina spinning in an open box in my memories.
It's shut now. Right atop all the dusty yearbooks.
Dusty…
I shove past Lemon and tear the music box from the shelf, opening it up to reveal a note inside. The ballerina turns to *Edelweiss* as I scan the crumpled parchment.

Always your fan. I'll never stop watching you dance.

"I knew it was him. Full of it back then, too." I shake

my head and shove the note and the box back into a crevice. It doesn't quite match what I'm looking for, but it's always been him.

I just don't know where he gets the audacity to act like we're teenagers, sneaking around an app like old love notes, instead of admitting he has feelings and is too scared to try for anything real. And how is that fair to me?

He *rejected* me mere hours ago.

He can kiss me but not be with me? He'll send secret messages to thwart my plans with others but not choose to be the one to take me home?

He fucking *is* home to me. I thought I'd made that clear.

"Are you okay, Shana?" Jeremy scootches to his knees beside me on the carpeted floor. It just reminds me I'm nothing like him. Or Lemon or Devyn or any of my friends.

I'm still sitting here playing patty cake with childhood trinkets on the bedroom floor of my father's home, hymen more intact than my actual sanity as pathetic as that is…and I don't want to tell them any of this.

We said no more secrets. But how do I explain twenty-something years of holding a single breath?

My body hums when I find the dog-eared page in my senior yearbook.

The year the notes stopped coming.

> *To my sister's only tolerable friend, I can't believe*
> *you didn't have anyone sign this. What gives?*
> *It's not the yearbook's fault you hate attention.*
> *Always watching out for you.-Dusty*

Does it mean I'm an absolute psychopath because the molten lava from before is now a pool of hot, sticky need between my legs?

Is this watcher the same man I kissed only hours ago?

Has he been watching me all this time?

My clit shouldn't buzz at the thought.

What is wrong with me?

My mind reels with the possibilities, and I hit the call button beneath his name before I can think better of it.

"What are you doing?" Lemon's eyes widen. "Who is that? You don't call a match!"

I need to know.

The phone rings. I'm a nervous mess, but this isn't anyone. It's Dustin Campell.

I feel it.

Someone picks up, but all I hear is breathing. I grind my teeth, furious at him because I know what this is now.

He doesn't want me on Flinger because he doesn't want me with anyone. But I'll be damned if he keeps pretending he doesn't want me for himself while he leaves a trail of breadcrumbs to nowhere.

"Look here, *Watcher,* which is a stupid name, I watch too. True Crime. So, I know how this works. You try to woo me with your weird watcher stuff, I fall fifty shades of freak for it, and suddenly edible arrangements shaped like my face are showing up with notes made from toe-nail clippings, and honestly, I just don't need that right now. So, send your needy little death plants to someone else. There is nothing special about me to like. *Someone I know* made that extremely clear tonight!" I slam the phone to the bed and huff.

Lemon snatches up my phone. "What the hell is this? Why is someone named Watcher messaging you?" Her eyes harden as she scrolls. "You're replying to him?!"

Jeremy pries the phone from Lemon, his voice void of its usual singsong, "Why didn't you tell us about this?"

I run my hand over the back of my neck, thankful that they care, but annoyed that they think my sexual innocence translates to having no street smarts whatsoever. It's not like I gave this guy any personal information.

He apparently already knows it. He's watching, right?

Plus, it's Dustin.

But they don't know that. And with the way they reacted earlier, I'm not sure I want them to know.

The notes. The heartbreak.

It's too much to explain.

And I hate, more than anything, that it turns me on to know it's him. Am I that pathetic of a person to pine for one man the entirety of my life when all he will ever do is push me away?

If I leave the blinds open as I undress?

To be bare to someone so obsessed with me, they're content to simply *watch*?

"Dad thinks it's harmless. He saw him. It's the same guy who sent me flowers, I'm sure of it." I don't mention that Dustin is likely both people, as I gesture to the crumpled flora and consider that it *does* look thirsty. "Anyway, Dad recognized him. It's someone we know." I clear my throat and pretend to look at makeup palettes.

"Wait a sec." Lemon narrows her eyes. "You mean to tell me that in this one, solitary week, you have: acquired a stalker, received flowers from a gentleman caller, and kissed Dustin-Fucking-Campbell, who has *apparently* been calling you *the moon* for a 'long time'—your words not mine—and your best friends know not a single damn thing about it?"

Jeremy snaps his fingers with a "Hmph," before standing to gather the discarded dresses. I haven't seen him this mad at me since I called Triple A to tow my truck instead of him.

But it was his day off. I don't like to burden people.

"Come on, Jer. It's not like that. Yeah, I didn't tell you guys, but it's not like I told anyone else."

"That's the point, Shay." Lemon throws her hands to her hips. "You didn't tell anyone. Were you going to tell either of us about the date tonight? Even for safety reasons? I mean what if your dad couldn't speak and you went missing. He's the only one who knew, and you know how unreliable his memory is!"

I shrug, my eyes dropping to my feet because…emotions and all.

Lemon paces before me.

"You don't tell anyone anything. You let things fester inside of you until there's nothing left but huge balls of emotion hurling around and ready to crash. You weren't even going to tell Devyn about your dad's health. Your best friend from childhood and she had to move back and find out with her own two eyes. You want to do it all alone, but we're here, Shana. Your problems are coming our way too, whether you like it or not, because we care about you. Your friends are here for the good, the bad, and the scary. We're here for your dates…your kisses."

"Definitely for your stalkers," Jeremy says, drawing a smile from my lips despite the situation. "Let's get some blush for these cheeks before your date, okay?"

"Do you guys forgive me for…hurling my balls at you?" We all burst out laughing.

"We do." Lemon powders a makeup brush. "But no more secrets, okay?"

I smile at my friends, grateful for their support. Even when I feel alone, they remind me I'm not.

But guilt slithers over me as I slip to the bathroom. My phone pinged minutes ago, but I wanted to be alone for this. Even if I did just tell him off. Even if he does say we can't be together. Even if he makes me want to scream with his indecisiveness.

I feel them.

Fireworks and butterflies and explosions all combine for this man who sees me, his response to my rant, '*there's nothing about me to like*,' heating that lava right back up to the point of shame.

Watcher: Liar. I like you in red.

Chapter Ten

DUSTIN

I feel like a lovestruck teenager, sliding my phone into my pocket. I replay what I witnessed earlier, hiding behind my favorite tree in her yard.

How she touched herself in red, opening her blinds for me. She knew exactly what she was doing.

Does she know it's me?

Or for her watcher?

I did watch, even after all I said in the studio.

Because I'm fucked in the head.

And this is among one thousand other reasons why I shouldn't entertain things with the woman I obsess over, no matter how she looks in red.

Or black.

Skintight dancewear in my fantasies, sprawled across my bed, peeled from her body, piece by sparkling piece.

Fuck.

I'm letting it get too far.

The bell chimes, and I bring my focus back to my job, as a familiar face stares back at me.

"What can I getchya, Abe?" The old man who owns the feed store orders a chocolate shake with whipped cream and malt, once a week. It never changes, but I always ask him anyway.

Abel's eyes crinkle at the corners as he browses the menu above my head. I'm never sure whether he's attempting to read the thing or if he's just putting on a show. Either way, I let it play out and sigh in relief at the familiarity.

At least something makes sense today.

I ready myself for his usual order, left pointer finger on the button for shakes and right-hand hovering over the cups. I've done it so many times it's muscle memory, and I sink easily into the comfort of predictable moments like this one. It's the first time my heart's stopped pounding since she kissed me.

"What's got your coon dog's howling, son?"

"What? I'm fine."

"Nope." He leans in closer and squints, nodding his head like that's that. "You're in love."

"How could you possibly know that in two seconds?"

"Ya' just got that look." He shrugs. "I don't make the rules."

"Okay, let's just say that were true—"

"It is."

"Whatever." I squint. "So...are you saying I have no choice but to go with it? Destiny? God's will?"

"I didn't say that. You did. But if that's what you need to tell yourself to make it work, then say it however ya like."

I thread my fingers through my hair and tug. Nobody in this damn town can ever come flat out and say what they mean.

Fuck, I sound like Dad.

Who expects me to meet him in the city in less than a week. To a gala, of all things, with the '*Business Elite.*'

Shana would have taught me to dance at the damn thing, but that was *before* she kissed me. Before we said what we said. Now I'm not sure I can be in the same room with her without imagining her lips popping open.

The roundness of a perfect o as she came over her own fingers in that red velour, moans spilling from her open window and landing on my cock.

It hasn't stopped feeling her there since.

Doesn't make it right. And it certainly doesn't qualify me as worthy of her. Glorified creeper is what I am. I shake my head at Abel in protest.

"I get what you're saying, but—"

"What *you're* saying," Abel corrects.

I throw my hands up. He knows what I did.

"This isn't a movie. This woman. Jesus, Abe. She's untouchable. God, fate, whatever you want to call it, they wouldn't choose me for her."

I wouldn't choose me for her.

"She deserves better than—"

"Than the man who helped renovate the town bar, free'a charge so it wouldn't close down?"

"What? Abe, that was forever ago. And *everyone* was helping out."

"How 'bout the brother who drove to the city twice a

week, makin' sure his sister never had to face therapy alone?"

"I know what you're doing, and I get it, but this isn't the same—"

"Someone better'n the young man who saw three girls in desperate need up in those woods and saved their lives, Son?"

I move to speak, but he stops me, shaky hand up as he leans against my counter.

"I don't give a shit what happened to those boys you saved them girls from. They weren't the first, and they wouldn't have been the last to try what they did. The whole town was better for it, you hear?" He follows my gaze, even as I try to look away. "Do you hear me? Do you think she will find someone better than the man who ended that misery? That stopped her—"

"Yes, Abel!" I slam my hands against the counter, thankful as hell for the lack of patrons, but he doesn't flinch, just sets his jaw and tightens his grip on his cane and the counter between us. And *fuck, I'm so angry*, but it's not at Abel, it's at myself. I hate that I'm even here at this crossroad. Dad is fucking right.

"She can find hundreds of someones better than me. I may have saved people, yeah, but I fucked people up, too. Do you know what that feels like?" I drop to a whisper, pain and remorse prodding upward from my veins, poking out of me like blades. "To know your honor comes from another's suffering?"

Abel closes his eyes and breathes. Slow. A memory crossing over him as he tugs a veteran cap from his back pocket and sets it atop his head.

"I do. And I know what it's like to spend the rest of your life pushing everyone you love away because of it. Now let me ask *you* a question. Do you know what happens when you let the love of your life pass you by? Because I do."

I clench the countertop, my fingertips white and crinkled with the weight of the question I dare not ask.

Abel pulls a crinkled paper out of his pocket. He doesn't show it to me, but I know it well. We all do. It's one he's held onto for as long as I can remember. Since I was a little boy chasing ducklings through his Farm N' Feed aisles in spring.

He presses it straight to his heart, his eyes locked on mine, glistening. "What happens," he says, knuckles tightening around the parchment, "is you spend the rest of your life loving them just as fiercely as you do at this very moment. And they never love you back." He folds the paper back up, slipping it into his trousers, just below the suspenders.

Like he's done my whole life.

He's loved her this whole time, whoever she is.

"What am I supposed to do, Abe? I…*I* told her we can't be together. For years, I've told her she's meant for someone other than me, and now she's finally taken my word for it. She has a date tonight for fuck's sake. She's probably there now. And you know what?" I shake my head, ashamed that I'm even considering she should love me, sending her plants and asking for dances meant for another. "She's better off that way. I hear what you're saying, but this isn't about what's best for me. It's about her, you know?"

"I can't make that decision for you, Son. All I can do is tell it like it is. Shana's a special one. Won't be long before she finds someone to love her back. Will it be you?"

"Damnit, Abe, it's not like I can barge into her date and…wait. How did you know it was Shana?"

The old loon smiles, saying nothing and everything at the same damn time.

The door chimes as a family walk in, and my eyes move toward the sound, relief consuming me. I need to focus on something other than Shana, so I crack my knuckles and throw some straws into my apron in preparation for the weekend rush.

At least we'll be busy all night, and I can ignore the thoughts of her with anyone else.

Someone who isn't me.

And they never love you back.

The woman with two little ones on either hip clears her throat, the smaller baby flopping to the side and swatting the ice cream display as she bounces. My mouth curves up, wondering what Shana would look like with our little ones.

Our little ones?

Fuck.

All I can think of is Shana.

Her eyes

That kiss.

Of the man who will steal her body tonight.

"Better yet, my fling can do me!"

"I'm sorry, ma'am, I'll be right with you." My throat constricts me with regret.

"I got her!" Abby comes from the kitchen, noting my discomfort.

"I thought Emily was on tonight."

"I am!" Emily pokes her head around.

Great. I've over-scheduled servers for this shift, likely because of my inability to concentrate on anything other than how Shana's lips tasted on my tongue. I'm not only paying three of us to be here for a fraction of the revenue, but we won't be as busy as I hoped.

I turn my attention back to the old man, still judging the menu like it might take shape and fly off if he looks long enough. "Do you want your usual chocolate, Abe?"

"You know what?" He smiles. "Feels like a root-beer float kind of night, don't you think?" He winks, handing me a crumpled five-dollar bill, and hobbles to the very booth she kissed me in less than six hours ago.

"I hear Cowboy's Paradise is nice tonight," he calls out as he walks away, "if you happen to be overstaffed."

He waves at the girls behind me, who giggle and curtsey, a running joke he's got with the ladies of the town that they're all royalty to him. I turn, unable to suppress my grin when I see the joy he brings them. The whole town really. To these people that feel like *my* people.

I wonder what made him push away the love of his life? And if he's so sure I shouldn't do the same, why did he?

I clean the edges of his cup with a fresh cloth, spinning it in complete rotation like I've done every day since I started here, then I plop a cherry on top and turn back to face him.

But his booth is empty.

And I'm left here, overwhelmed, overstaffed, with Shana Holiday's favorite drink melting in my hand.

Well played, Abe.

I try to come up with any single reason why I shouldn't, but the woman with the baby smiles down as tiny fingers she created wrap around her own. Her husband watches her feed the toddler a sundae, pretending each spoonful is a starfighter and must be eaten before it destroys the ice cream shop. He smiles at the woman he clearly loves, being unapologetically her, and I lose all will power.

I do what I've wanted to do for longer than I can recall, and I dig up lost time.

Watcher: Tell me about your first kiss.

A nano second goes by before she replies, and in seven short words, Shana Holiday owns me completely.

I finally understand.

I've been the idiot who saw none of it, all this time. And whether it's smart to act on it or not, this feeling in my chest means something.

I am hers and she is forever, unmistakably, mine.

"Em, lock up tonight, I'm taking off."

I don't even wait for a reply before I tug off my apron and slip into my office. One glance at my phone and my heart feels exactly how it always has with her.

Fated.

DancerBaby69: It was my only kiss. Until today.

Chapter Eleven

SHANA

I'm sweaty. Worst of all, there's giant paddle fans here. It's part of the Cowboy's Paradise aesthetic…the one Dustin helped create. These are his handcrafted tables we're sitting at, after all. The very bench my butt rests on right now was once sanded by his own two hands.

Oh my God, why did I think that, get ahold of yourself, Shana! "You're on a date!"

"Huh? Yeah. We are." My date raises an eyebrow, because I'm freaking *weird*, talking out loud when I don't mean to, but in about twenty minutes with the wind percolating above me, I'll probably be a popsicle in a tiny red dress that I never should have let Lemon and Jeremy talk me into. I tug at the hem to stretch to cover my nether regions, and I wonder how Lemon doesn't have an entire harem by now with these outfits.

I glance over my shoulder, certain I feel someone watching me, but there's nobody there, and it's not healthy the way my heart sinks to the bottom of my stomach as I scan the crowd and see nothing.

I like you in red.

The words float across my brain.

Airy and light, everything they shouldn't be since they come from a self-pronounced watcher. That should scare me, but nothing scares me anymore like the idea of Dad leaving me.

And here I am, back to the thought I can never strike from my brain no matter what deranged situation I may be in.

Like a date. I smooth out my dress as I try to focus on what Lawrence is saying.

He's handsome. In a Kentucky Derby, goes-to-church-but-might-still-have-a-couple-DUIs-his-daddy-paid-to-cover kind of way.

If you like that sort of handsome.

Which I don't.

There's a certain familiarity in the way he bounces his knee when he speaks, as if his excitement drives his every move. I can't place where I've seen that sort of energy before.

His mouth moves as he speaks about something legal and boring, and I imagine a sliver ring right where his teeth scrape his bottom lip.

Damn it.

"You know what I mean?" Lawrence takes a long swig of his overpriced chardonnay, a drink I hate but let him order for me anyway because he seemed like he really wanted to show off his platinum card.

But shoot…what was he saying?

"Yeah, that's crazy," I lie, offering a half laugh incase that's appropriate for whatever he just said. I'm not even sure if it was funny or serious.

"Right!" He nods his head in agreement, so I must have hit the mark conversationally, but holy moly I'm bad at socializing with people I don't know. When did listening and staying in the present become so hard for me?

Probably when the present became about Dad dying.

"I'm sorry…did I say something wrong?" Lawrence sits back in his chair, the sparkle in his eyes just a moment ago replaced with a desperate despondency I feel an immediate need to remedy.

"No, *I'm* sorry. I just…remembered something. I'll deal with it later." Second lie.

How many times will I lie to this man I might sleep with?

I shiver as he inspects me, and I hate that there's nothing there when his eyes are on me.

I want there to be.

But there's no thrill like Dustin.

My watcher.

My insides heat replaying how I touched myself in the window. Knowing he was there. Knowing he wanted it. I was so mad at him for rejecting me at the studio, it felt powerful to be the one in control up on my balcony, the moon lighting me like a wanton Juliette in the sassy red dress I wear right now.

At least Romeo had the balls to show his face when he came in the night.

My phone goes off, a loud twinkling chime that makes me jump. Lawrence looks annoyed. "Sorry, I forgot to turn this on silent. I like, never get messages, so it could be… I just need to check this."

He fake-laughs, barely masking the manufactured sound of it and eyeing me with something that feels a lot like regret.

Regret going out with someone like me, when he could have *Miranda*, or whoever Dustin was with the other night? Girls who don't blank out half the dinner conversation because they're thinking about men they'll never have?

Probably.

"Sorry, it'll just be a minute." I begin to worry it's about Dad and my heartbeat picks up, my hands sweaty as my fingers slide across the lock screen. Relief fills me when I see it's not Lemon or any of the health team.

It's a number I don't recognize, though.

If it's not spam, they'll leave a message, so I tuck the phone back in my purse and return my attention to my date, who has resorted to stacking the Stevia packets in tiny rows to keep himself occupied, humming a tune I faintly recognize.

I'm boring him, too. I sigh. "I've been a terrible date," I tell him, sliding the Stevia by the ketchup. His eyes flick to the movement and back to me before he finally offers a smile, one that doesn't seem to do anything for me, unfortunately, but here we are. "I've had a lot going on, but I want to be here. I promise. Tell me more about your work."

"Right, where was I?" He bites his lip as he muses, and I'm not even annoyed there's no sparkling ring between his teeth when he lets it pop free.

Just me over here, super interested in men with frosted tips who wear blue suits and brown shoes, and…ew, is that a golf tattoo on his wrist?

I'm not even gagging.

"So, have you ever heard of split-liability? I won this massive suit in Valley a couple years back between a tractor trailer and a circus train, and you would not *believe* the amount of property damage you have to claim for a herd of baby elephants. It was…"

Lawrence drones on about assets and mediations, and the rather extreme length his poor paralegals went to securing statistics from seventeen zoos across the country on the average life expectancy of a rare, white Bengal tiger…and I want to stab my ears out. Dramatic, I know, but like, *holy actual moly,* I was a dance major. And he is…a money maker.

Everything he's talked about this entire night has been a dollar sign, assessing values and risks at every corner.

"This is worse than my root canal."

My eyes widen as it slips out, and Lawrence draws back, disgust and surprise etched across his features.

"I'm sorry, am I boring you, *Miss Dancer Sixty-Nine?*" He spits the words at me, and even with sticks and stones, they sting. "I thought you were a sophisticated ballerina. I got us tickets to *Swan Lake* and everything. I *thought* I matched for a classy date."

"At the Sugar Stable? Cowboy's Paradise?" I don't mean to sound ungrateful, but like, it's Flinger. We all know what we're here for. And *Swan Lake* performed by the regional ballet is literally the direct competition to my own studio's classes, plus I've already seen it twice to scout dancers for next invitational, something he may have learned if he'd asked me a single thing about myself the entire hour we've been here.

"You know, I had higher hopes for you."

If I had the confidence to hit someone, this entitled asshole would be my first choice. Instead, I clench my chair, unable to move as each insult he hurls becomes a weight crushing the air from my lungs.

"If you just wanted sex, you should have told me you were *that* kind of dancer." He spits, raking his gaze to the apex of my thighs. "A lap dance would have cost me less."

What did he just say?

I want to speak, but I come up with nothing. My lips are dry, my throat is dust, my hands are the only thing that seem to be leaking sweat from my body like I'm a witch and water is my chosen element, and worst of all, I can't *think*.

I can't think because I can't be here.

I *shouldn't* be here.

I should be at home with Dad.

With my dying father.

My breathing quickens and it feels even tighter in my chest. "I…I'm—" The words are ragged. And I want to cry, but it burns as I inhale.

Doubt floods my mind as I think of how I put myself here, and I hate it. I want to go back to my studio, under my hoodie, to a dark room where I can spin and spin and spin and forget the world around me exists apart from the gravity holding me down.

If it weren't for spinning, I'd float away.

"The fuck is wrong with you?" Lawrence snaps his fingers in my face, but before I know what's happening a flash in the corner catches my notice, an arm reaches over me and a large hand wraps around Lawrence's gold-en-glad wrist. The man squeezes, until Lawrence screams, turning red in the face and arching his body, pinned to the table. "What the fuck! I wasn't going to touch her! Let me go!"

I whip my head around, my body sizzling with an energy I wish I could say was fear for my date being assaulted—even if he was a jerk. But it isn't. It's a feeling I can't describe. One I only feel when…

"Dustin?" I shove from the table, watching as he swings his gaze to me for a split second, green eyes angry and penetrating, like I've seen them only one other time in my life.

"I wasn't…to touch…touch her!" Lawrence gasps between a smushed windpipe, still writhing on the table as locals gather around. Nobody questions Dustin.

Not in this town.

"You're damn right you weren't." Dustin's grip tightens around my date's hand until actual tears spring from his eyes, spilling down his reddened cheeks. "Leave."

"Okkk- Okay!"

Dustin looks my way as he lowers to my date's ear, his voice a whisper I'm not sure was meant for Lawrence at all. I open my mouth to stop him, say something, but I'm not sure what.

Because the truth is, I like Dustin Campbell's crazed green eyes on me far too much to say a single thing that would ever break his stare.

So, I let it happen.

I watch as he slays my dragons.

I listen as he climbs towers.

"She hates Swan Lake."

It takes a lot to make your body do the opposite of what it wants, but I do. As tears fall down my face that came from God knows where, a place inside of me that will never stop wanting him, I suppose. A place that holds years of flames we've kindled and refused to let die for the fuel we continue to feed them, I swipe them away on the backs of my hands, and I defy my body's desires.

I run.

Because I'll never have this man who fights for me, who knows me like no other, not in the way I want. And it's not the first time I've faced that fact.

Chapter Twelve

SHANA

THIRTEEN YEARS AGO

Y ou gotta drink now, cutie."

My fingers curl around the plastic red cup, and I blink up at the boy who just said something to me, Thomas. He's a grade above me, but we don't share any classes or friends, so I know very little about him. Only that Dustin hates him. Sworn Devyn and I away from him or any of his friends.

Why am I with him?

"What did you say?" I rub my forehead. "I think I spaced out." I scan the field party I came to with Dev and Ash, my eyes zoning on the large oak with a funny branch I remember seeing on the way to the clearing.

Only, I don't see either of my friends.

And when did I get this cup of—I sniff the half-full beverage and my stomach rolls. "Is this beer?"

"Jungle Juice." Thomas winks, a slow smile creeping

across his face as he leans in around me, putting his arms on either side. With my back flush to his and my front shoved against the beer pong table, I have no means to free myself when I feel his lips touch the back of my neck. My skin prickles, but not in a good way.

"Get off me, please." I shove him back, but his hold tightens, and his height gives him the advantage to keep me right where he wants.

"Shh, we don't have to go all the way, Holiday. I know you're a good girl," he whispers in my ear as my body tenses. "Everyone here knows."

What does he mean, everyone?

"I could help you with that, you know. I'm good too. You hear me singing in church? I was praying for your tight little…" His hand drops to the curve of my hip.

"Thomas, please. Let me go." I shove him, thrusting my backside into his pelvis, but he's too wasted and *likes* it, groaning a twisted approval. Tears prick my eyes as he holds me there to wiggle himself against and I want to vomit when I feel the hardness.

I shift my weight onto my spotting foot and twist, trying to wrench free from his grip. I pray my strength and flexibility are enough to break out of his bulky hold, but his hands are like iron, his fingers digging painfully into my sides. A scream tears from my throat, drawing every eye in the field.

Eyes who don't help me. My heart pounds as I search the crowd. Who are all these people?

Where is Devyn?

I'm still fighting against Thomas as he wraps his other arm around my waist and feels for the hem of my dress, and just as I think I've become powerless, he's thrown to the ground. A loud thud is all I hear before five flesh hammering thwacks sound through the field.

The crowd closes in as Dustin Campbell pounds his fist against Thomas' face, an explanation following each punch.

"One," he says, lifting Thomas by the collar and shoving him against the barn, "is for Ava, who never smiles because of you."

Punch.

"Two," he growls, "is for Tiffany, who never laughs because of you." Fist meets flesh, and Thomas' lip bursts open, blood spattering Dustin's face like a painting.

I gasp, my heart beating so fast I'm unable to catch my breath. Talk. Move.

But *he* can move. And he does. Not just the punches and the punishing, either. He looks at my ruffled-up shirt and his eyes soften.

He nods once, licking Thomas' blood from his bottom lip before an instant shift in personality and a hard, fast, left hook to his jaw. "Three is for Sarah, who will never trust again."

"Your family signed an NDA!" He chokes on the blood streaming out his bottom lip and spits a tooth to the ground as he whines. "My father will put you behind fucking *bars*, Campbell!"

I draw in a sharp breath of air as I watch it unfold before me, but my best friend's brother isn't done yet.

Dustin could never say who, but one of the boys got away with what happened the night he saved those girls.

Not a single streak on his record, assault and rape were wiped entirely clean because this family had connections. Meanwhile, Dustin was sentenced to juvie for almost killing them in the girls' defense.

He traded his life for integrity.

He changed.

But he saved those girls.

I move my attention to Thomas, pinned against the wall as Dustin, the same boy who sent him into a coma less than two years ago, found him trying the very thing he said he'd kill him for if ever caught doing it again.

Dustin's voice booms through the field, echoing through the open expanse. "Four is for the months I spent locked up for righting your wrongs." He punches him in the gut, sending him doubling over and holding his stomach as he cries for mercy.

He receives none.

Certainly not in the green eyes I see before me. Ones that visit me in my dreams, in a softer, secretive way. In those eyes right now, there's only anger and sadness, and I feel for Dustin Campbell, in a way I never have before.

Does he see those girls the way he found them when he closes his eyes? Is that how he saw me just now? Why his eyes keep finding their way to mine throughout the fight?

He checks if I'm okay with a nod, even as he's the one covered in blood. I nod back.

I'm here for you like you're here for me.

The wind picks up, matching the energy in my soul, blowing around the field and whipping my long dark hair around me. A wild storm, precisely what this night has become. And just before he slams his fist one last time into the boy who almost took from me what he's stolen from three others before—Dustin's eyes flick to mine and settle in the very place I don't want them while he drives his fist against the bleeding pulp of my almost rapist.

Right between my legs.

So, I run, before I can feel or act or think any more on the reasons behind it. But not before I hear the words he speaks to my tormentor. And Sarah's and Tiffany's and Ava's before me.

The last ones Thomas will ever hear without aid.

"Five is for Shana. Try it again and you won't live to feel six."

Chapter Thirteen

SHANA

PRESENT DAY

Memories flood me, until all I can see, hear or think, is Dustin.

Dustin kissing me.

Dustin fighting for me.

Dustin *watching me.*

My stomach drops like a freefall, because I knew it.

Dustin Campbell *is* my watcher.

I race to the bathroom and slam the stall door behind me. The lock slides into place with an audible click, and finally, I can think straight. But the more I contemplate this new scenario, I come to terms with only one possible explanation.

Dustin and my secret creeper have always been the same person. Now *and* then.

It explains the flowers.

He knows where I live and could see me cry from his shop. It explains Dad recognizing him.

And it certainly explains how he was in the right place at the right time to crash my date. *To the actual ground.*

My heart soars further than I'm proud of.

I was having a panic attack back there with Lawrence, and Dustin saved me.

Because he was watching.

...is he always...watching?

It shouldn't make me want him more. Why would he push me away as himself, but draw me in as the watcher?

Dustin and Watcher.

I want them.

Even if they are the same person. I want each of them separately and both of them together, and I know that makes zero sense, but that's how screwed up I am.

My body hums with electricity, nipples tight against the dress as I slide the lock and emerge from the stall, making my exit and my plan.

Dustin won't let himself have me.

Will the watcher?

I slip out the back before anyone can follow. I assume so at least. If he's a decent stalker, he already knows where I'm headed.

I have a plan.

All it took was one date on Flinger to know what's not for me.

I've been using this app all wrong. It's time *I* started watching.

"Lem, it's me. I need your help."

Chapter Fourteen

DUSTIN

It's been three days since Shana has spoken a single word to me. Or the watcher.

And that should be exactly what I want. She's far away from me. I'm far away from her.

But she hasn't come in for her root-beer float, and I never anticipated how my chest would ache seeing her usual booth void.

Three days.

I've tried my hardest in those seventy-two hours not to watch her. Sure, I've gone to my tree, but the window's been closed. I followed her behind the train tracks on her walk home, but only because it was dark and she chooses the sketchiest paths to take.

She tempts me to follow.

Ironically, these last few days every rustling of a branch or the faintest snapping of a twig has me convinced someone is watching *me.*

My fingers stumble along my phone on their own it seems, checking notifications I know won't be there.

This isn't what I want. I don't *want* her to be far from me, and I certainly don't enjoy the idea of an eternity far from her. A future where I'm the old man, leaning on my rickety stool, telling the youth to take their shot at love while they still can, re-reading every text I've ever sent her like it's that damn paper Abel holds against his heart.

"Hey, Emily."

My twenty-two-year-old server skips toward me.

"What do you think it means if, say—for example of course—"

She snorts. "Okay, *for example*." She puts the word in air quotes, rolling her eyes as she leans against the counter, toying with her necklace.

"Never mind."

Emily lurches forward before I can go back to my office and pretend to reconcile register drawers.

"Nope, you don't get to never mind me. It's slow as shit tonight, and you've been sulking in your office since yesterday listening to awful nineties rock."

"Oh, come on, it's *Nickelback*. It's a classic."

Her nose scrunches, and it reminds me of Shana.

"Fine." I lean against the counter, lowering my voice so no one can hear me. "What if you went on a date and then your ex…well, not really your ex, because you never dated, but it *feels* like an ex, you know?"

Emily is staring like I'm a lunatic but fuck it. I think I *am*.

"Look, I'm crazy for this girl. Some asshole crossed the line with her the other night, and I…"

"You what?" Emily presses.

I take a deep breath. I have nobody to talk this over with. I can't tell Hunter because he *will* tell Devyn, and I love my sister, but she's more fragile than most people know. She and Hunter have too much going on right now to risk scaring her off.

Not like I can go to my father.

Emily's all I've got right now.

"We all do crazy things when we're in love," she says. "I mean, I wouldn't know, but I'm sure at some point everyone fights for their special someone."

"I didn't just fight him, Em. I fucked him up. He said degrading stuff about her dancing, snapped his fingers at her…it reminded me of…*shit,* I just lost it. I think his hand will heal one day." I rub my head; still not sure I believe that. "Not like he was a surgeon or anything, but I just—"

I look up to Emily's wide-eyed, jaw-dropped expression.

I'm just now letting it sink in, too.

I am crazy for Shana Holiday.

But I'm also just crazy.

Broken.

Easily and willingly ready to tear apart injustice when I see it before me. And I'm not a lick sorry for it.

"Um…" Emily pushes off the counter as she chews on the corner of her lip. She frowns, pointing a finger at me. "How did you know she was on this date exactly? Or that he was being shitty? Are you *spying*?"

No, I wish I could say.

"Yes."

"How long?" Her eyebrows narrow in judgement, but I'm beyond exhausted hiding.

I look out the window, yards away, and read the lettering across her studio, Holiday Dance. I trace it in my mind, like my tongue on her lips.

"Somewhere between flashlight tag and water balloon fights."

Hushed eye-contact across crowded classrooms.

Giggles over kitchen tables.

Not a lick of makeup on her face, and an oversized hoodie with frayed holes for sparkly blue thumbs.

"She stole my heart a long time ago."

"Oh my gosh, that's the most romantic thing I've ever heard. You love her!" She jumps to her feet and paces the floor. "Okay, so now you're worried she's mad?"

"Right." I kick my toe at the already scuffed tile.

Emily whips her phone out. "You're wrong. She loves you back."

"You can't possibly know that!"

"It's Shana, isn't it?"

"Does everyone know? Is it that obvious?"

"No." Emily laughs. "But I do see you every day of my life. You're my boss. It's my job to notice when you're broody, moody and extra snooty, and don't think Abby and I haven't noticed the bigger tip shares you give us on days Shana sits in that little corner spot and shimmies for you." She winks like we share a secret.

"She does not shimmy for me. I'd know if she was shimmying."

Emily bursts out laughing and walks to the back, plopping herself in my office chair and holding out her hand for me to sit opposite. She doesn't bother to check if I follow.

I do, reluctantly.

"Step into my office, friend." She spins around in my chair triumphantly, petting an imaginary cat.

Fuckin' Gen Z employees.

"Can we get this evil plan of yours over, so I can get back to my bad nineties rock?"

"Hey, you're the stalker. I'm just helping you clean up your mess." She snaps her fingers and points to the chair. "Tips are welcome, sass is not."

I throw my head back in defeat as she taps and swipes, sliding her phone across my desk.

"That's her, right? DancerBaby69?"

My body fights my will, thinking about Shana, and it's all I can do to keep my eyes away from the phone screen. I don't want to see the blue match number displayed in the top right corner.

To know how many men have slid their greasy fingers over her body on their screens, fantasizing about the real thing between their legs.

I slam my fist on the table and don't even register I've done it until Emily jumps, a yelp exiting her lips.

"I'm sorry." I jerk away and run my fingers through my hair. "Yes, it's Shana. Yes, it's *always* been Shana. And no, I don't want to know how many fuckers on that app are better for her than me, because I can tell you they all are."

"Is that really what you think about yourself?" Emily rounds the corner of the desk and sits at the edge of it. It's platonic. Supportive camaraderie that I'm not used to receiving. When you let feelings in, they take over until everything goes wrong. People get hurt when I feel things for them. But Emily has worked with me four years now. She knows me better than most, Sugar Stable being where I spend more time than my own home.

I nod.

That's all I can handle.

And she sighs, putting a hand on my shoulder. "You know, most of the people in this town, especially my generation, have grown up knowing of you as a hero. An upstanding citizen who makes cool shit for the local shops, upgrades park amenities, employs half the youth each summer…" She looks me in the eyes, and she doesn't mention the other stuff. The girls, Tiffany specifically, her older sister. But she says it all the same, the silent thanks I get from those who wish men like Thomas Remington didn't exist.

Who wonder why those same men are allowed to walk the streets after their sins are squeezed away by years on ankle bracelets, as if that prevents them from commit-ting future atrocities.

That's why there's people like me to fuck them up for what they're worth.

She pats my back, and I sigh into her embrace. I know she's right. I am those things. I do those things, but still, I *feel* unworthy inside.

"You should talk to her. If it were me—"

The door swings open.

"I have to talk to you."

Emily slides off my desk, and Shana's eyes dart to mine before she looks her up and down with a gaze so sharp I fear it might cut.

Hurt and anger radiate across the room.

"Never mind."

That's all she says before she storms off, keeping whatever she wanted to tell me inside, locking it up bedside my stolen heart.

The old me would have told myself that's fine. That whatever is meant to be, will be.

But that's bullshit, and we all know it. Whatever is meant to be is not what the fuck I want it to be. And very rarely does it become what I want without trying.

I want to try.

"Shana, wait! Shay!" I yell, scrambling after, but the door to the Sugar Stable slams shut behind her.

Chapter Fifteen

SHANA

I can't believe you've been hiding this from us!" Lemon falls onto my bed, floating blissfully on a cloud, a wide grin taking over her face as she scrolls through my messages from 'the watcher.' I roll my eyes at his façade.

Jeremy re-reads the note that came with the sugar plum flowers, which are half-crumpled in the corner window of my room. They do seem to be doing better since giving them water.

"*I'll be watching…*babes, this is creepy. How did your dad not think this was creepy?" He folds the note back up and sticks it in the plant, touching it as little as possible, as if it might be contaminated, or potential evidence.

I sigh at their antics and flop onto the bed, wrestling my phone back from Lemon.

She whines in protest, but she's read each message a hundred-million times now.

"It's not like they're changing as you read them."

It doesn't matter anyway.

99

"You know I'm right, don't you? The watcher *is* Dustin. And if that's the case, what was he doing with that teenage trollop the other day? I'm good enough to stalk but not stick?"

"That's rather slut-shamey of you. Emily goes to my church," Lemon assures me, starting a braid in my hair. "She's twenty-two, not a *teenager,* so don't go starting rumors you don't want following you. I say this from experience, you know."

I roll my eyes but forget she's looking in the mirror and it earns me a snug hair pull. "Ow, okay!"

Lemon smiles. "Good, because Emily told me Dustin's done nothing but sulk all week. He's worried you hate him for breaking that guy's hand. He was crying for advice over *you,* Shay. It's not what you thought you walked in on."

"Well, that's a relief."

"That they're not romantic?" Jeremy pokes his head out the closet.

"No." I shove off the bed. "That Lawrence's hand is broken *and* Dustin cried. Two birds with one stone and all."

I walk to the closet as she follows behind, hoping she can't see my face, because despite what I said, it *is* a relief that Dustin and Emily aren't romantic. It's the biggest weight off my shoulders since I saw her on his desk and instantly wanted to burn it to the ground for supplying a surface on which she could touch the man that should be mine.

I wipe my face on my sleeve as I round the corner and find Jeremy seated on the vanity stool in the center, six of my fanciest dresses fanned around him.

Lemon's eyes go wide, marveling at the rows of elegant gowns lined with beads and sequins. I've been collecting them for a while, most of them making substantial hits to my bank account the year I got my LLC and signed up for the Business Owners Elite. The membership alone gets you into the galas and networking events, so it's worth the yearly price tag. I met my web designer at the last one I attended, before Dad got worse.

I haven't been to one since.

"What do you have these for? I haven't seen you wear anything except that hoodie and a leotard my entire life."

"Not true. I switch it up to a puffy coat in the winter." I wink, making us all laugh.

Lemon nudges me. "Be serious for once, you know what we mean. These are fancy."

"You and Devyn had pageants." I wave my hand over the dresses dismissively. "I had networking galas and award stuff. No big deal."

"Time the fuck out." Lemon purses her lips. "What do you mean *award stuff*? Have you received awards we don't know about and been going to fancy ass galas and shit and not telling us, because I swear to God, Shana, I will take back my friendship bracelet before the Shaylyn Tryst concert. You will have a totally naked wrist and look friendless."

I don't tell people about this stuff, because it's not their job to worry about me. I need to get used to dealing with life alone. Soon, I will be.

Still, Lemon and Jeremy are the closest friends I've got next to Devyn and Dad.

I exhale an image of a funeral. One where I stand alone at a casket, draped in a beautiful blue gown, lined with jewels that sparkle so brightly you can't see the shine of my tears.

I'll be alone forever if I stay alone forever.

"Jeremy, this one's a Claudette Charbonneau!" Lemon gawks. Her squeals pierce my ears as she picks up another. "You have an Antionette Matisse, too? She's…not cheap."

"I wore them the year I opened Holiday Dance Company. I was named Business Elite's Top Startup when I filled so many classes I had to rent the empty studio beside mine before our first season even began." I twiddle my thumbs, their unhidden pride cradling me with confidence. "The black one is special. I wore it to accept the award for Most Profitable Small Business in the arts division a few years back."

Jeremy beams until I see stars in place of his pupils. "Um, Ring, Ring. Hello? I didn't even know about business awards. I call dibs on being plus one at the next one. Pretend I'm your boyfriend. I'm *insanely* good at acting straight." He loosens his belt to sag his jeans before sitting on the vanity and leaning back on one elbow, legs spread wide with a bored expression across his face. "See? So straight you could snort me." He winks, as Lemon and I double over in laughter.

"Sorry, Jer," I say, wiping laugh-tears from my eyes, "I don't actually go to those anymore, but I'm highly impressed with your heterosexual impersonation, nonetheless."

"Is it one of those, you only go if you win it that year, sort of galas?" Lemon asks, picking lint from the hem of the black gown.

"Nah, I mean, I usually do win it every year...for our region at least, but with Dad, the commitment—"

Lemon slams a finger to my lips. "You have been winning these things every year and skipping them? Not telling anyone?" She's furious, but I don't see why. It's better this way. There is so much going on all the time, and everyone is always dropping off casseroles or calling from church with donations, asking me if I'm 'hanging in there' with sorrowful eyes.

Don't they see I'm sparing them the drama?

I don't know what to say, so I just don't, and she sits back beside me and squeezes my hand.

Jeremy nods at the dresses. "Not to change the subject while we're dissecting years' worth of mental self-Stockholming, but...are you thinking what I'm thinking?" He winks at Lemon just as her lips twist in a smirk.

"Oh no," I say, decoding their silent message. "I am not wearing one of those on my date."

Lemon and Jeremy groan, throwing inaudible thesis statements at me and chasing me around the closet with different dresses they want me to try until I can't hear or think a single thing.

"Oh, come on, Shana! These dresses must be worth thousands. One gala a year can't be the only time you wear them!" Jeremy shoves a deep green dress over my head while Lemon has me cornered, hanger still attached, and I turn to face him.

"Of course that's the only time I wear them, are you kidding me? I'm a walking billboard for attention in those." I peel the green gown from my head and point out the all-black one that cuts off just above the knee. Rows of jewels zip up the front in swirling patterns, curling around the bust to accentuate the deep, plunging neckline. "I get a lot of looks when I wear stuff like this."

"Of course you *get a lot of looks*. My God, Shana you have no idea, do you?" Jeremy scrambles to his feet and turns to Lemon. "She has no idea, does she?"

"No, Jer, she does not."

"I have no idea *what?*" I all but scream.

"Baby-cakes, you are an absolute *ten.*"

"An eleven," Lemon corrects.

They crowd in on either side of me and force us toward the vanity until we're all staring back at the same face in the mirror: me.

"Do you want Dustin? Because after my full inspection of your messages, I agree, he is most definitely your watcher. And he wants you, Shana. For whatever reason, he's just scared."

I know the reason, I can't tell them.

"So, what am I supposed to do? Keep going on dates until he breaks every hand on Flinger until his is the only one left to text me?"

Lemon stops playing with my hair and meets my gaze in the mirror. "Yes."

"What? No, I didn't mean—"

"No, it's brilliant. The oldest trick in the book. We make him jealous." She slips her phone from her dress pocket and taps her fingers in a frenzy. "I have an actor friend who owes me a favor, and I think," her smile widens, "I have a plan."

"A set up?" Jeremy asks seriously.

Warmth floods me. My friends are in on this like it's their own destiny at hand, and I love them for it, but… jealousy? "Isn't that kind of childish?"

"Honey, he broke your date's hand."

Buzz.

Dev: Heard something happened at Cowboy's Paradise last night, but nobody will give me details. Let me know you're okay. Love you, Shay!

Guilt spikes in my gut.

I wish I could ask Devyn what she thinks, but that's never felt fair to Dustin. She doesn't even know we've kissed. How will she react when I explain I've loved no other man since I was thirteen and he taught me about tampons?

I've been lying the whole time.

Then there's Thomas and Dustin's second run in with the courts. He didn't want his sister to know about it. She was going through so much already when she was whisked away to the city, the year before we graduated.

She was broken back then. As was he.

His father only fought for custody of one kid, and it wasn't him. Then he ripped them away from each other.

I always assumed Dustin didn't want to come between Dev and me. But I think back to what he said in the studio, about how his dad could be.

Dustin has been protecting himself, too.

Lemon scrolls Flinger, silent for longer than I imagined she could even be, a determined glare on her face as she types a message to someone just minutes before I get a ping on my own phone.

"That should be him!" She paws for it, but I swat her away, opening the notification to the prettiest man I've ever seen in my whole life on the screen before me. *Haans.*

"That's his whole name? Just Haans? No last name? No number?" I scratch my head, not even sure how that happens. There must be a billion Haans' in the world. "How long ago did he make a Flinger account that he's got his own first name as a screen name? Is he like fifty?" I narrow my eyes. "Do you have a sugar daddy, Lem?"

"Several." She snatches my phone while Jeremy rolls his eyes. "But Haans is not one of them. He's an actor I met on this photo shoot in—"

"Wait, you were an actor? I thought you were a bartender before you became a nursing assistant."

"Lemon is a chameleon." Jeremy shrugs before he goes back to my closet for shoes to match the black gown.

The. Black. Gown. I doubletake.

"I'm not wearing that to meet Haans, am I?"

"Yep." Lemon smiles, pleased with that fact. "Now, Haans is a pro at this sort of charade. He does side-work for reality television. Just be natural."

I nod. It seems simple enough. I go on a fake date with Haans, and…wait.

"What's the rest of the plan? We get Dustin jealous and worked up until he Hulks out? That could be problematic. Haans probably wants to keep both his hands." I look back at his profile picture. "I think I've seen him on that Blind Lover show."

"I know, right?" Lemon gushes. "Anyway, it's quite simple. We've confirmed Dustin is stalking you. So, he'll show up to watch you on your date, that much we can count on. Jeremy and I will be hiding in the parking lot, so we know when he shows up. And what your broody little watcher doesn't know, is that through this fancy little dash cam I stole from my father's driver, *you* will be watching *him.*"

"And then…"

"Then we play." She smiles a devilish grin as she links her pinky with mine. "Trust me, Shay. It will work. Dustin doesn't seem the type who likes sharing his toys. He just needs to be mad enough to admit it."

"Ew!" I yank my pinky away and swat her shoulder. "Too much. I'm still an innocent, remember?" We meet eyes and she gives me a look that settles it.

"What's it gonna be? Hoodie or Hottie?"

"I'll do it," I decide.

"I can't wait to torture him." Lemon beams. Maybe that should be examined psychiatrically, but I let her hold my hand instead. "By the time the night is through, Dustin Campbell—*the watcher*—will have all eyes and thoughts on you, Shay."

Snug in my black dress, with my friends already off to stake out the parking lot, I finally have a moment to myself.

Dad's been sleeping lately, but as I look at my reflection and take in the dress my friends have pasted to my body as bait, I wish he were present. It all feels very *Much Ado About Nothing,* tricking Dustin into admitting his feelings over another man vying for my affections. And even though Dad isn't awake to recite it, I hear Shakespeare loud and clear, *"Of this matter, is Cupid's crafty arrow made."*

I curtsy to the mirror, proud of identifying the play without Dad's help. Maybe I'm a bit like him after all. Maybe I won't lose him, not wholly. Not when moments of his spirit are fractured through my days.

My eyes flick to my laptop screen, *six-oh-three.* I adjust my breasts, stunningly below-average, A-and-a-halfs, and wrinkle my nose at the girl before me.

The one who's going for it, for once.

"Time to *tame this wild heart into my loving hands,* even if he has *been a dick.* Get it? *Benedict?"*

I laugh into the silence as my eyes meet my own, because that's how it will be soon.

Just Shana Holiday, the last of her kind.

I'll miss you, Dad.

Chapter Sixteen

SHANA

The fox has left the den!" Lemon's voice sings from my Bluetooth.

"You don't have to use codewords," I snort. "You're not on a multi frequency radio, Lem."

"Well, what's got her panties in a twist?" Jeremy's voice filters in from the background. I can almost see the pouty look on his face from the tone.

"I don't *have* any panties," I whisper into the phone. "You wouldn't let me wear any with this dress." Or the last dress they put me in, for that matter, and I'm trying extremely hard not to think about the leather of the barstool flush with my lady parts no matter how much I reposition. *Ew.*

This outfit was meant for standing and mingling, not table-sitting.

"My nether bits are sticking to the chair!" I whine, about ninety-two percent ready to forget this whole ordeal and live out the rest of my days with a brooding, hulking, friend-with-no-benefits who breaks every hand between me and eternity.

"Oh, hush. You're being as dramatic as Jeremy," Lemon chastises. "Haans texted me. He's on his way in. Maybe we can see Dustin's reaction if we pull closer, but—oh, my God! He's getting out of his car, Shana. I repeat," she yells into the phone, panic lifting her to a high-pitched squeal. "The Fox is on the hunt! I thought we'd have more time to tease him than this," she hisses, but the sound becomes distorted until it's completely cut.

"You still there?" I shout, forgetting I'm in public. The bartender turns my way, arching his eyebrow. "Sorry! I'm fine."

"You are, aren't you?" His eyes tangle with mine.

It makes me nervous to have someone looking this way. Eyes feel invasive, scrutinizing. Unrehearsed feels unclothed, and I feel the need to perform.

But the look in this bartender's eyes is an attraction.

I imagine the only other set of eyes I've caught looking at me in this manner and shiver.

The corner of his mouth tilts in the barest hint of a smile, and Jeremy's right, it feels good to be seen the way you feel inside.

A throat clears behind me, like clockwork. Attention from a male that isn't him and he's practically summoned. It would be laughable if it hadn't come to this one too many times before.

"Dustin." I swivel to face him. "As you seem to be aware, I have a date. And while we're on the topic, I'd like him to keep both hands if I'm to make proper use them later."

I say the last part aiming to cut, more surprised than anyone that it came from my own mouth.

He visibly winces, his hand clenching by his side. I drop my gaze to his fist, knuckles so white he's likely digging fingernail slits into his palm, and I suddenly hate myself for toying with his emotions. "You should leave."

I spin back toward the bar and away from him, my heart pounding so hard in my chest it might rip my dress in two, but that's crazy, right?

Dustin ripping my dress in two?

Shit. No, no no no no no.

"I want to talk about the other night." He slides into the seat beside me and tugs at his hair. "Shay, when I see you with someone else, I just…"

"You sabotage it?" I say it like it's a question, but we both know otherwise.

"I didn't mean to do that. If you'll give me a chance, I'll—"

"You'll what, Dustin? You'll still push me away as if we've never been an option, but what? *Not* break my date's hand next time?"

He grimaces but takes it.

My words, his actions, after all.

"You deserve better than assholes who degrade your profession, Shana. He snapped his fingers at you for fuck's sake." He shakes his head. "But you also deserve better than me."

He reaches to brush a strand of hair from my eyes, but…*fuck him.*

I want it there.

It's mine to hide behind. He doesn't get to cut a knife through my flesh and watch me bleed on his terms.

I belong to nobody but me. I make the decisions of who I want to love. And even if it feels like ten hours of pointe work on blistering, bruised up toes, I will love him every damn time.

But I'm tired of waiting. This time, he comes to me.

This time, he fights because he wants *me*, not because he doesn't want anyone else to have a chance.

"You still don't get it, do you?" I laugh, but it's hardly jovial. It's a soft, defeated breath, hanging at the end of my sentence like a ghost, too dead for this world but unable to cross over for the baggage it won't let go of.

I look at him, this man whose eyes have been pained for as long as I can remember, deep, dark, green orbs that match my best friend's, eyes I trust in my memories, and in my heart. The face around them has changed over the years, grown into somewhat of a masterpiece, but I'd be willing to bet the stars and all their constellations that God designed this particular face especially for me.

I run my hand down the side of his jaw, and it flexes beneath my touch before relaxing into it.

I tell myself I don't like it.

That I don't love the feel of him baring the weight of his body on mine, even if it's not pressed between my thighs or sliding across my lips.

I pull back almost immediately, our connection suddenly raw and electric.

But he's still not ready. Not yet.

"You say we can't be together, but you call me your *moon.*" I lick my lips, my pulse racing as I find the words to reach him. "Well, if I'm the moon, you're the stars."

His eyes light, but I'm not done yet. This isn't a happily ever after, and if he keeps pushing the possibility of us away, there won't ever be one.

Not for me. *Not without him.*

"You're all around me, Dustin Campbell. My whole life, this vast expanse of darkness just beyond my reach. But it's heartbreaking being the moon."

His eyes water. Nostrils flare, but he says nothing.

Absolutely nothing.

Just stares at me with those pathetic, sad eyes. Ones that beg to love me but refuse to see clearly.

"Do you know *why*, Dustin? Why it's heartbreaking being the moon?" I grind each word so sharp it could etch his skin.

"Why?"

"Because the moon can never touch the stars. It will watch them burn, tantalizing flecks of flame dancing around in its path for all eternity, but it will never share their light. It will remain on its own forever, surrounded by glowing reminders of sparks that never died out."

"Shay. Look, I—" Dustin reaches for my hand, but I yank it back, drawing every cell in my body that harbors even the tiniest shimmer of confidence to gather in my feet as I stand.

"No, you look." I point to the tall, chiseled dutchman walking through the door, arching an eyebrow in challenge, my last cork in the cogwheel before I go. "I have a date. And whether you like it or not, Dustin Campbell, if you break any of his bones tonight, I will never speak to you again. Love me or *leave me*."

Despite my body's protests, I walk away from the only man I've ever loved. The smell of hot fudge and waffle cones permeating my senses as I call myself a liar the entire way to the dining area.

We both know good and well I'll speak to him again.

Especially if he breaks bones for me.

Chapter Seventeen

SHANA

THIRTEEN YEARS AGO

"What are you doing here?" Dustin paces the corner of the courthouse, next to the prep-room. I slipped from it when I saw his head through the slit-glass window. "I told you not to come."

"I had a summons."

He growls, digging his hands through his hair and fisting it at the roots. I worry it might split his scalp. I grab his arm before I know what I'm doing and bring it back to his side, holding his hand in mine.

It feels like it was made to fit there.

"You know we can't…" He holds up our joined hands, gently prying my fingers free. "We can't do this."

I shake my head. "I'm so tired of this, Dustin. It's *bullshit!*"

I rarely curse, but to hell with it all! I will curse from the mountain tops if he'll finally hear me.

"You saved me." I meet his widened eyes, tears welling in my own, and I catch the way his brow furrows. I couldn't miss it.

Why won't you let yourself love me?

Thomas' aunt and cousins stride past us, glowering. The youngest Remington child stares the longest. His eyes are the same pale blue I watched turn black beneath the fists of the man I love.

I slam my eyes closed and turn into his arms before I can stop myself. "Dustin, I thought he would…that I'd be—" My voice cracks as the tears fall over my vision, down my cheeks, across my skin like fingers, digging my flesh, lifting my skirt, the fear surging through me as Thomas' hands slid down my front and almost took from me what I've been saving for the very man in front of me.

I break like a dam, tears flowing faster than ever before.

"Fuck, Shay." He scoops me in his arms until we're sitting by the large, stained windows, hearts and daggers, ironically painted over broken glass. "I will never let anyone hurt you. Do you hear me? I will fight them all to keep you smiling. But I don't want you here for this. Being around that fucker has you in tears. You shouldn't have to see his face."

"I'm the only witness who was named, Dustin. That's why your lawyer called my dad, and why he agreed to let me be here in the first place. I'm your only option unless you want to be locked up for another six months, or worse, tried as an adult, because they *can* do that, Dustin. You know that? I ingested like six books on it this week alone. I'm not letting them do that to you."

I wipe my face on the back of my sleeves and sit up, scooting a few inches away when the opposing counsel walks in and sees us cozy. I want no reason for them to see a conflict of interest with me as witness, I watch far too much *Law and Order* to be duped by a technicality like that. I shouldn't even be talking to Dustin at all. He should be in his prep room, and I should be in mine.

"I'm a fuckup, Shay." Dustin raises his head to look at me, arms resting atop his knees.

"You're not."

"Yes, Shana I am. My dad thinks it, the judge thinks it. Even my own mother's stopped fighting for me, drinking anything and everything so she can't hear the things her friends at the club whisper about her once *prized* champion of a son. I'm not on the rodeo team anymore. I have no plans for college. I'm not even sure any of them would take me with my record. Hell, half the entry level internships for architectural assistants won't even consider me with the stain on my application. Do you want that life, Shana? Do you want a fuckup who can't control his anger and makes milkshakes for the rest of his life?"

Tears shine in his eyes, and I think he might cry. I wouldn't blame him if he did. The most brilliant creatures on earth can't escape emotion.

"Did you know an octopus can remember individual faces? And how they felt with each person?" I ask him, my body humming with something I can't place.

Encouragement, maybe.

Hope.

Salvation.

"When my mom died…" I fiddle with my cuticles. "When she passed, I spent every second I wasn't dancing at the aquarium."

A crinkle forms between his eyes as he listens to my story, and I settle back into the bench, closing mine as I picture her. Beautiful black hair, waves and waves of it, just like mine. It flowed down her back and shined in the light. I used to hold it to soothe my tears.

What would she say if she were here today?

She'd take one look at this boy, fighting my monsters and banishing my demons…*fighting for my honor.*

And she would thank him. She would wrap him up and rock him in her arms, praising everything he stood for.

Because he stands for everything *I* stand for, if only he could see.

I see you, a secret note once said. *I see the way you dance through tears.*

"She loved the octopus tank. If you don't remember, she was a volunteer. She'd take me there as a child. Dev came a few times, and the other kids whose moms worked there, my friend Lucy and her brother—I can't remember his name—but we had so much fun exploring that place. We'd sneak into the break room and use the sugar packets to build little houses for the hermit crabs, go to the cephalopod tanks and watch them swim around. Got to hold them a few times, too. They feel different than you'd imagine. Tentacles are *strong.*"

I smile, explaining the time one of them swiped mom's ring from her finger. I laughed and laughed, following him around the glass walls as he swam it to his garden at the very bottom. "The staff had a good laugh about it too, after they swam in for the retrieval that is."

Dustin's mouth tilts, and that fills me with purpose. I want to soothe his pain, to slay his dragons right back, even if they are only in his mind.

"Humans aren't the only animals to feel anger and hopelessness, you know. Truman the octopus—"

"Wait, *Truman?* Really?" He forces back a smile.

"Yes, Truman! What else would you call him?"

"I don't know, *Squidward*, or something."

"*Squidward* is a squid," I deadpan, holding his gaze in an unspoken staring contest. His eyes narrow. He wants me to laugh first, but I won't.

I will hold onto this moment where only he and I exist, debating reasonable invertebrate names forever, if it means I'll see his eyes this way.

Smiling.

But he knows how to bend me. Dustin flicks his tongue between his lips and drags it across the bottom until it snags on his piercing. He sucks it in and lets it pop free from his teeth with a tug I feel on every inch of my body, and he can tell. His eyes flare a dark, envious green that I want to brand over my skin.

"Okay, you win!" I sputter, laughter finally falling out of me.

He laughs too, the first one I've heard from him since he found those girls in the woods.

"Truman the octopus didn't like one of his handlers. He formed a bit of a grudge against her. He'd ink her path whenever she entered his space. Then one day, she left for college and didn't return for a long time. His inking miraculously stopped." I wiggle my eyebrows, loving this part of the story just like I did as a child. "But, when she came back, all it took was one step back into his tank and Truman blasted her with an ink stream, like she'd never left. He remembered her. And how he felt. His emotions took over and his grudge was unleashed. *Splat!*"

"Thanks for making me laugh." Dustin takes my hand and squeezes it. "I should have just punched him once."

"But then we wouldn't have known you can count to five." I point out, tongue in cheek.

"Ha-ha." He tugs my hair. "You know what I mean. I could have taken you away and he'd be fine. We wouldn't be in this courthouse waiting for—"

"Aren't you listening? I don't *care* if you ink up my waters, Dustin. I'll swim in the darkness for the rest of my life it means we're together." I lean in, and I press a soft kiss to his cheek. "You are a hero, no matter what it says on paper. No matter who got messed up because of it. Don't let this cloud you. You are strength and you are hope. And if I'm your moon, you're my octopus."

PRESENT DAY

Haans has a Dutch accent. He has appeared in three seasons of Blinded by Love, RealTea's hottest 'authentic' dating show. Apparently, those *authentic* people are all paid

120

actors and it's heavily scripted.

I must say, even for a fake date, this conversation is worlds more interesting than my last date with the letchy lawyer. But I still find myself wishing I were surrounded by waffle cones, coffee pots, and the brooding set of dark green eyes that haven't stopped looking this way since Haans fit his hand around mine.

What are you gonna do about it?

My breath catches in my chest at that thought. It feels wrong, this taunting. I want him to want me for the sheer fact that he does, not by manipulation.

"I can't do this," I tell Haans.

I don't want to make him jealous or angry.

"I love him. Even when I wish I didn't." Even as I'm practically begging him to love me back. "What is wrong with me?"

He drags our hands under the table and winks with a head nod toward my watcher. "People only see what they think. You don't want to make him jealous? I like that about you."

I cock my head to the side. "You do?"

"It takes courage. I think you should ditch Lemon's plan and just tell him."

"Said by the actor who already got paid."

He winks, and we both laugh. It's affectionless, *platonic*, but it's the cherry on top for my stalker.

And just like with his previous messages, my heart does a timestep for his ping.

Watcher: What is your hand doing under the table?

His blatant jealousy and brooding possession fires something up inside me. I wish I could say it was feminism, instead it's a flirty, wanton, lust-filled Shana that wishes he'd stalk his way over here and do all the things from my dreams.

That's the Shana that replies to his ping.

DancerBaby69: You like to watch.

DancerBaby69: Dustin.

My cheeks heat, I feel the tingle spreading across my face as it glows with pride. I didn't know I could be that forward, but there's a whole new tenacity, clawing its way free with each text.

Ping.

Watcher: You know very well I don't want to watch this.

"Ask if he wants to do more than watch," Haans suggests. My mouth drops at the dirtiness of that, but it *is* what I want, and Haans is right. The whole point of this is to tempt Dustin to stop hiding behind his phone.

I clink my ice around in my water cup, forcing my gaze forward, despite my instincts. I want to turn. To check Dustin's face and read the lines etched across it, scripts to reveal how he feels since he only seems to communicate in secret text and purple prose.

And it works.

Haans' eyes widen as Dustin strides across the restaurant, his boots thudding against the tile floors.

"You should probably run." I wince, but Dustin just stops beside the table, nodding politely.

Not breaking his hands.

I release a relieved breath into the space between the two men.

"Can we talk, Shay?"

Haans stands and nods. "Good luck, Licht."

"Licht?" I ask him, but he just winks.

"Don't forget how bright you shine, even in total darkness." He makes it out the door just before the familiar Nautica permeates my senses.

Dustin watches Haans leave the bar, cursing beneath his breath.

I roll my eyes. Doesn't this emotional oaf know who I love by now? He's incredulous.

I don't have to see the wild storm in Dustin's eyes to know it's there. I feel every spark of his energy charge my soul like a circuit, and my hand curls around my phone as I smirk down at the ping that brought him standing here.

DancerBaby69: Then touch me.

Chapter Eighteen

DUSTIN

She's a magnetic force beyond my control, and we connect faster than her date can leave the restaurant. I slam my lips against hers, in a bruising pull of my passion against her own, and we fuse together.

Touch me, she commanded, and like a knight before my queen, here I am, kneeling at her call. She fits with me, a piece of my puzzle, every curve of her body clicking into place. My fingers thread through her hair, deepening our kiss, and it's only passion moving me now, my sole mission to memorize her feel and taste and touch.

And maybe it is.

Maybe we only have one job in this life, and it's to find the person who drives us to the darkest places of our minds, dangling feet over edges of what-ifs, long enough to make it brighter.

"I can't just watch anymore, Shay."

"Then don't."

I lift her at once; tight, powerful thighs wrapping around me seamlessly.

"Why me?" I ask, as her fingers rake my hair. "You're fucking perfect, Shana."

"I'm not," she starts, but I stop it with my lips on hers. "You are."

Our eyes swirl together with we breathe.

Think.

Plan our next words, perhaps, both of us aiming to win an age-old argument neither of us ever wanted to start.

"You could have your pick of anyone less fucked up. So, why me?"

My hands tighten around her thighs, holding her up, because I don't know what else to do with them. My heart tells me to run them back over her body until she's liquid in my arms, and I've filled her with so much of me she couldn't think of another man as long as she lives.

There'd be no room left.

But my brain battles with the concept, my father's voice replacing my thoughts, lacing them with doubt. I loosen my grip, and she slides down my body until her feet touch the ground. "I–I'm fucked up, Shana. You don't want this. You don't want what's in *here*." I point to my head.

We sit in silence, beat after beat, my finger pressed against my skull as sweat beads my brow.

The paddle fans blow above, and our hair tangles together with the wind, the universe demanding we entwine. It commands me, as if it's on her side.

"I already know what's in there," she whispers, prying my hand away from my head and placing it back in hers.

"You are *not* fucked up, Dustin."

We sit at a table I made to match the color of her eyes, whether she knows it or not, and those same tiger-striped irises flare now, a period at the end of her sentence.

"You are not fucked up," she repeats. "Do you hear me?" She kisses me, her voice softening when I release a nervous breath. "Of *course* I want you. Besides, dating is impossible for me if you haven't noticed. If they aren't boring me to tears, you're breaking their hands."

"It was only a few fractures." I grin.

I nudge her shoulder, and it's like no time has passed since childhood. I'm just a boy with no clue how to talk to the pretty friend at the dinner table, the one who became a permanent part of our home for the rest of my life.

She still feels like home to me.

Her smile masks the earlier doubt from my mind, replacing it with memories of camping and sparklers, of jumping over stones in narrow creeks.

"Not to mention," I whisper, "I'll bet none of your other dates know an ultra large tampon holds eighteen grams."

She twists her lips. "Well, I'm glad you're finally starting see your worth. That's what this entire night was about, you know?"

"Tampons?"

She swats my shoulder, and we both grin before her eyes drop. "I'm ashamed to say I let Lemon talk me into making you jealous."

"What? You?" I roll my eyes. "That's not news. It was comically obvious." I play with the dark hair falling over her shoulders.

"I know," she says. "But provoking you was wrong. I didn't need you to tell me you were the boy beneath the window." Her eyes burn a fire into mine. "I've always known it was you, I just wanted you to admit this thing between us exists. That it always has and never wont."

"It never won't," I say. "But you didn't need a fake date to know I want you, Shay."

"Want isn't the same as need, Dustin. You say you want me, but I *need* you. With every part of me."

"Shay—"

"No. Just let me…" She exhales, lifting her chin. "I wanted to know that you need me like I do. *Your words are mere words, no matter from the heart.*" She swallows, wiping away a single tear as she steadies her breathing. "Shakespeare wrote that." She wrings her hands together.

I grab them, holding them in mine.

"So, what will it be? Do you want me in words or in actions, Dustin Campbell?" She nods at our hands on the table.

It takes not a moment longer for the grin to slide across my face when I place our joined hands over my heart.

"As I've said before, you're *you*, Shana Holiday."

Her breath hitches and her brows pull in. I know what she thinks. That I'll say what I've said before to push her away, but I can't watch from the darkness anymore.

Not when it feels this good in her light.

"You're *you*…and I don't just want you…I *need* you. Your words, your thoughts, your mind…and this—" I kiss her. "Just how you are.'

Tears fill her eyes. "You mean that?"

"I do."

"Good." She smiles. "Because I don't have much taste for rich lawyers *or* handsome actors it turns out."

"Handsome?" I narrow my eyes.

I can hardly wipe the shit-eating grin off my face when I think about the lengths this woman went to get me here, acknowledging what we've always been.

On the other hand, she's made herself a target for strangers on the internet, even if it was someone Lemon may know, Shana's got a public profile, and she has no idea she's a walking wet dream to any asshole with eyes.

As we sit here now, her friends are staked out in Lemon's unmistakable bright yellow sports car in an amusing attempt to spy.

As if I didn't see them.

But not all spies are amateurs.

There are corners of the internet she has no idea exist.

And I've seen it, locked up right alongside those sick fucks. I know how they prey on their next victim…burner phones smuggled into the cells and internet tokens provided by enabling family. I've heard them bragging about the deranged shit they'll do to their next victim when their sentencing is through. The most fucked up part is they already have one picked out. They just wait, watching them from a screen until it's time, bragging to the others of fantasies that made me want to stab my ears out.

And Flinger? It's a buffet for their perversion.

I look at the flawless woman across from me, someone so pure I fear she couldn't see the darkness in the devil himself, and I know it's crossing every line imaginable, but none of that matters if she becomes a target.

Obsessive compulsive, Dr. Robins will say, *trauma-based fear.* They can call it whatever the fuck they want, but I followed my gut to the quarry that day, to the field-party years later, and it's my gut that leads me now as I shoot a quick message to my buddy, the agent during my sentencing who uncovered the truth Thomas' family tried to burry. When they tried to point fingers at *me* for the shit they'd done. And likely the only reason I cleared my name.

I attach the image of Haans with the words, *background check.* It shouldn't have to be this way, but women are not safe. Not anywhere.

Screams, crying, fingernails caked with mud.

"Are you okay?" Shana comes to my side of the table and sits on my lap, wrapping her arms around my neck.

"I am now."

"Yeah, okay," she rolls her eyes, "now that there's a half-naked woman in your lap." She tugs at the hem of her too-short dress, and I try not to laugh. She could have been in a potato sack, and she'd still have my dick hard as fuck.

"I meant, I'm okay because somehow you still want me. Even after…you know, *who I am.*"

"You really are thick headed, you know that?" She smiles, shaking her head. "I've wanted you since sand caked the bottom of my jelly shoes. Since my feet turned in and my crowns were made of plastic. Since I watched you shove a kid to the ground for peeking up your little sister's skirt…*and her best friend's.*" She cuts her eyes to mine. "I don't just want you, Dustin Campbell, I *have* you. In my corner, and in here." She takes my hand and presses it over her heart this time, and it beats beneath my flesh, steady and strong, just like her. "The real question is, will you have me back?"

She looks at me like nobody else in the world exists.

Like she'd be okay if that were true.

I bite my lip ring and watch her eyes fall to the motion. "If I *have* you, Shana," my lips curve, "you're mine. I take care of what's mine."

She blushes beneath my stare.

"Do you know what I mean by that?" I stroke my thumb over her lips, loving the softest fucking whimper that falls from them when I do.

"You'll protect me?"

I move my fingers lower, brushing them over her chest, down to the pebbling nipples pressed tightly against the fabric of her dress.

"I'll protect you." I nod, circling the tight buds with my fingertips.

She moans, but she doesn't move, challenging me to scare her away.

But she must know she's tangling with crazy. I can't be what I'm not. I'll always carry their screams. I'll forever be paranoid for the safety of the ones I love.

Of her.

"I'll watch you. I'll become obsessed."

She draws in a sharp breath as I lean into her ear. "When you walk home. When you wake up and sit by the window sipping your Gatorade because you can't stand coffee or tea…" She gasps, her pupils round as saucers. "I'll especially watch you from that bathroom window when you let your hair down at night…when you drop your robe." I nip at her ear, but she doesn't shy away… my sweet little seductress leans in. "You can't want this, Shay. You can't love crazy."

"Yet, somehow I do." She lifts her chin. "You say you'll protect me, but you already have, many times. You say you'll watch me, but I've seen the way the bushes rustle late at night. *I've always known it was you.*"

Now it's my eyes that go wide.

"Did you think I didn't see you out my windows all these years? First home, then work. You're already obsessed with me, Dustin Campbell…*Watcher.*" She sucks my bottom lip into her mouth, but a few celebratory hollers from random patrons remind us where we are.

In public.

"Oh my gosh!" Shana giggles and pull away. "Your sister could be here, and we wouldn't even know it. We have to be more careful until we figure out what we're going to tell her." She scrunches her nose. "What *are* we going to tell her?"

"That you're *mine.*" My tongue darts out over my lip, like it always has when she's around, sentient as fuck and completely insatiable for Shana Holiday.

Is it wrong to love the flush of her cheeks, and the way her dress tightens around her pointed nipples when I call her my girl?

"I'm going to need Jesus around you," she breathes. "You are sinfully inappropriate just by existing."

"Is this what you find inappropriate?" I flick my piercing with my tongue, and she studies it like a long-awaited relic she's finally dug up.

"I've been imagining what this little jewel would feel like on my lips for a long time."

"And?" I chuckle. "Did it meet your expectations?"

"I don't know." Her eyes sparkle. "I was imagining it pressed against my *other* lips."

And I'll be damned, but we're both gonna need Jesus tonight, because I'll be on my knees with my head bowed, but it sure as fuck won't be in prayer.

Chapter Nineteen

SHANA

My back hits his living room wall, hard and fast, but I don't even care. My body has never been my own. It belongs to the forces around me. The ones that make me move.

And he does it.

Dustin Campbell has always made my body free to feel and explore, to bend in ways both wanton and sinful. Ways that felt wrong with anyone but him.

Even in my mind.

I'd be lying if I said it isn't why I dance for him each night, his eyes glued to my body. He couldn't remove them if he wanted.

It isn't a choice, but a summoning, and I command it with a flick of my hips he's never ignored.

"I like when you watch me," I say, just before his lips crash back over mine, needy and forceful, painful and unforgiving. Just how I feel about him.

His tongue twists around mine, and he guides me down the hallway, stopping to feast on my neck and nipples he's freed from the one-thousand-dollar gown hanging around my waist. He sucks one into his mouth as he manipulates the other, twisting it and making it his own personal fidget, and I've felt nothing like it in all my days. Touching myself isn't like this.

My clit comes to life under his control.

"Oh *God*," I gasp, "I feel that in my—*ohhh!* Don't stop!"

He hums, with my nipple hanging from his teeth, the vibrations bouncing across my chest and drawing prickles over my skin. I try to cover my blushing top half, but he grips my wrists and pins them to the wall, leaving me gasping as I drip between my thighs at the rough and intentional impact, the way his eyes darken as he tastes my skin.

I want more of it.

His kisses brush my neck, tracing a slow, deliberate line across my throat, and my greediest parts lurch forward all on their own, pressing against him tightly as possible.

Grinding against Dustin Campbell.

It's all I can think, the rabid beast within me taking over and stamping the caution all the way out.

"Fuck me!" I beg him, cursing with actual curse words, because I have no idea who I am anymore. *Sheltered Shana* is gone. She doesn't exist in the presence of the man she loves.

"*Teach me.* I need—" I press into him again, my body pulsing, all the feelings one can bear, gathering between my legs, and I think I might die if I don't feel his bare skin against that spot right now. "I need—"

"Shh." He kisses me, swiping away the worry with a flick of his tongue across my lips, and he lowers to his knees, sliding my dress up my thighs, inch by painfully slow inch.

The crisp air assaults my slick center, before it's replaced by warmth. Hot, sticky, liquid fire, steaming me, until my legs are wrapped around his head, violently riding his face like the bull at Cowboy's Paradise. I always *have* been the strongest one of my friends at those, the one who could last the longest.

Gosh, that sounds dirty.

It *is* dirty.

I should be mortified, but I can't deny the sensations any more than I can the music when I dance.

Under the privacy of my sheets, in the secrecy of night, I've played out this very act with this very man, time and time again, but it hardly compares to the pleasure I feel now.

I clench my thighs around his head, shifting until I'm wrapped, hoisted on his shoulders. He slurps and sucks, sending pulses of pleasure throughout me, and I can barely keep it together as he licks my slit from the bottom up and slides his tongue across the spot between my lady parts and my…

"Oh my God, Dustin! That's my…my bottom!"

"I fucking know," he growls in pleasure. He sounds like he's eating his favorite freaking ice cream, swirling his tongue over my puckered hole, his grip tightening to an almost bruising hold around my waist as I wiggle.

I shiver when his eyes dart upward to mine with a devilish wink just before he buries his face back in my center and uses a combination of his beard and piercing on my clit until I'm bucking wildly against his head. "Dustin, please!"

His tongue slides inside. "Hold still, baby. Wanna taste every part of you."

"Oh my God, Oh my God, Oh my God!"

He hums against my most sensitive parts, as I clench around him tighter than seems safe. I ease back, but he growls, tugging me closer and lapping up my…*my arousal*…like a starved animal.

"Fucking miiiine," he rasps, right at the peak of my build up, sending me over the edge until my body quakes, and I'm left a panting mess wrapped around him.

He releases his hold, as we catch our breath, and I slink to his arms as we both lower to the floor.

"I-I didn't know it could be like that."

He cradles me, my mind reeling as I scan his shit-eating grin for signs this is all in my mind.

"Like what?" He smirks.

It's all Dustin.

Not a dream. Not a fantasy.

And he looks like he wants me to share my feelings.

An even crazier revelation?

I want to.

"I've touched myself," I try again, "but—" shame clouds my thoughts.

It's *dirty* and *weird*.

A virgin with kinky fantasies.

I shake my head, blowing out a breath as I meet his emerald eyes. They remind me of the earth we share, the natural forces holding us both to the ground.

Memories and time and…

Love.

They soften, a silent assurance I'm safe in his company.

I believe it, too. I've always been safe from judgement with Dustin, and he reminds me of that with a brotherly charm that feels nostalgic, even if it is taboo.

"There's nothing wrong with touching yourself, Shay," he whispers into my ear. "Was this how you did it?" He drags a finger through my wetness until I cry out, the shame I felt only moments ago, gone with one touch to my swollen clit. "Tell me."

"I'd pretend you were there." I gasp, my dirtiest secret tumbling free.

"Maybe I was."

I'm aware it's a red flag, him stalking me for pretty much all my life, but *if music be the food of love, play on!* I can't find it in me to run from the man who acts on the passion of his heart after years of hiding it so tightly beneath his sleeve.

"I always hoped you were," I say.

He smirks when my center grows slicker with my admission, and he slides his finger inside of me. "Does it make you wet that I watch you, pretty girl? Follow you."

My nerve endings pulse urgently, the praise of calling me *pretty* and the absolute taboo of the other things he says rubbing together like friction within me, and I'm desperate to feel the release he gave me before.

The darkness surrounding our secret, his watching and my…*letting.* It's lascivious.

Twisted.

Depraved.

And my body weeps for it.

"My dirty girl likes it when I know where she is, don't you, baby? How and when you *come*." He licks my bottom lip. "What these pretty pink lips look like while you touch yourself. *So fucking perfect.*"

Oh God! I feel like I'll implode with pressure as his fingers mix with words. "Yes!"

"Good girl," he praises. "Kinky virgins are my favorite kind." He teases me with the very labels I hate about myself, but I don't feel shame when he says them.

He seems to know that, too, smirking at the pool of arousal in his hand. He pumps two fingers in this time, and I clench around him as he groans in approval.

"So fucking tight, Shay. *Fuck,*" he hisses. "Saved this pretty little pussy just for me." His mouth finds my neck and he curls his fingers inside, scooping at a spot I didn't know could make me feel the way it does, *so full!*

It occurs to me, he has yet to be inside of me. He has yet to be touched by me. I have not even seen him undressed below the belt.

But he doesn't seem to give a damn if he can play with my body however he wants.

He simply aims to please.

"It's wrapped so tight and pretty for me. Like a fucking present." He tugs my inner labia, something I never thought to try, but my clit aches harder for his friction. A normal woman would say she didn't like the way he teases. When he calls me his, *"pretty little virgin."*

"Dustin!" I wrap my thighs around his hand. It feels too good!

He pumps his digits in and out, my climax from minutes earlier still throbbing on my clit, making each brush of his hand feel like a whole new orgasm.

Then he drives me right back over the edge.

"What do I say to you in your dreams, baby? When I take this pretty pussy?" He bites my ear, as heat and breath and dirty words combine. "Do I tell you you're such a *good fucking girl*?" He strokes his pointer and middle finger inside of me, curving when he reaches the back, and I beg him to do it harder, then faster.

Every single time he complies, until I'm teetering on the edge of an explosion

"God! Dustin!

Three of his fingers stretch me to capacity now, and I wonder how I'll ever take the entirety of him—*the sizeable bulge I've felt growing beneath his jeans*—I clench my muscles at the mere thought, screaming as I come completely undone.

He twists his lips in a devious smirk, rubbing his fingers in all the right places, and something must be wrong with me, because all I want is more.

"What goes on behind those hooded eyes when I watch you? Tell me what I do, baby."

I don't answer immediately. *Shy Shana* comes to bat. But he encourages me with the same smile from my childhood memories, and a kiss as the cherry on top.

It's a safety I trust with all my heart.

"You crawl through my window," I admit, breathless as I pull my lips from his, "sneak onto my bed, and—"

Doubt bubbles back up. "Oh my gosh, *I'm* the creep,

aren't I?"

"You're not creepy, Shay. People masturbate and have feelings. You don't have to be shy about it."

"But I am." I scan my arms. "See? I'm a freak. My whole body is blushing just because you said *masturbate*," I whisper the last word, despite the fact we're alone.

"And if I say *fuck*?" His eyes shine with mischief, skillful fingers back to brushing my folds. "Tell me, what happens next when you pretend your fingers are mine?"

I hesitate, but he flicks my swollen bud like an afterthought while his eyes stay locked on our conversation, and it strokes something wanton inside of me, the way he plays me like a fidget. "You have your way with me." I gasp, widening my thighs.

"Which way?" He licks his lips.

"All of them."

Dustin Campbell takes no time rising to his feet, lifting me with him until I'm wrapping my legs around his waist. His lips cover mine before I can finish, his tongue winding around my own with a satiated moan that calls to my nipples.

He maneuvers my body until I'm facing his front, legs wrapped around his middle. He keeps me wedged against the wall and uses one hand to explore my chest.

I gasp at his fingers on my nipples, and I shove my pelvis against him without second thought, the essence of chagrin nowhere to be found in this moment with the man who makes me shiver, even as my pussy heats.

"Fuck, Shana, I want to lick you up and swallow down over and over again."

"Do it!" I rock into him, but it's too much and not enough, the feeling of his belt buckle against my clit sending my hand under my dress to relieve the incessant ache.

But Dustin has other plans.

He grips my wrist lightly, eyes swirling with mirth. "Only I touch this pussy now." He groans, like he truly can't get enough of it.

"Oh yeah?" I giggle.

He's full of it.

He also knows I like it, wet for every command, just like my fantasies.

"I mean it." He hoists me higher and licks my nipples, and when he pulls away, a punishing stream of air assaults each pebbling point. "If you want pleasure, you come find me. Understand?"

"What if I can't find you?" I challenge, tingling at the darkness lacing his words, the possessive streak that calls to me even if it shouldn't.

"Then, *I'll* find you."

A chill zips up my spine. One that should scare me, but the beating in my chest only mimics catharsis…not fear.

Is it wrong to like this?

He smirks, as if he can hear my thoughts, fingerpainting my opening as I try not to buckle.

But I must, because before I know it, I'm limp in his arms and all I can do is grind and moan into him, pretzeled around his body while he fingers me with my own desire.

I scream my orgasm through the air, clenching around his hand as he rubs fast, wet circles over my thrumming clit. And after I've exploded into a dozen different pieces, one million different ways, he stares me down as he licks his fingers.

"What does it taste like?" My cheeks heat.

"Addictive," he muses, guiding me to the couch and dragging a finger through my wetness. He holds it in front of my lips with a wink. "Sweet."

My tongue darts out, and Shy Shana is no more when I suck it clean.

"Something like sugar." He grins. "Now, be my good girl and lay back. I want another taste."

Chapter Twenty

DUSTIN

My body jolts, and I'm awake in a single breath, on my usual edge, despite the journals Dr. Robins suggests.

It's useless. Nothing stops them but waking up. Sometimes, not then.

They *revolve* in my brain, replicating, each encroaching thought spawning seven more in its slaughter.

Flashes of cut knees pinned to muddy rocks. Blonde, sticky tangles fused with fingernail crescents when they clung to me and sobbed as I fought to pull them free.

A cracked skull. A shredded training bra…

And blood.

And blood.

And blood.

And blood.

In places twelve-year olds shouldn't be touched.

"HEY! STOP!"

My heart thunders in my chest, and all I see is red when I swing my next punch. Thomas stumbles back, hands still wrapped around the girl's waist, her skirt at her fucking ankles, and I want to shove him over, fucking kill him. But he's got her, and he knows it. I grab the girl's hand, pulling her forward just as Thomas' smug stare meets my eyes.

And I shove him over to meet his death.

Only it didn't happen that way.

He lived.

Thrived.

I think about it often, how I *should* have pushed him over, his psychotic friends, too…watched those fuckers bleed out every drop of life, gasping as they took their final breaths from the fall. How I would have supplied not a shred of mercy as they atoned for Sarah, Ava, and Tiffany.

For Shana, the only one I was able to save before…

The memories never leave me.

Not for anything but a spinning angel on a dark stage, tangles of hair and cherry lips I want to kiss.

I could kiss them now.

Wake up to her smile.

Block the images in my head with her touch, her taste, and her smell.

My eclipse.

She sleeps, draped across my bed, legs twisted around my sheets, and arms tucked under my pillows.

She looks exactly what she is.

Innocent.

Pure.

Curled in a bed of white and begging *me* to ink up her waters.

I brush a curl from her face, a conversation we had as kids replaying—one of many where I tried to push her away. I know my reasons were sound, and I'm aware they still very much are. *Fuck.* Who openly dates the woman they stalk? Who does this? Who watches a woman from her window half her life?

But after last night…

I can't go back to the way things were with Shana Holiday.

She's always had my heart.

And she wants *me*, the accidental hero, falsely glorified and perpetually plagued by the past. The one people point to under hushed whispers. The one you don't bring home to your parents.

But I can't find the strength to tell her *no* anymore.

Not when she's stretched across my mattress.

Not when she presses her body into mine.

I lie back down, filling the role of big spoon, a position I never thought I'd be in.

She relaxes when she feels me, pressing her backside flush with my semi-hardened cock. Shana Holiday has no idea what she does to me.

I brush my fingers over her shoulder, smiling when she hums in her sleep. I didn't fuck her last night…*for reasons, I'm sure.*

Just ones I'm beginning to forget.

"Do you have any waffles?" she mumbles before her lashes flutter open. A grumbling sound comes perfectly timed from her stomach, and we laugh.

"Think I wanna eat something, too." I kiss her lips, swallowing the whimper she lets out in response.

"You've eaten plenty." She giggles, scrunching her face when her stomach gets louder. "I didn't have actual dinner with you *or* Haans last night."

She sits up, hands moving to her stomach, and my breath catches as the light streams in from the window beside her.

It almost looks like…I can imagine her here forever.

In my bed.

As my wife.

It wouldn't be the first time I played it in my mind.

"I can still feel wine sloshing in my belly." She jiggles it, breaking me out of the spell, and I realize how ridiculous the thought even was. That Shana would entertain a relationship with me is one thing, but surely, she realizes how fucked I'd be as a father.

Not in the cards, no matter how you read them.

"I should have taken some of Haans' French fries when he offered."

Shana throws her arms above her head, wrapping her hair in an updo. The sleep shirt I gave her last night rides up her thighs, and glimpses of her bare pussy flash me with each twist of her bun, but something about seeing her perfectly pink slit lined up with the hem of my shirt doesn't sit right with me when another man's name is on her tongue.

I stroke her chin with my thumb, lifting her gaze to meet mine.

"I don't want to hear the name Haans again."

"Jealous?"

Her smile alone almost caves me.

Virgin! I remind myself.

Her eyes twinkle, a playful streak she's only just unlocked.

It's one of my favorite streaks so far, though I hope to discover many.

She reaches for my cock, and I'm inclined to lose my sack the second she does, because nothing in all my fantasies could have prepared me for the way she looks at me, like there's not a single other option for her.

I'm hers and she's mine.

The air in the room couldn't get any thicker as she gets to her knees and wraps her hand around my cock. "I can help with jealous." She winks.

Just as my fucking phone rings.

"My father," I groan.

She frowns, but settles back into my comforter, patiently.

"Good girl." I bite my lip as the blush spreads over her face and exposed breasts.

"We're not done here, though," she brings my eyes back up with two fingers. "I'm still mad you didn't deflower me last night. I asked nicely." She pouts so prettily, and I laugh at the sight of it. I know what she wants, but I also know what she's never had: *all* of it.

There are things she doesn't even know she likes, entire kinks she may not know exist, and fuck if I'm not the greedy asshole who wants to catalog every single one of them.

"You didn't seem mad when my tongue was in your pussy last night," I tease with my finger hovered over the button to accept the call.

147

Shana gasps, but giggles all the same, the sound, light and peaceful on my heart as she scoots out of the video frame. The blankets cover her body, and I immediately frown.

She smiles when she catches my eyes wandering past the sheets and shimmies them lower, sliding them back up each time she almost reveals her breasts.

It's torture, and she damn well knows it.

"Covers off," I command, curving my lips when she bites hers excitedly. "All the way."

She obeys, and this may be shy, sheltered Shana, but she's no stranger to performance.

I almost miss the call, accepting it on the very last ring to catch as much of my private dance as possible before it's tainted with, "*Dad*," I rasp.

I listen to the cordial hello, the small-talk— something about market rates increasing and the exorbitant price of eggs, but it's near impossible to focus as the most decorated ballerina in all of Pine Forest makes a show of doing goddamned stretches *in my bed.*

"Dusty, did you hear me?" He squints at the frame, eyeing my headboard. "Fuck, Son, are you still in the bed? This is the problem with your generation! None of you want to work. You just want the luxury that work provides. In my day…"

Dad's voice drones on, but I've stopped looking at the screen. Even if I did want to hear, which ten out of ten critics will report—I fucking don't, I certainly couldn't care less while there's a naked ballerina in my bed doing poses that seem a lot like my dick could fit there.

"Dad, I'll call you back. I have…" I lose my thought as Shana rolls onto her back, propped by her elbows as she splits her legs open in the shape of a V. Her eyes alone are enough to tease any man, but her dripping cunt is all I can focus on.

"*Jesus Christ*, I have…com-*company*. Dad, I gotta go."

"The hell? That stutter's returned. Are you drinking, Son?"

"Bout to drink something," I whisper, unable to peel my attention from Shana to look my father in the eyes.

"Okay, you little shit, whatever you're up to is your own damn nonsense, but what I called you about was Business Elite. I'll be in first class of course, but I've managed to procure you an economy ticket and a room on the fifth floor. Might have been able to get you into the elite suites on the eleventh…casino and all, if you'd attended just a single meeting like I asked and filled out the membership forms you've had all year."

"I don't want to be in the *Business Fucking Elite*," I tell him, finding the only bit of strength I have left to drag my eyes from Shana and focus on the conversation at hand.

The one where I tell my father for the thousandth time, that I don't give a shit about wealth or success.

I just want to build shit.

Is it that hard to comprehend?

And if he leaves me the fuck alone long enough, I can do that.

"Christ, Son, we've been over this. Come to the gala, get the damn membership, and you can have Mullins to fuck around with in your spare time while you make *actual* profits with Campbell Enterprises. The money is in the land. Hell, you can even work remotely. Manifest your own fucking destiny or whatever shit your generation is pissin' these days. Just do this one thing for me, Dustin. I'm trying to get you ahead. Help you cover up what you started with all that *mess*—"

"Does it come back to that every fuckin' time?" I seethe.

"Yes, Dustin! It does! It comes back to haunt you every fuckin' time when you have a record. And you should have thought about that before you sought justice at your own fucking hands!" His voice booms, vibrating my fingertips through the phone.

Until it drops lower, a voice from my childhood—a man with a belt and a buckle aimed to punish.

And it's fucking worse this way, because I see myself in his anger.

I feel his anger in me.

Shana stopped stretching, but my eyes aren't on her anymore. They're stuck on a memory of Thomas's battered face.

I'm fifteen years old and my name becomes synonymous with cold-blooded. *Vigilante,* they'd whisper.

I didn't even know the meaning of the word.

"People will let you where it counts down the road if you do what I say, Son! You think I'm this bad guy, but I wish my father had paved the way for me a fraction of the bricks I've laid by fuckin' hand for you. I'm giving you the entire ladder, shined and polished, Dustin. The fuck is wrong with you? Fuckin' climb it!"

Shana's eyes find mine, the weight of his words affecting us both.

"I'm sorry," I mouth, but she just smiles sympathetically, unsurprised with the drama that is my father, something I'm not used to.

I don't have to pretend, not for Shay.

She already knows who I am.

I snort when she rolls her eyes and puffs out her naked chest, wagging her finger at me in mockery of my father.

Her breasts jiggle, and we both laugh as she cups them.

"Is something funny?" Dad sneers.

Shana eyes me, cute as fuck with her cheeks puffed, trying not to laugh. But when my nostrils flare, we both lose it, and our combined laughter spills into the phone.

"Dustin, do you have a *woman* with you? Christ, I thought I raised you with more couth than that! To answer the goddamned phone! You know what? Figure out Mullins on your own. Helping you is a waste of an investment."

"Dad, it's not like that. It's—"

"It is exactly like that!" His chest heaves with air. "Don't play games with me, Son. If you'd rather spend your days with frozen custard and *cheap tarts,* be my guest. Just don't come crawling to me when the cream isn't as sweet with penniless pockets."

Cheap tart?

My hands fist the sheets. He's the only man on Earth who could make me go from laughter just now to the hate I feel in his eyes, a reciprocal cycle of goddamned madness, brought on by *his* father and the one before him.

And still, I want to rage, throw my phone against the wall until it shatters. Never in my life has anyone been so disappointed in my past and confident of my future all at the same time. Nobody except him.

And until now, nobody has ever told him off before, either.

Shana untightens my fist. I didn't even know I'd been clenching the sheets, and before I can register anything more than the feel of her skin on mine, of how safe I feel with her, she transforms into the confident dancer from the window.

"Cheap tart?! Mr. Campbell, you should be ashamed!"

"Shana Holiday?" His eyes widen.

She ignores him, and I shove my hand over my mouth to keep from laughing at the look of disbelief on my father's face as she does.

"And this coming from the man who only bought a program-level sponsorship from the Pine Forest Athletics Club this season? Ironic, to say the least. You know Perkins Global gave us thrice your donation."

Dad's eyes widen. Guess he didn't know she was on the board, and Shana rubs the salt right in his wound with a raise of her brow. "The thousand-dollar uptick to platinum-level was too costly for your profits this quarter, huh?" She flips her hair back. "It's okay, though. Nothing wrong with being *cheap*."

Dad presses his lips together, but I can see the proud smile just before he grunts, a warm, confusingly familiar sound he uses with my sister, not a laugh, but the closest thing he gets to endearing.

"Shana Holiday." He shoves back his chair, giving us a wide view of his office, adorned in awards and blueprints and a stupid fucking stuffed bobcat that'll be the first fucker I burn when he dies, and it becomes *my* shit in that box he calls life.

"Does Devyn know about this coupling?"

"No," Shana's voice softens, a genuine display of concern for my sister, "she has too much going on right now with the new job and…"

"Hunter." Dad groans. "Yes, I'm already aware of their little game of house."

"I don't want her to run again, Mr. Campbell. She needs to know she's got people she can count on here."

"People who keep secrets from her? I'm curious. Did either of you ever tell Devyn what happened the night she left you at that field party? Your *best friend*."

"Dad, that's enough!" I growl, reaching for the phone, but Shana shakes her head, keeping it angled on her.

"She would have blamed herself. Don't you get that I'm protecting her? That we are protecting her? The fact you're still trying to pin one sibling against the other is abhorrent. "Don't you care?"

Dad's silence stretches to anxiety inducing lengths as he and Shana have a stare off. Will he tell Devyn about us?

I'm not entirely sure, but he meets Shana's worried stare and breaks the silence. "I agree she's in over her head," he finally says. "Enough secrets for her to learn in that trailer town as it is."

I just wish he'd have stopped there, but of course not. Not when there's an opportunity to leverage his power.

"I'll keep my lips sealed." He leans back. "As long as my son is polished and ready to network at the Business Elite the end of this month and actively scouting properties for the company like the rest of the interns."

"I'm not an intern, for the fiftieth fucking time." I massage my temples, but it's inevitable. He won't drop it until I'm under his thumb doing exactly what he thinks will make me worthy again. Someone he can brag to his buddies about over cigars and shrimp cocktails.

"I won't tell Devyn," he reiterates, his office chair squeaking over the line as he leans forward, "but *you* should. And soon. Blood has always run thick between you girls, and I'd hate to see my dumbass son ruin that friendship. You should know by now he's not worth all that."

He says it as if he's joking.

All three of us know he's not.

Shana tenses, and I can tell she's torn. A daddy's girl herself, she wants to play the role of my sister's best friend; laugh, joke, make him proud.

But she's called to stick up for me, more. I've seen this exact look ghost across my sister's face my entire life. Every Christmas, every birthday, every B that I brought home on a report card or bronze medal at a rodeo.

And my chest tightens the same way it always has when I spiral over expectations I'll never meet.

Is he right?

I'm not worth all that.

"I beg to differ." Shana's voice cuts my headspace, bringing me back to the grumbling man on the other end of the phone and the scribbles of his pen.

"Will you be joining us at the gala, Miss Holiday? I think it best we reconsider the accommodation, if so. Can't have you flying economy just because my son's less than competent. Your father's always been a friend, you know. I hope he's—"

"He's dying."

Nothing is said for several moments, just heartbeats and thoughts. Nobody dares to speak, until he scribbles his pen across a pad.

"My deepest condolences. I'm going to send his nursing staff a donation for whatever they need to keep him comfortable. Let me know if anything more is needed and it's done." He slams his desk drawer shut, the familiar sounds of his haste to throw money at everyone's problems so he won't have to feel for them, prickles my senses.

Shana looks at me, biting her lip, probably still torn about the sister's best friend-brother's lover debacle, but she says nothing, and dad graciously fills in the silence. At least that's one good thing he's done for me.

"I'll bump you both to first class." He says it like it's already been done. It probably has, knowing him. *Money is power,* after all. Just the thought of that churns my gut inside out, and I want to take his checks and scribbles and shove them right up his—

"I can't do much about the hotel arrangements since my *offspring* refuse to network with the right sort of people, but perhaps I could pull some strings for a suite on the tenth floor. You'll get a decent oceanfront view and access to the private happy hour at the very least, but—"

"Dad, stop! She's not going." The words stick in my throat, but somehow, I manage, grabbing Shana's hand and using the power I feel in her light to tell my father how it's going to be, once and for all.

"I-I'm not going." My stupid fucking stutter rears back in his presence, words tripping over my thoughts, but it gets out. And it seems to be clear enough.

"What did you just say?" His voice is low.

Laced with something I'd call pain if I weren't certain he lacked a heart to feel it.

"I *said* I'm not going. I-I—"

I'm not you.

I'm not you.

I'm not you.

"I'M NOT YOU!"

He's silent.

Until he's not.

And as the opposite of silent whirlpools in my gut, I spin with it, his thoughts and words and judgement binding to me.

"Of all the fuckin' sons, I got the one with the thickest fuckin' skull! You know that, Dustin? Do you have any idea the sacrifices I've made for our family? I have paid thousands in legal fees to ensure you become something, *Son*, and I'll be damned if you throw it away to open a goddamned *Hobby Lobby* when you could take what I've built and grow upon one of the most profitable businesses in the tri-state area."

I don't reply. He said plenty.

And he fumes in my silence.

Good.

Even if I can't see his face from where I threw my phone during the word *sacrifice*, I can close my eyes and feel the backhanded slap across my jaw. Funny how it still stings even after all these years.

"Do you hear me, Son!?"

"*I* do," Shana interjects, disgust plastered across her knitted brow as she grabs the phone. But there's something else there too. A match lit, ready to burn.

"Dustin's *going* to the gala."

I open my mouth to protest, but she throws me a look, tossing her hair back before she narrows her eyes at the phone, and then she does something I've never dared to do in all my life.

She looks my father in the fucking eyes until *she's* ready to speak.

I'm pretty sure in this moment, I'll marry this woman.

This knight, who sits in a butterfly stretch, draped under plain white sheets, using nothing but virtue to fight my battles.

I love her.

Even before she puts the cherry on top.

"Respectfully, Mr. Campbell, I've seen you in plenty of expensive getups over the years, but entitled asshole doesn't look good on you, and you can keep your tenth–floor accommodations. Dustin's *my* plus one, now. And when *I* attend Business Elite, it's on the Twelfth floor, with the winners."

She hangs up, tosses the phone to the mattress, and lets the covers fall to her waist in one swift motion, straddling me with glazed eyes, flushed and gloriously naked skin. "I see why you needed those dance lessons."

"I can't believe you just did that."

"I'm sorry."

"Don't be." I shake my head in awe of the girl who just defended me. "Where was Shy Shana Holiday just now?"

She blushes. I can't tell if she realizes it's a compliment, though. The way she goes into her head and stays there until she performs is something else entirely, and I find the need to assure her it's not weird.

It's her own special power.

"It was amazing."

I pull her close, and she instantly nuzzles my chest.

It feels real. The realest thing I've felt in a long fucking time. My chest flips in ways it never did with Miranda or any of the others.

Only ever for the girl who spins.

"Oddly enough, it's not the first time I've stuck up for a Campbell sibling against that man who calls himself a father. Her jaw tenses, her loyalty to my sister unwavering.

"Remember when you and Dev snuck out the bedroom window for that dance team party your parents wouldn't let you go to?" I tease.

"Stop!" She buries her blushing face in my chest. "I can't relive the embarrassment that you saw me do that."

"Are you kidding?" I tickle her side, until she looks at me. "It's one of my favorite memories of all time! The two of you scaling up the trellis with pizza boxes. And do you remember when my mom caught you? What you did?" I grin.

"Don't make me say it." She sighs.

"If you want to lose your virginity you will say it."

"Not fair! That is such an exploitation of my desires! I could lose it to someone else, you know."

"You're cute." I arch a brow. "But I will break his entire body if he tries. I don't even care who this hypothetical is yet, he's already not a problem, baby."

She shivers, as her eyes sparkle at my mirth.

"Fine, I ate four slices of pizza in three minutes flat and then proceeded to vomit for two days!"

"It was so fucking funny, though. Why did you do that? I still don't understand."

"I didn't want her to get in trouble. Her calorie count…your mom, she was horrible, Dustin."

"Yeah." I never thought of it from my sister's perspective. Our mother ignored me after my transgression. But before that, she always seemed like the nice one.

Mom never hit me with a belt.

She whipped Devyn with words, though.

"She was."

Yet another reason to tread lightly with this secret.

Dad's right about one thing, I'd never forgive myself if I came between my little sister and her best friend. Neither would Hunter, and he's *my* best friend.

We really have made a beautiful fucking mess, haven't we?

"He's a pretty tough adversary," I tell her, mocking Dad's demeanor with my lip down and chest puffed triumphantly.

Shana shoves me back into the mattress, laughing and falling into my body with a kiss on my cheek.

"Seriously, Shay, where did that come from?"

"I'm not shy with people I've known my whole life." She shrugs, sifting her fingers through my chest hair.

"Oh yeah?" I place her hand over swollen cock, curving my mouth to a smile. "Prove it."

"I don't know how," she admits, as she wraps around it. "Is it…like this?"

My eyes nearly roll from my head when she squeezes my shaft. "Fuuuuck," I grind out, noting the pride in her eyes at my moan. She's always been eager to please… *perform*, even when we were kids.

The good girl.

I offer more praise, and each time I do, she gets better. "That's it, baby, slower. Like that." I wrap my hand around hers, guiding the tempo and feeling my cock harden in her grip, and even though I've no intention of going all the way with her yet, being fully seated in her sweet, untouched cunt becomes my main concern.

Virgin, I remind myself, again. *Keep it slow.*

"Like this?" She strokes me. Her lips hover just over the head, waiting for permission like the good girl she is. "I'll teach you if you teach me," she whispers against my tip.

This can't be real life.

Yet here she is, tongue over my cock, precum practically crying from the tip.

I planned to be gentle. *Soft.*

But her whimper sends me over.

Fuck it!

I fist the tufts of her hair, like handles, and she instantly shoves her hips in the air. "Please!" she moans over my length. "*Dusty, please!*"

The way she says my old nickname… I'll be lucky if I can make it through a fraction of this lesson without exploding right away. "Stick your tongue out, baby."

She lights up with excitement. It's so fucking cute I can't stand it, too sweet for my darkness.

But when she flicks her tongue over my erection, and it feels like the world might shift beneath my bed, I see hunger in her eyes. A need for everything to align.

I know because I feel it, too.

"You're doing so well, baby." I slide my length all the way in her mouth. She gags, but moans, her pelvis grinding even harder against me. "You like that, don't you, baby? When I tell you how good you take my cock in that pretty mouth."

She radiates with my words, lights up like the night sky when I stroke her hair as I thrust. "Suck as you go down," I rasp, tugging her hair up and down, moving her head over my cock.

She gets better as she goes, and I think I may be done for when she adds the second hand and says, "I saw this on a tutorial," twisting both hands over my spit-covered cock, sucking my tip like it's a goddamned lollypop with gum she hopes to taste at the center.

"Ohh, fuck. That's it, baby…*fuuuuuck.*"

She shines with the affirmation, moving her head up and down, this time taking me all the way to the back of her throat. I buck against her face, holding her there as I will my cock to obey.

She's sloppy, and not very good, but it's the woman of my dreams submitting her body to my pleasure, something she's given to not a single other man her entire life, and I might explode in her mouth any second for that fact alone.

That she's all fucking mine.

I grind against her, carefully. The last thing I want is to hurt her. I move her head up and down my shaft. "Fuck yeah, baby, keep your tongue out."

Before I know what's happened, she's fine-tuned the motions I've only just taught her. Her eyes meet mine, my secret ballerina. This is *her* dance now.

I roll her nipples between my finger and thumb until she cries out around my dick, and it sends me wondering just how vanilla my sweet girl wants to be.

"I'll do it." I stroke her hair. "I'll give you lessons if you give me mine. Show my dad where to shove it again."

She hums in excitement, pulling her head from my hold and letting my dick pop free from her lips as she grins like I hung the moon.

She forgets she is the fucking moon.

Bold and beautiful.

I'd do anything in the world for this woman.

And that's exactly why I set my parameters.

She said herself she saved *everything* for me. There's no misunderstanding here, she wants this. No doubt about that. Or that she's a grown, consenting adult.

Still doesn't make it right to rush through every first.

Teach her.

Fuck, is this wrong altogether?

With my sister's best friend of all time?

But she deserves this done right, and I may be able to watch a lot of things, but I'll be damned if I set by and watch another man, especially one from Flinger, take what I wanted since the first hushed giggle down the hall from my bedroom door.

Truth or Dare, Shay. Do you think Dev's brother is cute?

The way I waited by the cracked door for her reply.

I fell in love when it was, *Sure.*

"I've loved you a long time, Shana Holiday." I grin. "Watched you." She sparkles at the reminder, and I shake my head, still in disbelief that the girl I love is turned on by just my brand of crazy. "But I want to know what *you* love."

I guide her head back down to my lap until her cheek rests against my cock. It radiates with pleasure when she gasps.

Whimpers.

Moans.

She rocks her hips in the air, as I suspect she will. Just like with the praise, she enjoys the submission of power.

Does she even know this about herself?

"Do you like this?" I stroke her hair, keeping her pressed against my erection, the hardness of it shoved against her.

She doesn't reply, but her beautifully bare pussy wiggles in the air, coated with her arousal.

"I think you do." I smirk. "I think you want it pressed against you while I touch your horny little slit. Needy little virgin, aren't you? Teasing dirty old men in coffee shops with those tiny skirts, barely covering this tight little ass." I squeeze the perfect roundness in my hand and shove her pussy down harder over my leg, bending so it hits her just where she needs it, and I let her ride me there with her face still held against my leaking cock, contorted in a cirque-de-bedsheets only fit for a body like hers.

"You're gonna regret giving me this." I slap her ass to test, and she loves it, bucking against my leg, the vibrations of her whimpers pulsing against my cock and threatening to force my load across her tongue. "Gonna dance for me every fucking night right on this cock." I smooth where I just slapped, trailing my fingers along her center, until I reach her clit and pinch. "Aren't you, sugar?"

"Yes!" She gasps.

"Good girl."

She tightens her thighs around my leg, and I feel her come as she rocks and gasps, begging me to teach her more.

"You're *my* virgin now, sweet girl." I lick my hand and slide it over her pussy, rubbing the wetness around her opening and inserting one finger as she moans into my lap. I use my free hand to feed my cock into her lips, pumping it in and out until it's hitting the back of her throat, but she doesn't seem to mind.

No, my filthy little dancer is moving to the music of our bodies, making art from moments in time, and before I know it, I'm no longer in control. Her hand is stroking me up and down and my cock is flush with the back of her throat. She eases off and I take her in, this beautiful creature transformed before me, confident and strong.

"*Fuck me,*" she begs.

But I can't. Not yet. I've said it before, I'm not a good man. *I'm selfish.* And there's something about her innocence I won't let myself take yet.

I haven't earned it.

I'm not worthy.

But I will be.

I'll do this shit with Dad, buy the Mullins property, and I'll start my business, something my father didn't plan, something I'll do on my own. And fuck, now that I've had a taste of my girl, the only one I ever gave a fuck about, now that she's mine?

I'm all in.

There's something more than pride or reputation or my father's expectations lighting my path. And once I've got these deals in place, I'll be ready.

I'll ask her to marry me. Lemon can officiate at the house so Shana's father can be present. She'd want that more than a spring wedding with a fancy dress.

I see it in my mind, with the woman I love wrapped around my cock, pumping her head against me. *I feel other stuff all right,* but I still feel this. An overwhelming sense of purpose.

"Not yet," I groan.

She pouts in protest, but I reach out and grab a chunk of her hair in my hand, pulling her head back so I can meet those fascinating dark eyes, and they've never been as beautiful as they are right now, clouded with lust.

But her fantasies are the same as mine.

I press my thumb to her swollen lips, and I wonder how she'll want it, but when she lets out a breathy whimper and opens for me, I know. She'd let me do anything I want right now, and she tells me this with one look alone.

"Dustin," she whines around my thumb, "please."

"Shhh," I say, replacing my thumb with a kiss. "We'll get there. You're my virgin now, Shana Holiday, and I'll keep you that way until I'm good and ready. Now be a good girl and turn around. I wanna taste you from the back."

Chapter Twenty-one

SHANA

If I ever wondered what it felt like to shove an entire kielbasa down my throat, which I hadn't, for those keeping record, I think this is that.

I gag on Dustin's length as hit hits the back of me, possibly going down even further as I suck him in.

"Fuck." He keeps my head over his lap and pumps into me, holding nothing back despite the years he branded me untouchable and clean.

Is it bad that I like how he dirties me up?

My center throbs spectacularly as he fists my hair and uses it to maintain a sinful rhythm.

When he pulls my head back, his cock slips out of my lips. I gasp in a huge breath, the air filling my lungs as my frenzied eyes meet his dark, green, glassy ones.

"You are sloppy at head, little virgin."

"What?" A whip of pain snaps over me with his assessment, which I'm aware is likely accurate, but it's not like I've been given a manual or anything. "That's not fair. I've never done this before." I sit up on my knees and

shove his chest back against the headboard, mad that this giant broody muscle man has the nerve to be as attractive as such while slinging insults.

His eyes flash in surprise when his head hits the wood behind him, not expecting my sudden dominance, I'm sure. But with Dustin, I don't feel the need to hide my feelings.

And right now, I'm feeling like I want to straddle him. So, I do.

Buck naked, unchaste, and *probably desperate*, I climb atop him and hover my dripping opening over his rock-hard, spit-covered length. And I grin, having gotten him right where I wanted after all these years.

I could shift a mere centimeter, and he'd tear through my last shred of innocence.

I want him to.

I rock my body, grinding my clit and pussy lips against him the way I imagine I might if this were the real thing. I have nothing to compare it to besides my fantasies.

But it feels like that's what this is.

Me, Dustin, naked in his bed.

I lean in and press a kiss to his lips. Then another to his neck. I lick my tongue around his Adams apple, and he bucks, his erection shoving further into my slit, but not penetrating, *not yet*. But it feels so close. It feels…

"Are you playing just the tip with me?" He smiles into my hair before ravishing my neck with his tongue, our bodies picking up their pace below. "I never did this when I was younger."

Heat from his tongue and cock on my most sensitive parts transforms me, and I gasp my thoughts into the air, clapping back. "You never did *me* when you were younger, either."

"You little fucking minx." He laughs, grabbing me by the hips and flipping me over so I'm beneath him, and he's now straddling me.

"You know when I said you were sloppy, it was a fucking compliment, right?" He smirks when my mouth drops open.

He pins both wrists above my head, holding them down with one hand while he licks his palm, and my body heats as he meets my gaze, and he fists his slick cock at my entrance.

My breath hitches.

"Do it," I beg.

His mouth curves, and he shakes his head, goading me.

"Stop teasing and devirginize me, Dustin Campbell, or I swear to God—"

He kisses me, cutting off my sentences, my airflow, and any concept of the world around me aside from this plane that only he and I exist on. My body molds to his when his tongue tangles with mine, but he flips it inside out and flops me free when he says, "Not yet, baby. You need to finish your lessons first. Learn your preferences." He kisses my neck. "Capabilities."

Okay, Mr. Mansplain.

"I don't care about being *capable*, I'm trying, very desperately so, to be *fuckable*, in case you haven't noticed." I gesture down my body with my eyes, my hands still immobile. And that thought right there just makes me even hornier, *pinned beneath his rock-hard body*. Are there normally eight distinct squares outlined on a man's abdomen muscles?

"You don't have to try, Shay. You are beyond fuckable." He thrusts his cock deeper into me, but not all the way. Still just the tip, and I fear I may explode on a noxious combo of desperation and desire when he sucks my nipple into his mouth and rocks his hips slowly.

I move too, my hips angling up to meet his gentle thrusts and crying out involuntarily each time his pelvis presses harder than usual, brushing my clit as he slides back and forth through my soaked pussy lips.

"No, the harder thing to do is *not* to fuck you. To show restraint just a little bit longer. Give you every first you never got until your very last." He thrusts into me, the deepest he's gone yet, but it's not enough to split me open and tangle with my soul. I whine in protest, but he shushes me, letting my wrists go free and using his other hand to pinch my greedy clit as he lowers his head back to my chest and moves from nipple to nipple, sucking and lapping each until I'm screaming his name and clenching my pussy as tight as it'll go. His cock is still hard and teasing against my swollen core, and I come for him, my body pulsing as he finishes me with slow, languid kisses between my thighs, and my eyes drift closed.

"Where are you going?" I sit up when he moves for the door.

He smirks, then, exiting the room and sauntering to offer me a towel.

His still hardened cock points at me in jest, but he lifts my chin to meet his eyes. "This is why I don't fuck virgins. They're so needy after intimacy." His lips twist, and I know he's just trying to get a rise out of me.

Pull my braids and run away.

Well, not today.

I slide off the bed and stand, fully exposed and arms crossed. "I am not *needy after intimacy*. I am *in need of intimacy*. Intimacy you'll only give me in small little snippets, despite the very apparent fact I want the full, unedited version with deleted scenes and all." I lick my lips, thirsty, defiantly. "I want to learn more."

My eyes drop to his erection, and he doesn't protest, so I lower to my knees, grabbing his solid length as he sucks in a sharp breath.

I summon the courage to mimic what I've witnessed in pornography, still in disbelief of my own actions. My heart races as I work up the courage to be like the girls in the video, but I want this.

I meet his eyes, and I spit directly onto the head of his cock.

"Oops, I got it wet," I say, with a sultry stare I copied from the aforementioned porno that Lemon basically forced me to watch, *the first time, at least.*

He wants to paint me as a good girl.

I want him to paint me with his cum.

I finally realize what my friends have been going on about all this time with their sex-crazed ruminations. It's exhilarating to love and feel loved. To crave someone that craves you back. To explore, touch and taste.

And it's not bad to want things like that.

Not with the one I love.

After a few strokes, he moans, threading his fingers through my hair. I spit on it again without a second thought, meeting his eyes in a teasing smirk. "Uh oh, it's getting dirty." My slutty words soak me to my core, and he groans when I rub my fingers through the arousal.

"Is that so?" Pressing his lips together in a coy smile, he leans down to kiss my lips before quite literally feeding me his cock, a protective yet commanding whip to his words that sends a thrill right through me. "You better clean it off then, baby." He spanks me, and while I thought the praise was orgasmic before, the pleasure zinging over my pussy while his cock slides down my throat, has me moaning around it, thrilled and turned-on as he absolutely degrades me.

Oh my God, what is wrong with me?

His teasing words surge on me, and I shouldn't like it, but I do. "More!" I gasp. "Talk to me like that more."

"Like what?" he teases, fisting his cock and slapping it across my open lips. Lust drips from my tongue, falling onto his flesh as he squeezes my cheeks together with his other hand, a gentle, yet immovable vice, holding me in place on my knees before him.

This man could tell me to lick his body from toe to tip, and I'd do it in a single breath, unable to dissuade the quickening heartbeat gathering directly in the apex of my thighs.

Dustin paints my lips with the head of his cock, my own saliva the gloss he layers on to his liking, and I shiver, my nipples hardening as he studies his work.

"There. When you come to your lessons, I want you just like this. On your knees, hard pointy little titties stuck straight out, and slick, wet lips. Both sets." He winks.

I light with excitement at the filth of his demands, and somehow still want him to talk like this, even if it is taboo and wrong. It feels like a performance or a dance.

One where I don't have to overthink my feelings, hiding in my hoodie for fear of other people's reactions or opinions. It's just these sordid roles we're both playing out. And I find myself leaning into the character as soon as that clicks, sticking my breasts out like he says and batting my lashes as I await his next command.

"Yes, sir," slips from my lips without thought, and even though that might normally mortify me, right now with Dustin, playing this role…it doesn't.

I'm not a shy, emotionless, stunted virgin.

I'm *me*.

I'm exactly who I want to be, doing exactly what I want to do, and that's okay.

Dustin's eyes flare when I utter those words and he smirks then, silently accepting my invitation to this new game we're starting.

"Good girl," he whispers, still rubbing his cock over my lips. "You will call me *sir*, and you will do exactly as I say since you're such a filthy, kinky girl. So desperate to get your cherry popped you'd do anything, wouldn't you?"

"Yes, sir," I smile.

He groans at my submission, maneuvering me by the thick ropes of my hair as he lifts one of his legs to the bed and covers my mouth with the bottom of his shaft, his balls dangling and hitting my lips and chin. "Coat them with your spit, baby."

Thick and tight. Massive like the rest of him. His

flesh slaps across my face, as I tongue parts I didn't know existed, his body tensing in pleasure when I do, strong hands holding me at the back of my head. And he's into this. He's so into it that I'm into it. We're kinky and stupid and feral, and melding into one.

"Stick your tongue out while I fuck your face like this. Yeah, that's right. Like that." He groans in pleasure as I pant for breath with my tongue out like a dog.

Somehow, this makes me feel electric.

"That's right, baby. Keep that tongue out and mouth open." His balls dangle into my mouth. "Oh, fuck yeah. Lick them like you want me to lick your pussy."

I nod, unsure if he can even see me beneath his eight-inch third leg, and his balls tighten on my tongue. Is this what it feels like just before he comes?

He continues with a steady stroking of his shaft while I suck beneath it, licking and swirling deeper and longer when I feel him tense and hear his breath hitch.

Finding what he likes is surprisingly thrilling; getting him to come becomes my unofficial mission.

"Fuck, baby, your tongue feels so good between my legs."

I luminate with his praises, the contrast to his rough, bruising words a new side of intimacy I didn't know I needed. This push and pull. And I want the absolute most of it. That same praise kink I've seen and read about, but never come close to experiencing for myself, it's right here and now.

"Come on my face!" I blurt, surprising both of us.

His commanding tone slips, and my hackles rise. "Are you sure?" My mind swirls with doubt about my preferences and kinks.

I'm the weird one.

I want the weird sex things, don't I?

Shame consumes me.

Being good is righteous. Perfection keeps us safe.

"Hey, it's okay." He brushes sweaty and slick strands of hair away from my cheeks as I stare up at him, my unconcealable innocence joining the party as I kneel awkwardly.

I'm still half turned on, but I'm not sure I should be.

Dustin brushes my hair from my face. "Don't be embarrassed about what you want. I only asked because I don't need that kind of thing from you unless you want it. You don't *have* to do that for me. I know you think I have a type, but Shay, you're my type. No matter what. And if you think you like that kind of thing and really *do* want to try it, then don't be ashamed of that either. But don't do anything just to please me. All I want is what you desire."

Are you allowed to swoon and cry during oral?

"Tell me." He wipes a single beading tear from my reddened face and meets my gaze head on, forcing me to spill my thoughts free like he's done for decades.

My watcher.

"When I was younger…" I pause, taking Dustin's offered hand and sitting on the bed beside him, legs dangling next to his—and it feels safe like this. Safe to tell him this thing I hold inside of me. "At the funeral for Mom…back when we were kids, there was this friend I had, her father was a donor to the aquarium." My eyes shift to Dustin, making sure I'm not overtalking or this isn't weird, but it isn't. I can tell because his focus never leaves me, even though this has got to be the strangest string of events in his life. "I was gargling your ball sack two seconds ago and now we're doing therapy or whatever this is."

His eyes crinkle. "Did you mean to say that?"

"This time? Yeah."

He kisses me on the cheek. "I'll let you gargle them again if it makes you feel better." We both laugh, and I find my body zinging back to life again, humming for his nearness. His touch.

Acceptance in Dustin.

But only if he knows the whole me. Maybe Lemon's right. Maybe it's time I didn't keep it all in.

I'm not alone.

I don't have to be, at least.

"Lucy lost her mother a few years before me. We bonded over this shared loss, I suppose, and even though she was across the river, Dad drove me to play with her from time to time that summer."

"I remember that." Dustin arches his brow in thought. "Devyn went to pageant boot camp or some shit that month and missed the funeral. I was so fuckin' pissed at her for leaving you alone like that. It's why I—" He stops, eyes flashing with remorse before shifting to the ground. "Sorry, go on."

I study him. Calm as a cucumber on the outside but clenching onto the mattress, white knuckled.

"It's why you asked me to that dance at her grave?"

I let my question float there between us.

Until I pop it back down.

"Yes, it was that month," I say. "Lucy, was different than anyone I'd ever met. She was poised, I guess. I was a dancer, but she was a *ballerina*."

"You are a ballerina. Fuck, Shay, I might be your biggest fan, and you have no idea the extent I mean that, thank fuck, but I've *seen* it. The way your body becomes part of the music. Part of the whole world. For two or three minutes at a time, when you allow yourself to be free, it takes over space and time. It's magical."

Dustin's eyes swirl when he describes what he sees when I'm dancing, and chills spread, my father's voice falling softly over me.

"But boy, when she was at the aquarium in her element…I'd stop and stare all day long."

"You really do love me."

"A little."

I nudge him and he makes a show of falling off the bed, but quickly returns, crawling to the other side to rest against the headboard. He opens his legs for me, sexiest thing in my entire life, and beckons me to come lay between them, back flush to his against his beating chest, held in place by arms that feel natural wrapped around me.

"Tell me more," he whispers into my hair, kissing the top of my head. "Do you stay in touch with her now?"

"She died, too." I sniffle back my sadness. I've cried over my losses enough for one lifetime.

"I'm sorry, Shay. I didn't know."

"It's okay. You wouldn't have known with her age… it was a fire."

He wraps his arms tighter around my body, as if he can push the leaking bits of me back in, but the only way to grieve is to remember.

This much, I already know, so I push back my tears, and I force myself to remember. "Lucy did everything perfectly. Not Devyn kind of perfect, wanting to impress people for attention—you know what I mean." I crane my neck to make sure he isn't offended by my clip at his sister, but he rolls his eyes in agreement, and I snort.

We love Devyn, but she's a lot.

"Lucy was different from most kids I knew. She said please and thank you, got straight A's, was hand-picked for solos, her lines and angles perfectly constructed for elegance…and do you know why she was like that? Why she toed the line in every area of her life?"

Dustin considers this, before surprising me.

"Maybe she felt like if she didn't mess up, life would be easier for her dad? Without her mom around?"

"Wow. Yeah, that's…" I peel away from his arms, turning to face him fully then, considering for the first time that this man I'm wildly obsessed with is oddly poetic. And perceptive. "You see a lot but say so little, don't you?"

"I could say the same about you." He smirks. "Hoodie girl."

I grin, wondering how I got so lucky with this man. The thought flits through that maybe I'm not lucky yet, this being new. Me being weird. Him being…him, but if he loves me in my hoodie the same as he loves me in my ballet slippers, then isn't that all that matters?

Maybe Dad's right. Love makes you see things about a person in a way you wouldn't see them in anyone else but that one other soul swirling through the wind in just the right pattern to tangle with yours.

To dance.

"I was the best dancer I could be after meeting Lucy. I studied harder, practiced for hours a day. And most importantly, my one personal mantra I tried desperately to never upend: I didn't break rules."

"What happened when you did?"

"I'd beat myself up. Worry people would die because I got a B. After that pizza debacle with your mom, I went home and practiced my aerials until my wrists were bruised." I sneak a peek at his expression, an angered frown, and I flush. My eyes whip away from his, mortified. "That sort of thing. So, sex?" I blow a raspberry into the air on the tail end of a self-deprecating laugh, and Dustin narrows his eyes, looking straight through me.

"You're telling me you aren't a virgin because you saved yourself for me all these years, pining for the thought of my one-of-a-kind cock? A virginity only I could coax from the stone? I'm not Sexcalibar?" He shoves an invisible stake through his heart and drops to the side.

I smile, smacking his shoulder and launching onto him, until we're tumbling in laughter and bed sheets.

He brushes my hair away from my face and plants a kiss straight to my trembling lips.

"You don't have to be perfect, Shana, not for anyone. Besides," he grins, "I think I like you good *and* bad."

Maybe rules are meant to be broken.

Chapter Twenty-two

SHANA

And pas de bourrée and leap and turn! Great job, ladies!" I skip to the stereo and flick off the power switch. "Now," I spin to look each one of my talented girls in the eyes, because everyone can improve—something I'm learning two-fold lately, "if I look out and see your toes aren't pointed at competition, I'm going to point them for you, got it?"

Giggles and tired sighs sound through the studio as I tell them goodbye and sweep the floor for my next class, kinder ballet. Sometimes it can be a lot, five-year-olds and all, but they appreciate movement at its base level. They explore ways of turning and leaping that come directly from impulses. Their curiosity of the world is a vessel for song. It might be my favorite class, even if it isn't very technical.

And I might feel a tug at my heartstrings when they run to my side, barely reaching my knees, and show me their triangle shaped first positions like we practiced.

Would my son or daughter dance? Would they be like me and discover the world through rhythms and patterns?

I shake my head, dispelling myself from the odd fantasy. It's not like I want to be a mother. I've never felt like I would be good at being someone's caretaker.

Even if I *am* responsible for my grown father and thirty children at a time most days, they aren't mine in that sense. In the end, I'm not the one shaping them, bringing them into a world they didn't ask to be a part of and filling it with people they love, only to feel the marring loss when they're taken away.

My smile slips, until I close my eyes to dull the thoughts. Dustin replaces them. His blazing green eyes, his devilishly handsome lips with that sinful silver pierced through them, just how his very essence seems to pierce through my heart. It pumps into my blood stream until it's all my body can feel, and with the thought of him, I'm instantly needy.

I want his words. His filthy phrases. His commanding presence. The kinky role he plays for me so I can do things I feel like I shouldn't. So, the power of that choice is taken from me and instead, I'm given a new choice.

To give him all of me.

We haven't gone all the way, yet. But as the days have passed, I've found myself tangled in more than just his sheets. Each nightfall brings a new lesson in deviance. Kissing, tonguing, fingering, sixty-nine being my favorite so far.

But every time I ask him to…you know. The answer is always the same.

"Cherry goes last."

I lick my lips at that word—cherry—and desire flashes over me, my body heating, nipples hardening beneath my leo in response to the mere thought of Dustin Campbell's breath across them.

Jesus, I need to get laid.

"That was a funky look," Maisy says, propped against the studio door frame.

Annoyance prickles me, but only for a moment. For a dance mom, she sure is here a lot when her kid is not. But she's the most helpful mom of the entire team, and I'm certain none of the costumes would get sequins without her, so I let it slide, even if she *is* a gossip queen.

I swipe my hoodie from the floor, wrapping it around myself in armor. "I was just thinking about things." I move to pass her, but she blocks my path on the threshold.

"Do *things* have anything to do with Dustin, *Hunk of Muscle*, Campbell walking around with blueprints of the building and inspecting the crawl space?"

"What? He's here? Now?!"

"Yeah, he's in there now, babycakes. If that's what those eyes are searchin' for." She winks, but rolling my eyes at her again won't help my situation, so I give in and drop the act, since she's the only mom in the vicinity. I wish I had mine right now.

"Okay, *yes,* Dustin is the thing! But I'm all sweaty, and I have greasy hair! And this leo is one size too small, but I wear it anyway on Tuesdays since I only have little kid classes and you do *not* want to wear an unflattering outfit in front of the middle school girls, trust me, so anyway, do I have a wedgie in this?"

I turn so she can look at my butt, and then it hits me that I just asked this dance mom to look at my butt.

I'm certainly not the weird one like I worried. Not at all.

I take in her amused grin and promptly swipe my hood up, ceremoniously tugging the strings around my face. "Just ignore me. Never mind. None of that was said."

"Hah!" Maisy chuckles, tugging me back in the studio and clicking the door shut. "You are adorable, you know that? I think the girls on the team might have more experience than you do some days."

"They sadly do."

My teenage students are confident with who they are. Weird how I'm always preaching that to them, yet don't believe it myself.

"Honey, it's not rocket science. Just go out there and talk to him." She fans herself, eyeing the door before shooting me a sly look. "Not gonna lie to you, he looks pretty damn sweaty, too, and that is not a sight you wanna miss if you know what I mean." She walks away, swaying her backside.

She's probably right. I should just go out there and talk to him. Say something normal people say…like…

"Hi," a gravelly voice says from behind me. My eyes lift to the mirror, and his reflection stares back at me. My breath catches in my chest when our eyes meet, and the thoughts and feelings and stressors of the moment before vanish in his presence. Until his eyes dip, and I watch them through the mirror, landing square on my ass, likely noting the too-small scrap of spandex lodged between both cheeks.

He catches me watching and smirks, wrapping his arms around me and toying with my nipples through the fabric.

"You look sexy in this." He kisses the crook of my neck and hums. "Even your sweat tastes sweet. Wanna take you in front of this mirror so bad."

All the things I was self-conscious about are the very things he makes me feel good about. I swear, when Dustin's close to me like this, when he is all I can see and I am all he feels, the world around us just stops.

We are thieves in love and time is ours to steal.

"Yoohoo!" Maisy knocks, sticking her head through the door opening. "The kinder babies have started to arrive." Her eyes sweep to Dustin, his large, unconcealable cock proudly erect beneath his skintight jeans, and she clears her throat. "Should I…um…let them in?"

I pull away from Dustin's embrace, feeling very naked in public like this. Where everyone can see that I'm…I don't know…happy. In love?

When Dad is dying.

He knits his brow, no doubt noticing my shift in energy.

"My class ends in an hour. Do you…do you need something?" I ask him formally. It feels weird when my pussy was just shoved against his beard last night. Like we should be past formalities and stolen glances in public, yet we aren't.

Or maybe it's just me that feels this way.

Shameful in love.

"Yes, actually, I need the keys to this closet." He tongues his cheek.

"Why?"

"Did you fix the leak?"

My lips press to a thin line. "No, I did not."

"Well," he shrugs, whipping out his tape measure, "I'm fixing it, like the lawnmower in your backyard. It's working now, just needed to flush the carburetor."

"You did that?" My heart is a giant melty mush.

He nods like it's nothing. "Gonna fix this, too. Today, hopefully. You can't let it go on and on forever, Shay, you'll get a mold infestation." He scratches his beard and frowns, "I'm concerned you might already have one."

"Mold?" I ask, knitting my brow. "It could be that serious? It couldn't close the building down, could it?"

He looks skeptical, and I don't like that.

"Dustin, this studio is my *everything*." I grab his shirt collar and tug his tall frame down to my level. "Tell me this won't shut my studio down."

"Look, I can't say what it is until I check on what it is, okay? I just know that it looked bad the other day when you were trying to hide it from me." He gives me a chastising glare. "Which I'm still pissed about because you know I do this kinda stuff on the side. I could have helped before it got this bad if you'd walked across the courtyard and asked."

Lemon's words ring in my ear.

"You don't tell anyone anything. You let things fester inside of you until there's nothing left but huge balls of emotion hurling through your atmosphere ready to crash."

"Guess my balls are crashing, huh?"

"What?" Dustin laughs. "You are funny, Shana Holiday."

"So you've said." I step closer, despite the nerves that build within me when I'm in his presence, and I back him up against the closet, lifting in relevé to kiss him. "Thanks for loving the funny girl."

His eyes scan mine and he laughs, incredulity draping his features.

"Did you just thank me for loving you?"

"Yes?"

"It's not a choice for me. Just as much as dancing isn't a choice for you. We are the way we are because we feel something tugging so strongly we have no other option but to explore what comes from giving in."

My heart does just as he says and tugs at his words.

"That's where I've been wrong all these years," he continues. "It's not about controlling your emotions. It's about living through them and finding out what's on the other side. Giving in to who you are and what you want."

"What if I don't know who I am?" I ask.

"Then I'll remind you," he says softly. He kisses my hand and moves me to the mirror, his body warm and supportive behind me.

"You are the funny girl because you make people laugh. You're the weird girl because you don't play on trends. And you are the good girl because you care so deeply for those you love. I've watched your whole life, Shay, and you might be all those girls at some point or another, but you know which one I care about most?"

"Who?"

"*My* girl. And I like her exactly how she is."

Chapter Twenty-three

DUSTIN

My little virgin is tormented by thought.

And it's eerie how similar they are to my own.

Am I good enough?

Have I done well enough?

Will the sky crack apart like a weathered deck stain and flake off in sections until there's nothing left but colorless, splintered age and nothing to stand on because I made the wrong choices?

I'm not a therapist. Wouldn't claim to be one, either. Half the time they're as a crazy as the rest of us. Like mine, suggesting that if I'd stop noticing the woman I love, I'd be happy.

She was wrong about that, at least.

Because when I peek in the open studio window and see Shana teaching toddlers to spin on one foot, I *am* happy. They tumble to the floor in a fit of giggles and sparkly tutus, and for a split second, I let myself imagine our own tiny dancers twirling at my feet. I could teach them carpentry. Natural grace and craftsmanship, they'll be unstoppable.

But I shake it away just as fast, my father's voice echoing in my ears.

You can't fix crazy.

My eyes shift to the leaky-closet door.

But I can fix that.

FOURTEEN YEARS AGO

"Shana Holiday, Son? That's who you're asking to the dance?" My cheek stings from Dad's slap, his voice a sharp whip against my defenses "She's your sister's age for fucks-sake."

"Only t-two years."

"After what you did last summer, rearranging faces with your fists at the quarry, immobilizing three of your peers! Do you really think Randall wants his daughter to hold those hands? She's a good girl."

"I know she is. I-I really like her, Dad. I-I—"

"Y-Y-You." He twists the knife he wields even deeper into my heart before he yanks it out and guts me. "You do not like her. You see, when you decided to break the law on your quest to be a fuckin' hero, you forfeited your rights to make decisions. I am your decision maker now. And you will not be going to some stupid fucking dance."

"Dad, I said I'd be there for her!"

"Not after the stain you caused on our family name. For what? Heroism? I will not have you cast out of the upper crust like my father. You almost killed the mayor's son, for fucks sake, Dustin!"

"They were hurting them! Screaming for help! They were *touching* them, Dad! What if it had been Dev?!"

I tear my face from his chest and force my gaze to his eyes. "What would you have done? Would it have mattered who his f-father was if it was your own flesh and b-b-blood lying there?"

I'm not sure it would.

"What would you have done?!" I slam my fist against the wall beside his head.

He doesn't flinch, just eyes my fist with an arched brow and tosses the leadership conference packet to my feet.

"Not put someone in a coma."

PRESENT DAY

"Is that a screwdriver in your pocket or are you just happy to see me, Dustin Campbell?" Maisy Trotweather, mother of one of my niece's friends, bats her orange eyelashes, fanning herself dramatically, which suits her entire personality, unfortunately.

She's about ten years my senior and knows everything. Or so she'd have you think.

"Ehem." She clears her throat, her voice raising an octave. "I noticed you and Shana looking cozy. Are you two a thing?"

I turn with a surprised look, and she smirks.

"It's a bit obvious, hon." She plops down in the rolling chair behind the counter like that's the end of our conversation and flips through a dance wear catalogue.

I wait for more, but I gather she's dismissed me when she circles a third leotard without once looking back up.

"What do you mean *obvious*?"

She cheshires, slamming her catalogue closed, the papers rustling beneath her fingers. "I *mean*, I can see you glaring less than a hundred feet away beneath the streetlamp every night, frothing whip cream out your dang ears. And if I can see it," she points to the glasses on the bridge of her nose, "the whole block can, honey bunny."

I really thought I was stealthier than that. *Shit, has Devyn seen?*

She studies me, tapping a pen against the desk. "I think it's good for Shana. She acts like she doesn't need anyone, but she does. She doesn't talk to anyone about her father. I doubt she even tells her friends. But if she has you, then I know she'll be all right."

"Why do you care?"

"I'm a mom," she deadpans, as if I'm the crazy one.

"And?"

Maisy studies me. "Not everyone has a false motive, Dustin Campbell. I care because she needs someone. She needs you."

I don't know what to say. I'm no savior. Shana doesn't need a savior. She should believe in *herself*. Hell, I believe in her more than me. I've done nothing noble here. Nothing but stalking my sister's best friend for a decade and then playing kink-master, withholding sex from her like a fucking fetish, getting her all worked up over my father's bullshit when she should be worrying about her own father's imminent death.

"You have it wrong," I tell Maisy. "Shana doesn't need me. I need her."

"Well, then," Maisy arches a knowing brow, "commit to it. Someone like Shana deserves to be more than a secret beneath a lamp." She winks.

Maybe she does know everything.

"Besides, I like you better than that other fella that came around. The lawyer with broken arm."

She lets that hang there until my jaw flexes.

"When?"

I slap my hand on Maisy's catalogue when she refuses to look back up after dropping such a high caliber bomb, and I swear I see her smirk.

"He came asking about her during the competition team practice last night, but she was busy." She winks. "I suspect she'll remain pretty busy if you play your cards properly, huh, Mr. Campbell?"

"Please never call me that." I choke on my father's name, just as Shana appears, waving to parents and children as the kinder dancers skip away. She bounces between Maisy and me. "Is everything okay?"

"Seems like it will be." Maisy winks before seeing

herself out. Her opinions still linger in the air though, and what she said irritates me. That ass wipe from Flinger tried to see her? After the things he said?

I fixate on the idea that Shana is going through losing her father, and there she was telling mine off the other day for me because I'm not even brave enough to speak up.

I can pick up my fists, but when it comes to speaking actual words, explaining how I feel, I can't take a swing.

And with one phone call, Shana Holiday knocked him out cold.

"I need you, Shay." I drop my head, unable to meet her eyes as I confess. "I need you in so many ways, and that's not fair, because you should be relying on someone right now, not the other way around. You're the strongest person I know, and somehow, even though you think you're this camouflaged rock in the dirt, you shine your brightest under pressure."

"Dustin, do me a favor." She holds up a hand. "Stop glorifying me and I'll stop glorifying you."

"What?"

"We have too much past." She sighs, dropping to the floor like a child and sitting in a butterfly stretch. It makes me laugh, because it's so fuckin' Shana it's not even funny, so I join her in the same stretch.

Poorly, I might add, because my legs don't do *that*.

"You fought my demons when we were kids, and I glorified you for centuries."

"Decades," I correct. "Well, actually just one decade to be exact, but—" Her pursed lips silence me. "Sorry, go on."

"Just like your sister, I swear. Anyway, for *centuries*," she clips, "I thought of you like a celebrity. You saved my life."

I suck in a sharp breath because it wrecks me, replaying those days in my mind. The summer before my freshman year with the first three girls I found victim to the Remington crew. And my senior year, when he tried it again with Shay.

"I'd have killed him if they didn't pull me off. You think I'm a hero, but I-I lost control." I didn't even see his face anymore, just a target with a death wish, a dark soul I could spare God the chore of wiping clean. I would have delivered him to the devil with my own hands, and gladly, if they hadn't stopped me. "Y-You know that, right?"

"Yeah." She licks her lips, silence and beating hearts filling the space around us. "I know."

My body eases its tension the moment she wraps her arms around me, resting her head on my chest. "And the boy who did those things? The one who saved me?" She buries her nose in my shirt and inhales, sinking into a comfortability neither of us seemed to know we needed, before lifting her eyes to mine. "I love that boy. For exactly what he did. Exactly how he is."

We don't play our games or roles tonight. But she comes to me when her business closes and mine locks up. Not to kiss or talk or dance. No, she strips us down, first her clothes, then my own, and we lie there, bodies flush.

She's the big spoon, tonight.

I only hope I'm enough to fill it.

Chapter Twenty-four

SHANA

A cherry pops between Lemon's teeth, juice flowing over her glossy lips as she tells us about this employee of her father's whom she detests and is *not at all concerned with.*

I snicker over my root beer. Turns out, I'm not the only one with an unconventional admirer.

"And then he sat there and just…*watched.* Can you believe that? Sure, it was hot, but who does that?"

I choke on my drink, hardly able to catch my breath between Lemon recanting her polyamorous experience with exhibitionism, and Dustin in my plane of sight behind her, making a muscle show of his waffle cone crafting, hands down by his waist as he slides a metal rod into a mold…*stuffing and flexing and twisting.*

Devyn pats me on the back, shaking me out of the spell, and Jeremy motions for the server to get us some napkins while I use the sleeve of my hoodie to wipe my chin.

Per usual, our weekly pageant directors' meeting has morphed into a vent and gossip session.

But this week, my friends are just as frustrated with intimacy as me. Lemon is in complete denial about her feelings for a much older gentleman, *a whole other story*, and when Dev tells us about living with Hunter Isaac, Pine Forest's very own thirst trap, and goes way too into detail, I actually *want* to know.

I'm not cringing or hiding my reactions, trying to save face over completely normal parts of adulthood.

There's no worry or fear enveloping me as I listen to them unload.

Not anymore.

My root beer float melts as I listen to my friends, and Jeremy nudges me, offering a throat lozenge. "You got quiet again. Just wanted to make sure you're okay. Coughing fit or, ya know. Whatever." He nods to Dustin while Dev isn't looking.

"I'm fine," I assure him. "Just forgot how easy it is to choke when it goes down."

My eyes widen then, and my friends' do too. Even Devyn whips her head my way, a laugh curving the edge of her lips.

It's nearly impossible not to blush when her eyes match her brother's, and all I can picture is what I was choking on of his last night.

She's going to flip when we tell her.

Old Shana would have hidden in her hoodie with shame, but a smile tugs at my lips when I realize, for the first time ever, it's not *if* I tell her...I'm thinking about *when* I do.

Because the possibility of a future with Dustin isn't just a fantasy.

I take that entire concept in and break it down. I'm whole, even as I'm still gathering the bits I might not see, parts of me that are forming day by day. Parts he brings out of me by being the safe space for my confidence to bloom.

The innuendo still hangs thick in the air, and Jeremy's cheeks are puffed up with air to the point he may blow.

I know what they expect from me. From shy, sheltered Shana Holiday, but she's changed for the better.

And the new Shana rolls with laughter, joined by her friends, in her favorite booth, under the watchful eyes of the man she loves.

I steal a glance at the man in question, wiping a table nearby, and just as I suspected, his eyes are already waiting for mine. He smiles.

I wink at my watcher before I twist back to my friends, Jeremy exhaling in relief.

"Not gonna lie, Shay, I was gonna be so pissy if I had to keep that laugh in until the parking lot."

Lemon shushes him.

"I didn't mean it like that. "Jeremy rolls his eyes. "You're *you*, Shay. You're a good girl, and that's okay. We don't like to make you feel uncomfortable with our wild ways."

He's not being rude. It's simply the truth.

I *am* that girl. The weird one. The shy one. The one still struggling to find herself amid the world around her.

And these are exactly the people to share that with.

I stop Dev before she rushes to my side like always, fighting my battles just like her brother.

This is *my* life. My battle.

My choices.

No matter what happens to, or at, or around me.

Regardless of who dies.

This is me.

I nod at Jeremy, tears filling my eyes before I swipe them away and replace them with a smile.

I'm not sad about this. Not anymore.

Jeremy smiles, too. All my friends do. And when he waves Dustin over for our check and sees the way I melt for his smell alone, he clinks his glass to mine one more time before exiting the booth with the others. "Bout time you stopped hiding what's in your heart."

Twist.

The lock clicks. The last thing I suffer watching Dustin handle, jealous of everything his fingers have gripped tonight that isn't me.

And now, everything else falls away.

I take off my converse and lace up my jazz shoes right in the middle of the Sugar Stable. Can't say I ever imagined a moment like this when I was standing in this very spot ordering swirly cones as a kid.

I can barely breathe beneath his gaze.

"Stop staring at me like a half-cooked waffle cone if you want to learn how to waltz," rushes out of me.

"A…what?" His eyes shine brighter than before. He even stretches like I taught him, and I lick my lips like he taught me.

Both of us have been different since we started these secret rendezvous of ours.

Happier.

Hornier, if I'm being honest with myself.

Maybe it's because I'm still a virgin, even after dozens of 'lessons,' or perhaps it's because we're still a dirty little secret few are privy to, but my cheeks heat when I register his eyes raking me up and down. Need pulses in my center.

"A waffle cone." I step forward. "You look like you want to lay me flat and fill me up." I bite my lip.

He stares at me, floored at the forward remark I may or may not have recited in my mind seventeen million times before this, touching myself to the brink in my bed last night. It's all I can do to shove my legs together at how hot it makes me, playing it out in real life.

Is it too weird? The thought flits across my mind, but I grab the condiments around me before I can stop myself and pour them directly into my cleavage.

"Oops, I got dirty."

He drags his teeth over his bottom lip and swears under his breath, setting his jaw and narrowing his gaze on my chocolate-covered breasts.

"Fuck, I love it when you talk ice cream to me." He grins, launching between my thighs. "Pretty little cherry sundae, aren't you?" He gropes my hips, tongue swiping over my nipple. "Fuck, baby. How'm I gonna keep from going all the way when you taste like the final course?"

My body breaks into goosebumps when he plays along with my silly fantasies. When he talks about sex in this blatant manner.

But his words concern me.

I don't want him to *keep from going all the way.*

Not this time.

"I want you to fuck me," I tell him. "I want the final course." I wrap my hand around a can of whipped cream to my side, and I squirt it into his mouth before he can say no.

Dropping the can to the floor, I go on relevé and slam my tongue between his lips, taking what I just gave right back. "Do you want it, Dustin?"

"Yes," he whispers, eyes swirling with questions.

I answer every one of them with a single nod.

I'm ready.

He stills, both of us breathing and waiting, and the whole world seems quieter than normal while we share our eminent exchange. Will it be like always?

Or is he a new Dustin, too, like I'm a new me?

Is it only me that hears my heartbeat?

I can't stand it.

"For fucks-sake, you creeper, stop watching me and—ahhh!"

"C'mere." He smirks. "Turn over." He motions to the counter.

I stare in confusion. "But I thought—"

"Calm down, waffle cone. You're too sweet to tear right into." He kisses me, cream and syrup twisting around our tongues. "Need to enjoy you slowly. Savor the taste."

He teases my nipples between his fingers and teeth, tugging until I'm hissing at the pain. "Need to warm you up first." He flips me over, and I'm turned on beyond my wildest fantasies. He hoists me until I'm on all fours, my most intimate parts close and personal with his face. Hot breath coats me in arousal when he grumbles against my pussy.

Then lower.

"Gonna take this tight little ass one day, too. You're gonna beg me for it, aren't you sweet thing? Dance for me until I fuck this tiny hole?"

"Oh!" I cry, my hips wiggling at the feel of him there, the deranged promises of his cock where his tongue now flickers drawing my hips harder against his mouth, my clit grinding over his lip ring and voice singing to the heavens as my pleasure rolls up and down my body.

Dustin's wide hands grab me, angling my hips just how he wants before he shoves two fingers in to accompany his tongue's wild lashes. He sets me over the edge again and again, until my thighs are clenched so tightly around his head and hands, I fear I'll bind him to my bottom half in a smeared mix of cream and fudge, and my own desire.

He flips me over, hooking his arms beneath my knees and yanking me across the counter so my center is in line with his cock.

And then he frees it.

I know how large it is…I've seen it, *sucked* it…but nothing could prepare me for how it feels pushing into my center, slick with his spit and aching with my same need.

He fits it against my hymen, and it's already stretching me far beyond what his three fingers ever have, but my body pulses, my clit practically banging down the door to be let in.

He lowers his lips to mine and whispers, "*Relax,*" and my legs fall open around him.

My head hangs back as he trails kisses over my skin and his bottom half presses in, tearing through my folds and pushing slowly into me, so deep I can feel him in my stomach, I'm sure of it.

"Ohhh!" I moan, stinging at first, but settling into the zing of pleasure as he works himself in and out, the head of his cock stretching me wide and hitting a spot inside me that feels far too perfect for words.

I want to keep him there, in that exact rhythm, even as the soreness increases with each reinsertion of his engorged shaft through my torn and stinging muscle.

I wrap my legs around him and force him even deeper to the place that has me reeling, pulsing, pumping my own body up and down in tandem with his, the slickness pooling from inside me. "Oh my God! I'm going to! I need! Dustin, please!"

He shushes me with his lips. "Look at you take me, baby. See how your perfect little pussy stretches open and squeezes me?" He thrusts harder, right into that same damn spot that makes me scream. "Such a good little virgin taking me whole."

"Oh! Oh!" I scream, the buildup almost too intense. The words he speaks like darts, assaulting my folds along with his thickness.

"Yeah, you like it, don't you baby? Gonna let me do whatever I want with this sweet little cunt. It's mine, isn't it, sugar?

My body electrifies when he growls against my ear, and I whimper, *I love it* and, *yes,* and *yours,* shaking around him in pleasured waves.

He pumps in *and out and in and out,* and it's too much. *Holy shit. It's so full.*

"I knew it the first time I saw you in that tankini. I wanted to feel this tight little cunt around my dick before I knew what it even was. So fucking warm." He groans, his other hand wrapping around my neck, and hell if this isn't wrong and sexy all at once. "So damn sexy, baby. Always been mine, haven't you?"

"Please!" I beg him, unsure of what it is I'm even asking. But no, I do know. "Make me come, Dustin! Oh!"

He slams into me, rubbing circles over my clit until the pressure builds so high within me that I burst, colorful language and sinful promises flowing from my mouth as fervently as the gushing stream joining the space between my legs and his glistening cock, wet *from me.* From the soft ripples of ecstasy pouring out of my soul.

Dustin kisses me then, swiping sweaty strands of hair from my forehead and wrapping them into the mass of darkness fanned around my naked body, his eyes memorizing every dimple and freckle of my skin if I didn't know any better.

"You're such a creeper. *Always watching.*" I poke him in the cheek until a smile forms.

"You're one to talk. That waffle cone speech was next-level porno material."

"You think?" I laugh.

"You're a talented choreographer, but I think you might have a knack for adults-only screenplays with that dialogue."

"You think that's how pornos happen? People write their masturbation fantasies? Not that I masturbate to you waffle-coning me or anything, but—"

Ohmygosh, I did not just say that.

My hand slams against my own mouth before I vomit more of my skeletons, but Dustin's there immediately, pulling it down and snorting back a laugh. His eyes crinkle, a grin across his face as he shakes his head in wonderment. "You are funny, Shana Holiday."

"You always remind me of that, but you know what's truly funny about this?" I pop a literal cherry in my mouth and press back a smile.

"What?" He smiles.

"*I'm* a next-level, screenwriting porn-star, and *you* still don't know how to waltz."

Dustin sighs dramatically, pulling me against his chest, but his smile stays put, dancing with mine where it was always meant to be.

Chapter Twenty-five

Not bad, Campbell. But remember your form. It helps in the turns."

"I knew it was gonna come back to my form."

Dustin's smile grows, as he plays along with my teasing antics on the video Lemon has watched on loop.

"Look how good my pizza position is now, though."

"It's called third position for the fiftieth time. You're such a goof."

I cringe at my girly giggle in the recording and cast an embarrassed look at Lem, but she hasn't moved her eyes off the phone screen since I admitted to my late-night meetings with Dustin and agreed to show her even a sliver of what we are. It was harder to hide from her. She's at my house whenever I'm not, taking care of Dad.

Not going to lie, it feels good opening up to Lemon, even if it is about feelings and emotions.

She's been here for most of them, even if I did think I was doing a decent job of keeping them zipped in my hoodie pockets.

"I love him for you." Lemon beams. "I still can't believe that is Dustin Campbell giggling and dancing with you on there. Never would have thunk it."

"I know he's not normally like vibrant and everything, but he's different with me. It's like…" I trail off in thought as I wander to the sugar plum plant by the window and pour in its daily dose of vitamin water. "He brings out the beauty in life, even the droopy, dark parts of it."

"And again, I still can't believe he was lowkey stalking you and sending you notes and plants and…anything else I missed?" She narrows her eyes accusatorily.

I guess I get it. I wasn't exactly open about what Dustin and I had in our pasts with my bestie. Any of my besties.

"Probably." I sigh. "I'm sorry I have a hard time opening up to people." Dad and I talk in riddles most of the time, neither of us wanting to face the reality that life has felt half of its worth since Mom. I'm not sure why I feel the need to explain this to Lemon.

Am I overcompensating?

This need to apologize to Lemon right now, this guilt for holding a secret…it has everything to do with my other best friend. The one who shares eyes with the man I see forever with. Anxiety twists that I haven't told Devyn anything about me and her brother. Even after all we've been through.

It's not that I don't think she'd approve, but isn't it best to tell her when her life isn't so complicated? Isn't it my job as her friend to keep her mental health cushioned?

Or are Dustin and I wrong for thinking she needs sheltering.

Sheltering is exactly the thing that's held me back.

And anyway, just because my life is all over the place, it doesn't mean she doesn't deserve to share this with us.

Devyn's text from earlier today burns the inside of my eyelids every time I close them.

DEV: What'cha up to this weekend?

ME: Business Conference, one of the fancy award ones you came to that one time!

DEV: Bet you won again, you dance diva!

ME: Just a little. <Angel Emoji>

DEV: Super jelly! Dustin's mysteriously away this weekend, too, and Hunter's moving a herd of cattle with the 4H kids. I'm gonna be bored out of my mind if Jeremy's working. Send pics to keep me busy!

I want to tell her he's with me. *Your brother is with me this weekend, and I hope forever.*

I love him permanently, just like I love my best friend. And that means this secret can't last.

Lemon elbows me. "Did he send you *all* of these?" She holds handfuls of folded paper notes, some old but most of them new, spilling from my old music box. More of them fall from my purse that's upturned on the bed. "Not gonna lie, babe, I know it's Dustin and that eases my mind, but this is a bit obsessive. Even for a familiar stalker. Don't you think?" She unfolds one and reads it off. I remember it from a few weeks ago. But of course, she'd choose the creepiest one. They aren't all like that.

"It's sweet." I shrug, plucking back the crumpled parchment that says, "Eye love you" and smiling as I remember the way I undressed in front of my window that very night.

"'*Watching you. Are you watching me, too?*' isn't creepy, Shay? Come on, you know that one is out right weird."

"Okay, well, yeah, I did kind of get shivers with that one, but it's also part of this game we play. I used to get little notes on my doorstep and in my mailbox as a kid… I suppose I always knew it was him. It's morphed though, Lem, it's more now…" I stop talking and widen my eyes, but she narrows hers and urges me on. "Kink."

"Oh my God!" Lemon jumps from my bed. "You didn't? You did! Ohmygod it was your first time, wasn't it?"

I nod, still mortified I'm opening up about it to anyone but feeling so very free now that I have. Giddy, even, and I can't stop the redness spreading over my face and chest.

"Don't be embarrassed, Shay! That's amazing. Plus, we all knew you were a virgin. You're obvious about it."

"Rude!" I throw a bathing suit at her and laugh. "Well, anyway, it *was* amazing despite painful…why don't they tell you how sore you'll be the day after? It was almost worse than the taking of the cherry event altogether."

Lemon snorts and falls over in laughter. "You did not just refer to your de-virginizing as if it were a fantastical Midsomer event, did you? Your father has you reading too many classics. I'm gonna start filtering in some of my smut." She removes my one piece and throws a tiny, red bikini into my suitcase and winks. "Now that you're a whore and all, you can wear this in the hot tub at the hotel. He likes you in red, remember?"

"Ahhh stop! You're so bad." I shake my head, grinning wide. "Horrible influence." I toss the red Lou Boutin's into the bag with the sports illustrated looking suit and wink. "Definitely shouldn't pair it with these at all."

"You're worse than me, now! I've created a monster!"

We spend the afternoon choosing outfits and formal wear for the weekend Dustin and I are just days away from finally sharing at the beach. Most of it will be in the hotel, at the gala and conference, but the bits in between…those are the ones I'm most excited about.

Something has been unleashed within me. A sexual awakening, but more than that. It's this feeling, like…for years now, I've been putting my happiness to the side for Dad's sake because he needed me. He never asked for it. In fact, all he's ever wanted for me was love.

"Hey babe, I hate to burst the happy little bubble you're blowing right now…yes, pun intended." She winks again, and I roll my eyes. "But you are on birth control, right? It's your business and all, it's just, I didn't know if you considered that, being a recent cherry-owner and all."

"Yes, Mom." I sit back beside her on the bed and nudge her with my shoulder. "I've been on a progesterone tablet for years, but you're smart to ask. I suppose most non-sexually active people aren't on something, but I get cysts if I'm not. Sometimes even when I am. This helps." I toss her the little blue packet from my purse pocket.

"Good!" Lemon smiles widely. "I just wanted to make sure. The last thing you need is a surprise you didn't want. My mom…well, I was a surprise she didn't consider. She maybe should have thought about that."

"I'm sorry, Lem. I didn't know." I touch her hand.

"It's all right. Super rich Dad who compensates for her lack of appearances with money, so it's all good, right?" She tosses her hair over her shoulder, and I can tell she's done, so I drop it for now. "But we weren't talking about me, we were talking about you and your new reason for contraceptives." She wiggles her eyebrows dramatically, and the irony isn't lost on my sense of humor.

"Dustin was there when I got my first period. It's so awkward thinking back, but…"

"But what?!" Lemon gasps, sitting up straight on the bed. "Don't stop the story when it's juicy!"

I cringe. "Don't say juicy when I'm talking about periods."

"Fair," she snorts.

"We kissed that day. My first kiss." I smile, twirling a strand of hair around my finger; a lovestruck cliché.

"All right, I've had it," Lemon says finally. "This is so sickeningly cute and perfect, I can't stand it anymore. I'm shipping you. You're shipped. You are meant to be together forever and ever, and the stars have spoken to you for decades." She scrolls her phone and her eyes sparkle as she lifts them to meet mine, the glow lighting her face. "A Taurus and a Virgo. I don't know how I didn't see it before, it makes so much sense. You're destined."

"Okay, Madame Psychic, take it easy. It's just a new relationship with a guy I've liked my whole life who happens to awaken me sexually and help me with therapy and is *sinfully good with his tongue…*"

"Mhm. He's helping you with therapy? Sex therapy?"

"Grief counseling!" I throw a pillow at her, and we both giggle as a bashful heat overcomes me. "He's kind of storybook perfect, huh?"

"Sounds like it, babe. Make sure you two get some alone time between the work stuff, got it? All work and no lay makes me sad for you."

I laugh, but a tension forms in my shoulders when she checks Dad's video monitor.

Should I really leave him for the whole weekend? What if he takes a turn for the worse and I'm not here for him? How selfish would I be if I were off waffle-coning my stalker at a fancy gala while he's breathing his last breath, *needing me?*

"Stop." Lemon snaps her fingers in my face, perfectly painted a light shade of lavender to match her witchy eyes. Ones that pin me in place, like the mother I no longer have. The one I need right now.

A true friend.

"Live your life before it passes you by, Shay. It's what your father wants. It's what I want. And babe?" She tosses a lacy teddy she procured from seemingly nowhere into my bag and zips it up with a grin. "It's what you need. Now get your cute little emo butt to the studio, and if nothing goes wrong, by this time tomorrow, you and Dusty boy will be tangled in fancy hotel sheets with an ocean view, while your father and I enjoy a riveting Benedict Cumberpatch rendition of Much Ado About Nothing. *Again.*" She scrunches her nose and we both laugh.

She's right.

What could go wrong?

Chapter Twenty-six

DUSTIN

Everything is wrong.

"Are you hurt?" My heckles rise faster than the tears that fill Shana's eyes, standing on my doorstep in the middle of the night. It's all I can do not to tear through the doorway and break whatever stood in her path and caused this. Because it's *my* heart that squeezes tight when hers beats this erratically. "Did someone harm you?"

"What? *Oh.*" Her eyes dart to mine from beneath soaked lashes and she sighs, upset with herself. "I didn't mean to alarm you. I'm not hurt. Not physically."

Her words ease me little when she still stalks about my living room in tears, swiping the evidence onto her sleeves and curling up into the smallest form of herself, legs tucked into her hoodie so only two white socks stick out beneath the worn black hem.

She pulls a letter from her purse. "He's selling the studio. The whole strip. It's not just my building that had leaks and mold. All the piping was old and in need of repairs. Since we all leased from the same man, and he can't afford the repairs to the entire strip, he's leaving it up to us. We fix it on our own, each of us individually, which most of the vendors can't even fathom affording on small independent business revenue, or he'll sell the whole strip."

"That's *fucked*." I pace the floor, livid at this property owner for his negligence to routine maintenance. Not only is it a waste of his own investments, but it's also a slap in the face to at least six…no, *seven* small businesses that lease along that strip. The one that's been across from mine for as long as I remember. Even Abe's Farm N' Feed is over there.

"No. Fuck that, Shay. That's not going to happen."

"It's not? How do you figure?" She wipes her face and blinks at me expectantly, and it feels like nothing I've ever known before…this confidence and trust someone has in me, of all people.

But I *can* fix it. I can take care of *all* the leaks, and we can raise funds through the town for mold cleanup and everything. Hunter and Devyn would host fundraising rodeos and pageants. Cowboys Paradise would likely match donations with a happy hour of some sort if they knew it was for Shay and the other businessowners we've grown up with.

These are our friends.

This is our town.

"We can do this."

I'll do this for you.

"Besides, whoever this dude is talks a big talk, but my dad's had me in these bullshit real estate workshops for *centuries*, as you like to say."

She twists her lips at my jab, but eases into my lap as I settle down on the couch. I wrap my arms around her and bury a kiss in her vanilla scented hair.

"There's not going to be any buyers willing to take on an entire strip that fast in this town. Especially one that has funds to invest in mold and water pipe repairs up front. It takes months for that kind of buyer to settle in."

"That's the thing." She sits up and twists her hair into a nervous braid. "There *is* a buyer willing to gobble the whole thing up, leaks and all. Had some lawyer already draft up the settlement documents." She blows out a long-winded breath and breaks my heart with the confidence in her tone when she suggests breaking her lease and finding a new home for Holiday Dance.

One that won't be across from me.

"Fuck that. I'll call my father tomorrow and get this figured out, Shay. He can investigate properties in a way we can't see without his company's programs. I'm not letting you lose your studio."

I think I've said the right thing. It's certainly the best I can come up with to help her, even if it does involve my father.

But she sighs, and her eyes cast downward. "You can't fight all my battles, Dustin. Maybe it's time I faced it and bought my own building, outright. I like to think things can be perfect. Dad and dance and *you*…but it's not always, is it? I've been pretending things are fine, when really, they've been breaking down around me. Even you. Fighting for me, ready to save the day. I need to be strong for myself. Now more than ever."

"I want to help, Shay, I was just—"

"No, Dustin, it's fine." She heaves a frustrated exhale and pushes off the couch. "Look, it's just me. It's my emotions. I get that. I just need… I don't know. I feel like I need some space."

"Space?" My chest tenses, twists, and beats faster than I've ever felt for the slow pulsing I feel inside my skull. My eyes find hers, full of stress and pain and still, I want to keep them in my view. To watch over.

"It's not what you're thinking. I just feel like I'm losing Dad, right? I'm losing the studio now, too, and… what if it's me? What if you're next, and I lose the only thing left that's good in my life, right alongside the rest?"

The beating slows with time as I process that.

"Me? I'm what's good in your life?"

"Yes, of course." She removes her hood. "I love you, Dustin. I just don't know how I'm allowed to have that. Good things *go*. Good things fail. They die."

"Everything dies, Shana." I kiss her, stopping her next words from emerging. She's too deeply swallowed by grief to see it now, but she can feel. So, I kiss her again. "Do you feel the way our bodies come to life when we touch?" I lean back on the couch, and she scoots down with me, until her head is resting in my lap. I unwind her braid with my fingers as she relaxes into me, the fireplace beside casting a warm glow over porcelain skin I brush my hand across. "Do you feel what it means to love me? For me to love you?"

"Yes." She gasps, as I trail my fingers across her lips and then flutter them down the front of her chest.

"Everything that has loved has lived. And everything that lives will die. 'Gather ye rosebuds while ye may,' right?"

"That's Shakespeare," she exclaims on a yawn, drifting to sleep in my arms while I rub her.

It is. I know it eases her, my ballerina. My artist. My…

…not mine, is she?

She's *hers*.

And that's what she's been saying.

I look upon the only woman I've ever loved, asleep in my lap and curled to fit just right against me, and I know what she needs. What I need, too. What we've needed together all along.

Confidence in ourselves.

And a reason to be loved.

My phone buzzes in my pocket.

I slide out from under Shana when I see that it's Dad. *Perfect timing.*

"Hey, Dad, I was meaning to call you about—"

"Dustin. I trust you and Miss Holiday have arrangements for tomorrow." He cuts me off, of course, has to be the one in charge of everything, even a conversation. But it doesn't bother me like it normally would. I'm not fuming from my ears at his voice, so that's progress.

"We do, but look, I've got a problem. Shay's studio had some water damage, and the landlord is threatening he's got some buyer willing to gobble it up if she doesn't make repairs. I was hoping—"

"Finally need me, I see. You still have a log in to the company's remote server. Look up the listing details and I'll have my lawyer send his real estate agent an inquiry.

While you're at it, do something for me." *Of course.* "One of my agents is on about some gold mine in your neck of the woods, the emails should be cc'd to you since I thought you'd be working in the city by now."

"Dad." I groan.

"Never mind. Look, start pulling your weight with family business and you'll be amazed by what rewards come to follow. Having connections has its perks, is that not why you need my help?"

I'm surprised he hasn't made me snap yet. I would normally throw the phone by now at the very least, but his jabs seem to stick less when I've got all the fortune in the world on my couch.

He's also got a point. He *can* help me because of his power. Without so much as worrying Shana one bit. She's concerned about her father and the future of her world enough as it is.

"Bring the details to the gala." He clips. "And I'll make sure everything's good for Mullins and take a gander at your girlfriend's studio."

"I'm glad you're finally turning things around."

Click.

I clench my teeth at his last comment. As if things were going the wrong way before? But the condescension hardly registers next to the other thing he said.

Girlfriend.

Shana's chest moves up and down, peacefully as she rests in my living room. She tired herself out from crying, but a few minutes on my lap with my fingers combing her hair and she fell fast asleep. A sense of belonging overcomes me that she feels so safe in my care.

"Girlfriend," I whisper. Her eyes flutter open.

"Yes, boyfriend?"

"I'm gonna move you to my bed so you can sleep more comfortably, is that okay?"

"Mhm." She drifts back to rest in my arms, and I find myself swelling with pride when I tuck her into *our* bed and cover her up. "Love you, boyfriend," she grumbles before rolling over.

I love you, too.

And I'll fix every leak her life presents to keep her happy.

Back in the living room, I'm too stimulated to sleep, pondering ways to get the town rallying around fundraisers for the square.

I pour a glass of brandy and twirl it around as my laptop loads the listing from my father, but when I take a swig, I almost spit it back out as the property before me is none other than Shana's very strip.

The goldmine Dad's agent is settling is hers.

And just when I think it can't get any worse, the plastic mouse cover cracks from the force of my grip as I scroll down the listing and find a name that has me ready to break hands all over again, the settlement counsel.

Coincidences like that don't just happen.

I send a text to the same friend who researched Haans and double the fee. I'll pay for as much information as he can dig up.

Because Shana is a target, just as I always feared.

I feel it in my bones.

What I don't know is why. But it won't be long before I find out.

This mystery mogul may be a lawyer, but I'm Dustin Goddamned Campell, the blood thirsty vigilante who sees right the fuck through evil like him.

And he's messed with the wrong ballerina if he thinks Shay will be lying down even remotely for whatever he's got planned. She's stronger than she lets on.

My eyes dart to the cracked bedroom door, to the peace I'd rather watch from afar than disturb, and I wonder if I'm doing the right thing keeping her from the darkness.

Fighting her battles…

But she's Business Elite's guest speaker. She's a successful businesswoman who's earned her moment to shine. The need to protect her consumes me, and my mind is made up before I can replace my mouse with another.

I resist the urge to track this man down in his sleep and remove his eyes so he can never rest them on Shana again, and I print the papers on my screen, slamming my whiskey on the table instead.

I'll tell her tomorrow night after the gala. We'll have a nice time. I'll clue Dad in on what's going on with the property and his so-called *buddy*, and we can resolve this without a fight, or worrying her any further than she is right now.

Leaving her own father for more than two days is something she hasn't let herself do in years.

Hell, if it hadn't been for the therapist I encouraged her to see, and Lemon giving her the push she needed, she may not have gone to the gala this year at all—and according to Lemon, it's something she used to love. I shake my head in amazement at the thought of my shy, hoodie wearing girlfriend spending hundreds on gowns to dance her night away. It's a part of her she finds shameful, like so many others. And it's time she got her Cinderella story.

No way I'm letting her miss that again. Not for this shithead with a boring ass job and a stupid vendetta.

I'm coming for this smug, money-hungry prick who's fucked with my girl yet again, and my first hit is in the form of an opposing bid on the whole entire strip of properties in Pine Forest Square. Might be close to my entire savings on the line, and a direct forfeit of my chances to secure Mullins, but I can win this. I just need something I never thought I'd have to ask for again.

Dad's help.

With everything I can muster, I hit send on my bid and effectively start the competition with the attorney working for my very own father.

An attorney I'd like to fuck right off to the depths of hell for the fact he even touched my girl at all. But I'll do it the right way this time, for her.

For us.

My mouse hovers over the name that makes my teeth clench and nostrils flare, before I slam the screen shut and head to bed with my girl.

Guess I'm breaking more than hands this weekend. Time to break contracts.

Fuck you, Lawrence Lawson, attorney at law.

Chapter Twenty-seven

SHANA

LEMON HEAD: Omg I said we're fine. Stop texting for updates, you're ruining the fifth act of Titus Andronicus, and shit is gettin' cray.

LEMON HEAD: HE MADE A PIE OF HER KIDS, SHAY. Did you know how dark this shit got? I def skimmed in English class. Did not remember this plot. <barfing emoji>

Laughter bubbles out of me. Dad *does* love tragedies, doesn't he? The bloodier, the better.

SHANA: Thank you for reading to him. It means the most.

LEMON HEAD: No prob, babe. I love this old thespian. He's grown on me.

She really does love him.

I never imagined, when I found out Lemon Perkins, my childhood best friend's ex-arch nemesis, took this position as my father's care tech, that we'd become like sisters.

Or that I'd be lucky enough to have someone who cares for Dad as much as I do. Isn't it important that he enjoys these last few months?

A tear slips from the corner of my eye and rolls down my cheek, but I wipe it away and smile when my phone buzzes back to life with a pic of Dad and Lemon snuggled in his bed with smoothies and matching sixteenth century bonnets, complete with feather quills and all.

LEMON HEAD: I lied. I'm not reading that big ass script. I borrowed a VHS from the library, filmed in like the 1700s by BBC. Papa Holiday ADORES it btw. Major brownie points received. I'm catching up to you.

Gosh, I love her. There's no doubt he's in amazing hands. I sigh a relieved bundle of nerves into the air and turn away from the window. To the large, burly man that makes my insides flutter, crammed in the seat beside me as he drives us over the land bridge.

"Everything okay with your dad?" Dustin asks, slowing as the department of motor vehicles worker flags us to the side lane. "Construction on the dam again? It's because they keep fuckin up the buffers with their bullshit apartment buildings that they even need to keep fixing the shit at all."

"Mad about it?" I tease, lacing my fingers over his, formed around the gear shift that he pushes into second as we come to a pedestrian's pace on the detour. He brakes when another worker with an orange outlined stop sign halts the traffic, easing onto the clutch with thighs I'm paying far too much attention to the thickness of as he throws our hands into first.

"Guess we stop here and wait until they open this back up." He leans back in his seat once we're parked, stuck in line with a bunch of other cars while they work on clearing the dam. "And yes, I'm very mad about it. Hunter and I used to play at this shoreline as kids. It's sick what assholes like my dad do when they buy up land and then all the sudden the place where you used to hide with the reeds and turtles, listening to cicadas sing, feeling tadpoles skim your toes, whittling bark into whatever your mind could think because there was actually a spot of nature available to still think in…is a fucking *hotel* now."

I frown. "I can see what that would do to your image of him, but can I ask you something?"

He nods, and I will my confidence to keep up with my mind, because he's helped me in so many ways in my life. With getting into therapy, which is going really well it turns out. When we were kids, and my mom died. Even now.

"Do you think you hate the man your dad *is*…or the man he *was*?"

"Ouch, Shay." He lets out a breathy laugh, but I can hear the truth behind his joking tone, and I squeeze his hand harder.

"All I'm saying is, I don't get a choice to love who my dad will be one day. To see how our relationship might change or grow. I don't want to be that bitch, but don't waste yours. People change."

"I'm starting to see the parts of you that must resonate with my bratty little sister now," he teases, but I throw him a serious look, and he gives in. "Fine. Tell me like it is, it's okay. I probably need it."

"It's nothing bad, Dustin. You care so much that you bleed out everything you have inside to make life comfortable for everyone else. But where's your comfort? If the relationship with your father is always a sore subject for the rest of your life but both of you are here and willing to make it different, begging for it to be so, what are you waiting for? An invite? *Death?* Because I can tell you, one may come sooner than the other, and it might not be what you hoped when you imagined your future with the only man who will ever be *that* man to you."

"Fuck." He rubs the back of his neck, jolting when several honks sound from behind us and the road worker knocks on his side window.

"Carry on!" he shouts, and my goosepimples prickle, body heating as a blush spreads over my bare legs and arms.

"Sorry if that was too serious." I fear I've takaen it too far, opinions being subjective and all. Certainly, where parental relationships are involved. But he simply squeezes my thigh, rubbing his hands over my skin to warm me up.

The goosepimples settle down, until he's massaging slow circles in the apex of my thighs and my head hangs back in bliss.

"I'm so lucky," he whispers.

"How do you figure?"

"Got the sexiest dancer in all the city in my passenger seat, legs spread wide and dripping, soaking through her flimsy leggings, just begging me to bend her over and slip inside, stretch her how she likes."

He rubs me to orgasm while he drives, and I can hardly handle how hott he looks with one hand on the wheel and the other between my legs. "You shouldn't be allowed to look this sexy," I mutter breathlessly.

"Oh yeah?" He puts his fingers to his lips and sucks them clean. "You shouldn't be allowed to taste this sweet."

My cheeks flush so brightly I can feel the heat atop my skin, but it doesn't bother me the way it used to.

Matter of fact is, I love this man, and I'll drip from his chin for the rest of my days.

"Can't I open them yet?" I whine, saltwater licking my ankles and feet. Thankfully, they're bare, because Dustin did give me that hint at least. I've been holding my sandals at my side while we trudge through the water's edge. "I know you said it was a walk, but you *are* a bit of a stalker, so I have to ask…you're not luring me to my death in some oceanic cave, are you?"

"If I were, I wouldn't tell you," He teases, dropping the blindfold to reveal a tall, stone building I know and love. One he looked deep inside my heart to carve out and put here before me.

"The aquarium where she…did you know this was the one my mother worked at?"

The Oceanside Research and Conservation Center for Aquatic Life. ORCCA for short.

"I did." A worried brow creases the center of his forehead when my tears start to bead. "Is it okay? That I brought you here? I asked your father if he thought it would be too much, but it's just a few miles from the hotel, so—"

"It's perfect, Dustin." I rise to my tiptoes and kiss him on the lips. "Just like you."

"Well, I'm no marine creature with multi-sentient limbs, but I'm pretty good, right?"

"You've studied up on cephalopods, too?" I grin wildly as I shake the sand from my feet and slip on my sandals, skipping through the large double doorway, lined with tiny carvings I used to trace with my fingers. Even now, as I skim the stone with my hand, I feel the peace and wonder this place used to bring me.

I feel my mother.

"Thank you so much, Dustin. Thank you!" I throw my arms around him, pushing him against the doors and slamming him with a kiss.

"Anything for you, Shay. I mean that." He nudges me forward. "I got us the VIP passes. It's empty today. Most people don't come at this hour, the lady told me on the phone, so…" He slides his tongue across a silver gem that's new as of today. It has a purple stone in the center that I can't help wondering about. Was it put there for me? Like the purple flowers?

"Show me some fish, Shay." He winks when I seem unable to move from my spot of elation here in the lobby and walks ahead of me, into a blue-lit tunnel, surrounded by jellyfish.

It's beautiful. The whole place. I remember my seventh birthday party here, with a cake and turtles we got to pet right over there. I can see her now, in the corner, walking in with my candles a glow, leading the birthday song as my friends gathered around. Lucy was there and her brother whom I still for the life of me can't remember the name of. The memories fade so fast. To think that neither Lucy or my mother are alive to see this place, and never will be again, is heavy.

"I miss her."

We walk around the exhibits for what seems like an hour, before we finally reach that place. The special one that haunts my happiness and tangles within my soul. The place she was most at peace, her very own dance floor.

I touch the glass I used to see my mother come alive behind. "She'd swim with them. She wasn't afraid."

"You remind me of her. What I remember at least." He wipes away my slow rolling tears. "You look just like her, beautiful. Brave."

"Hah!" I almost double over. "Me? Brave? You sure you're not talking about one of those Flinger models before me?"

He frowns.

Okay, that wasn't fair.

"I mean, I'm not brave. I'm the furthest thing from it. I'm insecure and worried and anxious all the damn time…"

"And," he brings my wildly flailing hands back down to my sides and forces my body to the tank, bracing me in front of my reflection like he did in the studio, "you're a successful businesswoman, an award-winning teacher, a talented athlete…and quite frankly a damn good fuck, waffle cone."

"Is that my new nickname now?" I twist my lips at him through the tank, and he lowers his to my neck in response, hot breath lingering in a place that feels connected to much more.

"Can't call you a virgin anymore, can I?" He licks a solid line down the side of my neck. "Not when I've felt the inside of you wrapped around me like a glove."

"That feels so good," I tell him as he guides us to a dark corner. "But won't people see?"

"Someone very *very* wise recently told me she likes watchers," he teases, "but we only have twenty more minutes to hotel check in, so we better behave, hadn't we, waffle cone?"

I groan, wishing he wasn't right. "Okay." Disappointment flickers through me at the idea of leaving a place this peaceful. This quiet darkness my mother once called her home away from home. The place my father watched her as he fell in love.

Maybe she's here now.

My grumbly poet of a boyfriend must see this, because he's on his knees in a flash, offering me his hand and bowing like a prince straight out of every movie I never bothered with. I was too busy dancing in front of the mirror.

But *this* prince seems to yank me right through the looking glass and spell me in all the ways I didn't know I needed. A guide, to aid me in my shift from complacency into something more. To break free.

Be the Shana Holiday that isn't alone.

Not the last of her kind.

"Will you dance with me, Shana Holiday?"

And we do, by the glow of the neon lights, surrounded by jellyfish and magic.

His skills have improved. My heart patters like a schoolgirl at the way he holds my hips, confident in his lead and strong in his moves. It's assuring as a teacher, but even more as a partner.

His partner.

"You're scarily good for this for a newbie." I throw his earlier words back at him, grinning from ear to ear so there's no mistaking my teasing here.

I truly am proud of him.

"Who knew six foot everything, bear-like country boys could be so swift on their feet? I'll have to start a beginner male dance class, so all the big oafs in town can show off their pizza positions."

"Are you making fun of me, my sweet, compassionate teacher? You wouldn't, would you?" He pretends to take a dagger to the heart, and I roll on top of him, tangling him in kisses and defense tickles as we fall deeper in love. I wobble a bit as I stand, Dustin catching me in his arms, but I came up so fast I guess the air left my lungs with my breath. "You're breathtaking?" I joke. "Just a bit light-headed suddenly."

A yellow octopus swims to the rock at our eye level and swats a tentacle at the glass, blinking at me.

"Feels like a sign," I say, "like my mother is trying to tell me something. Even in the darkness, our light will still shine. Love will still find us. We can grow together or…" I trail off, grasping desperately for a reason to confirm it's her, but before I can finish my sentence, the little yellow dude inks the water and darts away.

"Feels like Truman the Octopus," Dustin corrects, and we laugh about that one until we're back in the car and on our way to the next big adventure. Maybe it *was* a Truman situation. Or maybe it was her, giving me her blessing.

Either way, I'm doing it, this journey with the man of my dreams. And for the first time in my life, I'm confident about something that isn't dance.

Here we come, Business Elite. If we can handle cherry popping, waltzing lessons and an octopus inking, what *can't* we do together? Hope blossoms inside me that we'll save the studio, too.

"And I love that for us," I blurt out loud, weird and awkward as ever. Dustin presses back a smile, but who even cares about embarrassment at this point?

I'm *me*, after all. And I'm beginning to like her just how she is. Weirdness and all.

Chapter Twenty-eight

DUSTIN

God plays puzzling games with my integrity. Always has. So, it's He who will be at fault for whatever happens to the man across from me at the gala table.

Lawrence Lawson, in the flesh.

My background check on the asshole hasn't come back yet, but I don't need a cop with a computer to tell me what my instincts already have.

He smiles widely, beaming a sinister light at my girl, a woman who squeezes my fingers so tightly they tingle.

"I'll get us seated somewhere else. We can leave altogether if you want, just say the word, Shay."

"It's okay," she whispers, reaching up to pull at the hair she's used to hiding behind, but it's not there. It's high atop her head in a poised ballet bun, two thick braids twisting through it. The bright red dress she chose tonight is elegant and racy all at once, a long-sleeved bodice made of transparent lace roses and a slit so far up the side of her leg, my mouth waters.

"Did you wear this color for me?" I ask, aiming to ease the tension that coils around us.

Because not only is this a table with the very man who plans to ruin Shana's chances of salvaging her studio, and all the tenants of Pine Forest who run their businesses out of that strip, but also because aside from Lawrence here, I'm the only one who knows that.

Shana just knows her strip is being sold to a mysterious buyer. Dad only knows there's a property his random new buddy intends to help him buy, and this fucker Lawrence is the attorney ready to settle it all. I'd bet my left nut he's the entire reason for the sale.

He stares me down like a puzzle of his own.

Try it, buddy. Nobody can piece my shit together.

But I can see right through him the longer he sits here, a defense one picks up behind bars, to read people. And even though his face says he's all but ready to attack, his fingers tightly clenched around his water glass, white at the tips from the force of his grip, tell me this predator is more like a snake than a wolf.

It's not a hunt. He's only paying attention to me, because I'm starting to pay closer attention to him.

And I will wreck his chances of fucking Shana over and doing any dealings with my father or his associates, if he so much as tries to make a move against any of the people at this table I love.

Yes. I breathe a deep sigh, squeezing Shana's hand as I think. *Even my father.*

Because she was right about what she said in the car. I do hate who he was. But he isn't that man anymore. He may have moved on and divorced my mother—they had their shit, and he wasn't always there for me, but when times have required the type of support he knows, legally, monetarily…he's given it.

Does it excuse the man he was all those years ago? The one who saw a fighting boy and turned his back on the grounds of reputation? The one who pushed too hard?

No.

And it doesn't excuse his abrasive conditions now.

But I notice the crow's feet around his eyes, the grey streaks in his hair, and suddenly realize how long it's been since I last saw him in person.

Since I wanted to.

"Hey, Dad."

"Son." He nods cordially before easing into his chair like an old man, older than I thought he was. He grunts as he scoots into the table and folds a linen napkin over his lap ceremoniously. I marvel at that for a second, impressed really. I've always let my distaste for him run so thick that I never noticed how well he fits into this upper-class world, despite knowing he scraped bottles by the train tracks as a child for lunch money.

I'm proud of that, and I don't know how that's supposed to sit.

I've always seen him as soulless, a Scrooge, blinded by profits and the rise to be more…but he was a father in an unhappy marriage to an alcoholic.

He wound up living hours away from his teenage children, one of which ended up behind bars and…well, my sister had her own set of issues, didn't she?

Was he simply doing his best by staying away, sending money and securing us a future?

I notice a folder on the table beneath his hand labeled *1602 Mullins Road-Settlement Documents*, and I know he didn't do that for him. It's for me. Like I would for my own children, if ever given the chance.

In the same breath that I measure my father's trespasses against me, I begin to think over my own. I have also hurt others in the name of justice.

Shana squeezes my hand back, and I lean into her support, the support she gave me yesterday and the continuation today.

She's right. Maybe it's time to get to know my father.

This dinner has been surprising. Instead of fighting and grimacing, holding back words against my father like usual, I've been smiling and exchanging pleasantries. Shana, who was nervous about her acceptance speech up till now, has been relaxed into his company, as if this were a real thing between us. How we might be at a family get together or…wedding, even.

I watch my father and the woman I love laugh across from one another, recanting old stories from our childhood, and I like that thought. Marrying Shana Holiday and making her an official part of our family.

Telling my sister we share a best friend.

"You've been quiet. *Dusty*, was it?" Lawrence chimes from across the table, leaning back in his chair, spread eagle like he owns the place. Little does he know, Lemon owns the place.

Her father does at least. Every little venue or hotel on Boardwalk Avenue, including the snow cone stands are properties of Perkins Global Enterprises, and I'd like to wipe the smug elitist look off his face and tell him I could have him kicked from the premises with one text.

But I won't.

I grit my teeth while I look him over. I can't wait to get him alone with Dad and see the way his face drops when he learns nobody at the Campbell Firm will be contracting him again.

Borderline stalker, that's what he is, and he wasn't even nice to Shana on that date, just wanted to take her to stupid Swan Lake to get under her skirt. I know, because I legitimately *was* stalking her, as fucked as that is.

"Nothing wrong with being quiet," I say flatly. "I prefer to watch and listen. How about you?" I take a swig of my drink and down it all in one sip, clanking my glass on the table only a tad too hard. "You *watch* any, Lawrence?" I cock my head toward the surgery scar, three inches thick along the thumb of his left hand, put there because of me. "Doesn't look like you do much listening."

"You fucker!" Lawrence growls, slamming his good hand down, nearly knocking my father's glass from his station.

"Dustin, what is the meaning of this?!" Dad rumbles.

Shana's eyes bounce between the three of us, looking every bit like my little sister caught between one of our old throes.

"You're causing a scene." Dad cuts his eyes to Lawrence. "Both of you."

Shana begins to speak for me. Dad knows nothing about her history with Lawrence, or that he's targeting her, because shit, *she* doesn't even know he's still targeting her. *And I don't know to what extent, either.*

I fucked up.

I should have told her about all of it. I should have phoned Dad before today, too. I *am* a fuck up.

"You don't get it," I try to tell them, "he's—"

Shana cuts me off, exhausted and hard to read, but she doesn't seem mad. Not at me. Maybe, just disappointed I provoked Lawrence.

She knows who he is, she just doesn't know what *I* know. And before I can even tell her, she's hushing me. "I need a moment."

Dad grumbles, the disappointment I'm all too familiar with radiating from his body, ready to fire like a bomb if I say or do the wrong thing, like always.

"I would love to share a dance, Miss Holiday." Dad offers her an arm. "Congratulations on your accomplishment with the Business Elite."

She smiles, exhaling her worry and nodding politely back. "I'd love to. Thanks, Mr. Campbell."

Lawrence and I are left across from one another, locked in a stare-off that seems to intensify by the second.

Neither of us blink.

Until we do, simultaneously.

Lawrence smirks, crossing one puny leg over the other in a smug sort of prodding, but I tell myself to let it slide.

Shana will be back here soon, and I can control myself around this shit long enough to figure what he's playing at.

I think I can, at least, until he speaks again.

"She's elegant for a *dancer*, if you know what I mean."

I immediately want to break his other hand.

I know what he's trying to do, and I loathe that it's fucking working. "If I remember clearly, *you* were the one with the boring job. Not her."

"I knew you were listening on that date. I could practically smell your pathetic stench watching her from across the bar."

"Fuck off, Nemo." I crack my knuckles just to show him what working ones look like. "I can make the right fin just as lucky as the left."

"I could sue you for even saying that!" He spits, but he scoots his chair back all the same.

"Got proof I said it, do you?"

His nose scrunches in and he clicks his irritated tongue, dismissing me, I guess. What the fuck ever.

All I care about is apologizing to Shana. Making sure she's okay before they announce the speakers.

She dazzles, laughing and shimmying with my father as he twirls her around the floor. I beam back at them, waving as she teaches him a tricky step to a popular country song. Never did I think I'd see that side of him.

I want to snap a pic for evidence and send it to Devyn. *He can have fun and be free, see.* But my chest pings in a melancholy fashion when I remember I can't tell her. She doesn't know about us yet.

Our father, the grump in question, and Shana come skipping back to me, linking arms and using faux British accents to describe the taste of the fancy scones, and I grin at the possibility of the future playing out before me.

I want Devyn to know.

I'm ready if Shana is, *for all of it*.

Forever.

"That was extraordinary, my dear. I look forward to many more dances as you continue to court my son, I hope."

"I guess I'll keep courting him." She snorts, rolling her eyes to me.

"I'm sorry I got meat-heady," I whisper as she sits.

"It's okay. Your dad showed me a good enough time." Her eyes widen with mine as she hears her sentence out loud, and we both laugh when her arms break out in goosebumps.

My father does not hear the innuendo, *thank fuck*, but Lawrence does. "Passing her around the family, Campbell? I'd have thought better from a man of your morals."

"The fuck did you just say?" I growl, clenching the tablecloth to save face, and my fucking sanity.

"You heard me."

"Ignore him." Shana tugs my arm, her eyes glancing between Lawrence and my tightening fist. "He's not worth it."

"Oh, *he* will be worth it when you see what he has that you want. Only three more days until then." Lawrence stirs the ice in his glass, holding her gaze suggestively.

"What is he talking about?" Shana eyes me, like I'll agree, but I can't agree. Because I do know what he's talking about. I should clue Shana in right now, but I feel the need to set this fucker straight first. He's messed with my girl *and* my town.

But I can do this without a fight.

I can do this the right way for Shana.

I'm ready.

I unclench my fist and hold Shay's hand instead. I want to explain it all to her this instant, and I wish I had before, but right now what matters is telling this creep where to fuck off and keeping her safe.

"Have you checked the bids lately?" I smirk when I see his brow line bead with sweat. "Sometimes real estate can be hard to get your *hands* on. You've only got one good one now, so."

"Dustin…" Shana elbows my side. "What is this?! What is he talking about? What are *you* talking about? And why don't I know?!"

"Shay, I'll explain," I assure her.

Lawrence seethes from his phone. "You didn't!"

"I did." I swig my water, but Shana tugs at my sleeve again.

"What is *happening*, Dustin?"

She won't calm down with this secret in the air, and as much as I didn't want to ruin her night with this, she deserves to know about her studio, even if I do have it under control.

I remind myself she's not mine.

She's hers.

I clear my throat and turn away from Lawrence. This isn't for him. "He's the one bidding on your studio. On all the businesses there. For *my* father."

"What?" She twists her neck his way, but I ease her chin back.

"I didn't want to upset you. You have the speech and your father, so when I found out last night, I bid against him and—"

"Whoa, whoa, whoa. You knew about this last night? And you didn't tell me?"

"I didn't want to worry you. I have it under control. I was all set to rope Dad in on the plan, and secure the property *myself*, but…"

"But you didn't tell me, Dustin."

"I was protecting you."

"You were sheltering me! Like everyone has. Like I have to myself my whole damn life!"

Lawrence invades our space, poking his arm between us to slap a settlement contract down on the table. "This is what your father has already signed. Now that the bid is much higher, he'll have to reset *his*, which I'm all too willing to bet he'll do. What makes you think he wouldn't? After the same bullshit you've brought him time and time again… *Malicious Assault* and *impairment of a minor,* was it? Oh, I'm sorry." He crooks a wicked smile. "It was impairment of *three* minors. I know about your history of vengeance. Thomas Remington and his crew. Do you know he has to use hearing aids? For the rest of his life. Pity, really. He used to sing so beautifully in the choir."

"Who the *fuck* are you?" A growl rips from deep in my throat, so audibly the table beside us turns to stare.

"This isn't about land, Dustin. *It's power.*" Lawrence flicks his eyes over Shana's body, and I want to end him right there, even before he says, "And she's, after all, just a *dancer.*"

Shana stiffens beside me. Her fucking speech is in just a few minutes, and she's the goddamned winner of this whole night and this asshole is here bringing up *our* pasts like he knows us.

Thomas singing in the church…you'd have to be a local to know that. Even before he almost died at my fists, he and his crew had stopped attending regular service.

God knows when the Devil sits in his pew.

And I know when a predator's in mine.

"I wasn't kidding when I said I'd break the other hand, Lawrence. We both know my father is not going to sign that bullshit once he knows how it'll affect the Pine Forest community. You're just fucking with her at this point. For what? Because your date didn't work out?"

"Okay, this is going too far." Shana searches for my father to return from the restroom, but her name is called over the speaker.

"Shana Holiday of Holiday Dance Company is our Grand Winner of Business Elite's Small Business Excellence Award. For the Seventh Year in a row!"

Shana turns my way and pales as the announcer chirps on. "And how lucky we are! This year, Miss Holiday has been able to join us and accept her award in person! Congratulations, Miss Holiday. Please come share some words of wisdom or tips for the younger, newer entrepreneurs here."

Her face pales. "How am I supposed to go up there and speak when the two of you might kill each other?!"

Lawrence smirks., "Don't worry, honey, you're good with that mouth. Isn't she, Dustin?"

I want to slice his face open with my knife, but I don't. And fuck if that's not progress, so I'll take it. I do my best to block out the skeevy lawyer with a death wish, a mere foot away from his ending, and focus on Shay.

I know I fucked up, but she needs me right now. She needs me to be her light.

She blows out a gust of air and tears fill her eyes as I smooth my hands down her arms.

"Put all this away for now. It's my fault this got so far, but now is about you, Shay. Just be yourself. Tell them how to be better, like you did with me in the car. With my dad. My nightmares. Just speak from your heart." I wipe away her tears with my thumbs and offer a genuine smile. One I hope she knows means *I'm sorry.* "They'll be lucky for even a shred of what you give them."

My heart beats fast as she grabs my hands, tangled by fingers and fears. But she smiles back, and I can see the confidence shining as she lifts her chin. "You got this."

I meander back to the table and pray I can convince my fists they don't belong docked in Lawrence's eye sockets for just a few more minutes of this gala.

"That was gross," Lawrence says.

I sigh, hating him even more, but nobody said I couldn't fight with words.

"The only thing gross around here will be the negative number in your bank account when all your contracts start falling off. When my father and his network boycott your services." I turn away from him and face the beauty that is my moon, lighting up the stage before me. Not dancing, but possibly even better. Owning her light. Basking in her glory.

Letting herself live and love for the first time since her mother died and her father was diagnosed.

"Thank you for this award," she starts, the cadence in her voice a shaky squeak. She inhales suddenly, closing her eyes and then opening them back up and finding mine. Her words flow with the change, like a choreographed dance. I find it impossible to look away as she faces her fears and encourages everyone in this room to do the same. "I used to think success was about making sure nothing went wrong. But I'm beginning to learn that you can't control it all. And true success, whether in business or in life or *love*..." She finds me in the crowd again and smiles. "True success comes with reacting to the leaky parts. It's how you fix them. Who you choose to let in and ask for help when it all becomes too much. Even if they go about it the wrong way. It's about—"

"It's about love, it's about happiness and help...blah blah blah." Lawrence sneers over his whiskey. "Does she talk this much when she's sucking your cock?"

"Say it again!" I slam down my fist, knocking glasses on the table and halting Shana's speech. All eyes are on us, and I hate it. I didn't intend to cause a scene, but he's *here,* attacking her again. For what? To rile me up? To stain her reputation along with mine? "You say one more thing about her, and I'll—"

"What is the meaning of this?!" Dad scolds in a hushed tone.

"You'll what?" A sinister smile curves Lawrence's lips. "You'll deafen me? Paralyze my entire right side maybe? If I get to choose…" he muses, circling his chair. "I'll take what you did to the more fortunate of the boys…just a *really bad coma* for a while. Sleep through the memories of my mauling, if you will."

My chest tenses with his accusations, memories of what I did to Thomas and his friends as blood flowed from his eyes and ears slicing through my brain like a chainsaw, ripping through meat and bone with force and no compassion. Just power and pain.

"You know what?" He smirks. "I take it back, make me deaf," Dad stares at him incredulously, seeing him for what he is. "Then I won't have to hear her go on about my cock when she realizes she's too good for you."

"That's fucking enough!"

Heads from the other tables turn to face us, and I catch a second's long sliver of Shana's mortified face on stage just before Lawrence lurches across the table. He's on me then, tackling me while Dad pries my arms back so I can't swing them and shoves Lawrence aside.

"Stop it, Son! You're making a scene!"

"*I'm* making a scene?" I whirl on him as Lawrence cowers beneath my father's boot on the floor. "This fucker has been spying on Shana, Dad, tricking you into closing on her studio and a handful of other locals in the area, and for some reason he won't let up on the insults he likes to throw at her. Ones that don't fly with me when he knows as much about her as he does."

"I'm sorry." Shana's voice quavers over the speakers

just before she exits the stage. "Thank you for having me."

We all snap our attention to the stage as a round of apprehensive applause fills the awkward silence and Shana makes her way back to the table.

She doesn't look me in the eyes. Any of us.

"This," she says quietly. "This is what I was talking about. Everyone always wants to do things their own way. And if you're like me, that means being alone. But you know what being alone and festering in your own ways and habits does to a person? It makes them stagnant. It causes remorse and resentment, turmoil, and despair. Longing and hoping for nothing that changes because *change* comes with conflict. Change can win if you let it. You just have to work together. To trust. Don't you see?" She heaves a depleted sigh from her tear-streaked lips and directs the last words to me alone. "I thought you did."

My breath and my heart leave with her through the swinging ballroom doors.

I'm up on my feet to follow her before my next heartbeat can fire, but I'm halted.

"You!" Dad starts, and at first, I think it's at me, but it's *Lawrence* he yanks up by the arm and drags to his feet. "Threatening my family and their town? Shame on you. You will not do business with Campbell Properties, or any of our associates, ever again, Mr. Lawson. And you'll be lucky if I don't press charges for verbal and physical provocation. You were right about one thing…land is power." His eyes narrow. "I have a lot of land, Mr. Lawson. Are you familiar with The Honorable Judge Presley? Helped him close on a lovely estate last spring."

Lawrence spits at his feet, straightening his suit jacket and storming off, but not before looking my way…and smiling.

Fucking creep.

My eyes flick to the doors, the same ones Shana left through only moments ago, and the need to go to her surges through every piece of me before Dad wraps his hand around my arm.

I wince.

Then so does he.

"Habit." I clear my throat as remorse ghosts his brow.

"I'm sorry I've not been on your side in the past, Son, but know that I would never stand for this from anyone on my team. That kind of man is *not* my buddy…that's not me." His face reddened from humiliation and anger over the nefarious side of his new pal, Lawrence, sets in. His eyes are sunken, and I can't ignore how old my father has become when I see him this way, worried… caring. "If I'd have known the town wanted to restore that strip, Hell, I'd have offered leasing programs to the tenants directly. You know we can do that…does…does Shana know we can—"

"I know, Dad. I know that's not you. Shana knows you would never operate like Lawrence, okay?" I scrub the back of my neck, moving to a private alcove of the banquet hall. "She made me realize something this weekend." I cast a deflated laugh into the air between us. "We were different people when w-w-we—"

"Stopped trying?" He sighs, knowing what I'm saying without any further explanation needed.

He doesn't correct my stutter.

And it doesn't go unnoticed.

"I want you to know, Son. I've only ever done or said the things I have, to help secure your future."

"I get that, Dad, but *you* have to know something too. What your idea of forever looks like, and what mine are, those are two different things, and the only future I'm remotely concerned with just walked away from me in tears. And that's half my fault, if I'm being honest."

My eyes travel to the doors, no longer swinging.

That's what got me in this mess in the first place, not *being honest.*

Dad nods, a smile forming just before he does something we've not done in a long, long while. We hug.

"You *aren't* my father," he says. "You may have a temper and a record like him, but no matter what you've done or what you do, you are nothing like him. You are my *son*, and I am proud of you. I regret that in my efforts to… I thought you needed…w-well—"

"Who's stuttering now, Pops?" I smirk, earning a groan and a chuckle as he shakes his head.

He's trying.

"Well, to Hell with it!" His nostrils flare, a subtle rub to the pocket-watch my grandfather gave him before he was sentenced—when Dad was just a kid—and he exhales as his sincerity shines through the tears in his eyes. "I do not wish to be a stranger to the man I raised. Not like I was to the man who raised me."

I don't know how to react. He's bleeding his heart out, but years of resentment I harbor for his choices lord over me, even if they do feel a few pounds lighter on my chest with his remorse.

Will they always be there?

You can't erase what's been written in blood.

But when his eyes crinkle at the corners and he gives me a look of pride I've only seen him use on my sister, one I've waited my whole life for, the pencil doesn't feel so out of reach anymore.

We can't erase it, no, but nobody said we can't keep writing.

"You have always been worthy, Dustin. Now go get her."

Chapter Twenty-nine

DUSTIN

Percussion. That's what it feels like.

Heart bouncing and feet scrambling up steps, two at a time.

Then three.

The elevator was taking too long. This is now.

She is forever.

I can't take back the things I've done. The secrets I've kept from her. The past, where I hid in corners to catch a glimpse of her light, or current, where I withheld vital information regarding her studio, despite knowing all she wanted was my integrity and honesty.

But for the first time since I was a child, using my *father* of all people as a compass, I know what to do.

If he can atone, so can I.

Each passing moment I'm with her, my tinted view of the world…of what could be, is forced to the light.

Shana Holiday does that, *a song with a body.*

A body with a soul.

One that fits perfectly with mine.

And that's exactly what I'll tell her when I see her. That I never want to be apart, and the only fight I want to be in, is the one for our future.

I reach the twelfth-floor master suite, *Business Elite's Finest* across the door on a golden plaque, and I take a deep breath before I knock.

Nothing.

Knock.

My hand raps against the door, harder this time, but again, nothing.

My pulse picks up, barely having slowed at all from my ascent to the highest tower in the tallest building.

But there's no princess here to save.

Reluctance be damned, I pry the key card from my back pocket. I don't want to bust in on her if she prefers to be alone. But then, the thought of her falling asleep crying…tears streaking her pillows from the unrest of earlier—that thought *stabs* me.

If she's asleep, I'll lie beside her.

We can talk in the morning, when she's ready.

Hell, I'll let her deck me as hard as I did Lawrence, curse me if she needs it. A sad smile crosses my face with that thought, shy little Shay with a swear word on her lips, and the love I have for her fills me with confidence. Not in myself, but in our relationship.

Our mutual, unconditional love.

I turn the handle, hopeful this will all work out. I've never been so sure about a thing in my life, but I'll fix this.

We need each other.

I push open the door, but the breath I'm holding is

yanked from my lungs.

Not with what I see…but who I *don't*.

I scan the room, but it doesn't make sense. If she'd run off to the restaurant or bar after the fight, sure, but her *dress* is draped across the bed, the very one she wore downstairs only minutes ago. Her earrings sit fresh on the nightstand.

My brow crinkles as I process it's barely been twenty minutes since the incident downstairs. Not nearly enough time for her to change and vanish without crossing paths on the way up.

Unless she took the elevator.

It's the only way I'd have missed her.

I grab the keycard I've placed on the dresser and pluck an apology flower from the hospitality bouquet, but my breath wooshes away like I've been kicked when my eyes drop to the floor to see Shana's phone cracked and wedged between the fire extinguisher and the wall, *by the exit.*

My throat tightens as I bend down to pick it up, hands shaking. Something doesn't sit right.

We fought, *yes*, but Shana's not the type to be irrational. To run off and leave her phone behind, wandering alone on the boardwalk at 11 p.m., let alone shoveling her way through massive convention crowds in the hotel restaurant or bar.

I slide open her phone, entering 5678 and unlocking the screen. Second time my therapist's been wrong about my creeping on her being unhelpful, and even though I want to smile at that, at how the girl of my dreams and hopes became the girl who hoped and dreamed for me right back, worry is all I can feel or think.

Where is she? And why is her phone still here?

Her home screen lights up with texts and missed calls. *Seventeen of them.*

I'm not sure what's going on, but Lemon's been desperately trying to reach her for the last ten minutes, so I dial back from Shana's phone, immediately putting it on speaker.

If something happened to her father, maybe she left too fast to realize she dropped her phone.

But the car keys are still in my duffle. How would she have driven? The name on the screen eases me only slightly, and all I can do is pray they're together.

"Oh, thank God you're all right!" Lemon shouts in hysterics. "I was about to start calling Dustin. Don't fucking *do* that to me, okay?"

She's not with Lemon.

It's not about her father.

Terror streaks through my mind.

Blood.

Tears.

Limbs

> *And*

>> *Hands*

>> *And*

>>> *Clinging arms.*

"Fuck! Lem. This *is* Dustin. Where is Shana?"

"What?" Lemon's voice cracks. "She's…she's not with you? She was going to find you, but her phone cut out, and she…Dustin, she screamed!"

"*When?* Where was she going?"

"To you! She was coming to see you, but—I don't know if I should tell you."

"Tell me."

"She was…*shit!*"

"Lemon Perkins, you tell me whatever the fuck you know, do you hear me? Her phone was by the door *cracked* and—Lem, I fucked up."

"She was going where you told her in the note, but then she screamed out of nowhere! Don't fuck with me, Dustin, is she with you or not?"

Impatience forces its way through my lungs until I'm growling into the phone, swiping it on video. "What note? I didn't leave a note." I circle the room with the phone to show her I see nothing by the bedside.

Lemon rolls her eyes in annoyance. "Well, I guess not, stalker. You leave her so many you can't keep up with them." Her eyes widen at something on the bed behind me. "Check her purse! That's where she keeps them."

"Lem—"

The words crumble on my tongue.

Lemon's brow pinches over the screen as she takes in the confusion that must be plastered over my face. My heart threatens to pound clear out of my chest, my body is weak, my throat is tight.

I dump the contents of my girl's purse frantically, through shaking arms and swirling vision.

I cannot breathe.

"What the fuck are these?"

Every hair on my body stands on end, pins and needles

stabbing me from the inside out, as *dozens* of folded foot-ball papers spill onto the bed from the bag. One note is unfolded and crisp, penned on hotel parchment.

Lemon squints at me like I've lost my mind. "The creepy notes you leave her. You know, like the one with the plant? *I'm watching* and *See you soon*. That kinky watcher-shit you two do."

Fear claws at my senses, because it can't be…what I'm reading on this paper…

"Lemon, I've never sent her any notes."

My eyes fill with dread, tears falling, desperate for answers as I tear through the other folded bits of things I didn't write.

Undress for me tonight.

I clench my teeth and turn my horrified eyes to Lemon's. "The only note I *ever* left her was with the plant. Everything else was through Flinger."

Flinger.

My mind swarms with memories, clues hidden right in my face, and my eyes drop to a note on the bed. One with a pull tab that I yank open to find a sickening moment in time, stolen from her. From me. *From our relationship.* And with one look at the typed signature on this note, I know the thief too.

Dance for me tonight at your window.
*XO, **L**ove of your **L**ife.*

L.L.

"Lawrence Lawson."

"Oh my God!" Lemon shrieks. "Jeremy, call the police!" she shouts, turning her trembling face back to mine on the screen. "Go to the place on the note but be careful! Turn on your location, and…and I'll give my phone to the police to track you! It's our fastest bet."

"It's not far," I mumble, already locating the note. "I know where he's taken her. I'll call as soon as I know something."

"Wait!" Lemon chews her lip, heavy eyes set on mine. "I shouldn't be the one to tell you, but…" She swallows, terrified eyes piercing mine. "She's in more danger than you know."

Chapter Thirty

TWENTY MINUTES EARLIER

Broken.

That's how I feel. Torn in half, like a fragile sheet of loose-lief paper, crumpled in on myself because I thought we'd both changed.

He warned me he'd never be able to control that side of himself. The one that can't stand by and hold back.

Still.

I never should have let myself go on that stage and speak in the first place, leaving him alone with that scummy flinger-has-been, somehow resurrected from the depths of my memories and shoved in a suit and seat at our very table.

It felt odd.

I should have known there was something connecting him to Dustin's father and the properties when I saw him at the table by Mr. Campbell, but this?

256

In front of several hundred of my peers in the Business Elite, I've been humiliated.

I take the elevator twelve floors up to my suite, not even caring that I've wiped mascara across a thousand-dollar dress I imagined Dustin unzipping me from only hours ago. I slam the door behind me and promptly tear the heels and gown from my body to change into one of Dustin's oversized shirts and some dance shorts.

In an instant, I feel safe. It even smells like him… *Nautica,* that stupid glass bottle I'll always go gooey for because of him.

Because it brings me back to our roots, and that reminds me what we really are.

Forever.

As long as I have memories, Dustin's been in them. And I never want to think that will change, even if I am bummed some other parts of him seem to be holding on steadfast and *not* so amicably.

Mainly the fighting. The unnecessary urge to stick up for me. To solve it all.

But I guess it goes both ways. I have an unnecessary need to bundle up my woes. And he knows I'd have tried to handle it completely on my own had I known what he knew about my building and Lawrence Lawson.

Still, I'm angry for the secrets. All they do is cause people to hold onto feelings for centuries, like me and Dustin. I smile at that memory.

But I guess I haven't been so truthful either. Not where secrets are concerned, at least. The biggest one of all being the one Dustin and I have been keeping from his sister. From everyone except Lemon and Jeremy, really.

"I want to tell Dev," I tell Lemon over the speaker phone. I dialed her up a few moments into my ruminations and threw on a face mask to cool off my puffy eyes. "I'll talk things out with Dustin and lay into him for sure…but still. After all that, I want this secret, and all secrets, put to rest. Everyone knows everything from now on."

"No more hurling balls, then?"

"Guess not." I sigh, reaching my hands above my head and knocking into the shelf above the hotel headboard. It's fancy up here on the Twelfth Floor, *Elitists and all.* I roll my eyes as Lemon bursts into laughter over the phone, but then I see something that pulls my mouth into an instant smile.

"He left me a note!" I squeak happily.

"Over your anger already?" Lemon shakes her head in faux disappointment, but I can't help myself.

I *am* mad.

But I also love him.

So, I unfold it and read aloud.

Seeing you in fancy gowns has nothing on the stars
we saw before. Meet me there when you see this.

-XO, Your Octopus

"Uhh?" Lemon squints up close to the screen. "Does that mean something to you because it's weird, per usual."

"It does." I swoon, recalling our dance around the aquarium only a few hours ago. "He wants me to meet where we went earlier today. I know I'm supposed to still be mad, but…is it super weird if I just want to hug him and make sure we're all right?" Even if he *was* in the wrong for giving in to Lawrence's shit, which he one hundred and twenty percent was, life is better with that grumbly milkshake man. And I *am* proud of him for showing quite a bit of restraint tonight. The old Dustin would have thrown a punch before appetizers had been served.

I smile at that. At the progress he and I have both shown in our own lives.

"You're worse than Hunter and Devyn," she teases, but the smile stays in her eyes when she assures me I'm not a total relationship moron. "It's normal to want to make up. *I think.* I'm no expert in *staying* in relationships, as we all know, just starting them." I hold back a snicker when she gives me a serious look. "But you and Dustin have clearly been a match for—"

"Centuries?" I offer excitedly, and she nods in agreement, her support and friendship wrapping me up like I didn't know I needed. Because we do need our friends, as much as it hurts to lose the ones we love, loving them at all is worth it for people who are there when you need them most.

"Hold on, Lem, I didn't see I had a voicemail from before I turned my phone on silent at the gala, but I still need to figure out what to say to him when we meet. He can't be totally off the hook, ya know?"

"For sure, babes. I wouldn't dream of letting him slide easily if I were you. Groveling and oral at the very least for punishment if you're asking for my honest opinion." She clicks her tongue sassily into the camera as I laugh in agreement.

"K. Hold on, lemme click over."

The recording plays in the background, and I recognize almost immediately it's from the Pine Forest Health Center. The therapist I've been seeing has been working to get me on meds to help with the anxiety surrounding Dad's situation, and that eases my mind a little.

"Miss Holiday, this is a notification from the after-hours nursing staff at Pine Forest Health Center. Because you have signed authorizations indicating we may relay health information and lab results to you via phone or voicemail, we are exercising our right pursuant to…" blah blah blah, the bored-sounding nurse recites her script on the message, and I don't want to wait any longer to find out my doom. I just want to leave this room and find Dustin.

"Recent lab results show that you are not a viable candidate for benzodiazepines, therefore your prescription will not be filled as previously discussed with your healthcare provider. Please call our office for additional information or check your health portal for test results. Thank you for trusting the staff at Pine Forest Health with your—"

I end the call, immediately dialing the doctor's office, but it's almost eleven on a weekend.

Of course they're closed. Ugh!

I switch the call back to Lemon, who is still on hold, the amazing friend that she is, and every scary thought rolls out of my mouth at once. "What if it's bad? Why can't I be on an anxiety medication? What if—" I can hardly speak it. "What if I'm like my parents, Lem?"

"Stop it!" Lemon snaps. "Look me in the eyes."

I do.

"Go to your health portal and pull up your lab results. We'll read them together. Okay?"

I do what she asks, taking her off video to log in and promptly clicking the newest attachment. "I got it." I study the document, confused and equally frustrated. "I don't know what any of this means!"

"Look at the key on the right as you go down the list," Lemon explains, "If it's out of normal ranges, it should show up in red."

"This one does." My breath leaves my lungs. "It says positive, hCG >36."

Lemon gasps.

"Shay, you're pregnant."

Sadness, happiness. Fear and apprehension.

All of them course through me like an injection to my heart. I rummage for my keycard, leaving my purse on the bed. We'll be back here soon, because I refuse it to be any other way, needing more than anything to be with the man I love, regardless of what happened at the gala. None of that matters now—meaningless fights and grudges.

Our family is what could *be*.

I yank at the door, rushing my thoughts to Lem, my fears, plans, hopes…whispers of words that don't make any sense at all as they stumble directly from my still-blown mind and out of my mouth with no filter.

My future.
No, our future, Dustin and me.
And this baby.
Not the last of my kind.
"I'm pregnant."
But speaking it feels like a *sting*. That can't be right.
I shake my head, colors and light spinning around me as I try desperately to maintain the truth I just held so close, one where a life now lives inside of me.

But the sting *is* a sting, pinching at my neck. Alarm censors beat from my chest as I use all the force I can muster to slap my hand against the entry point, and I feel it there.

A needle.

A scream rips from my chest; the last thing I manage to get out before my body hits the ground.

Chapter Thirty-one

SHANA

My ankles scrape against a coarse surface, prickling threads pinching when I pull.

My head pounds before I can peel my eyes open, and I vomit as the blackness falls again. I drift back to here, wherever that is, and yank my feet forward, but nothing gives. My vision flutters, a firefly blinking, sometimes close until it's far away again.

"Open your eyes, Shana!" a voice hisses, deep and musky, but forced like it's being shoved out of a tube it can't quite fit inside. But that makes no sense.

My head pounds, and it reminds me of my monthly headaches, which reminds me of my period, which reminds me of...

"The baby!" My eyes spring open, but it's so dark where we are, I can hardly see the other person across from me. It's patchy, and I'm wobbly.

I didn't notice the hangover until my eyes tried to focus.

On Thomas Remmington.

"Thomas?" I attempt to shove back, but forget I'm stuck in place. Tied to a chair.

Tied like Thomas.

It's dark, but the lantern hanging above us glows enough. It's unmistakably him.

I'd know that voice anywhere. It's the one that splintered my confidence.

A date.

A drink.

A fizzing white pill you'd never notice across a beer pong table in a field of people.

"I didn't want this!" he sobs through a twisted fabric gag, stretching his mouth. "I'm not who took you." Thomas' eyes drift to the floor, feeling the footsteps beneath us before I can even hear them. "Pretend…" his sentences become panicked and half-spoken, "sleep!"

I watch, aghast, as he slinks into his chair and closes his eyes.

"The hell is going on, Remington!?" I yell, trying to buck my chair forward. Instead, I earn a slow clap from the last man I ever expected to walk through the door.

"Lawrence?"

"Hey, honey, I'm home. Did you miss me already? Uh-oh, your restraints are loosened." He bends down and tightens the ropes on my wrists and ankles, breath heating my exposed skin and churning my gut.

Or that's the baby.

My breath gathers in my lungs, and I heave it out steadily.

"Pity your old pal Tommy isn't awake to see the big finale."

"What are you doing, Lawrence, and why am I here? I know you and Dustin had your moments, but we didn't work out. You didn't like me to begin with, remember? You called me a stripper!"

"Your GUARD DOG BROKE MY HAND!"

The air releases from inside me like it's been knocked the whole way out, and all my hackles rise.

He smoothes his hair, a tic in his neck taking over and forcing him taller. He straightens his suit for the third time, then forces his skeevy smile on me. "I wanted you from the start. *I* noticed *you. I* asked *you* out on Flinger. We matched, Shana! *Sixty-Nine!*" His voice drops. "Don't you remember?" His eyes wander my face wily, a different side of Lawrence reaching out from inside and breaking through and taking over. "He *ruined it*, Shana!"

"Okay," I breathe, nodding, anything I can do to get him to move an inch away from me. Away from the threat that at any moment he could knock me over, punch me, kick me, harm this child—*or worse.*

My neck stings on the puncture wound of the drugs he injected into me, and for a swift second, I allow myself to pause on a thought. That maybe whatever he gave me already hurt the baby more than anything he could do now.

What if he killed her?

But, no! I shake my head, grinding my teeth in defiance of my own thoughts. I won't think that way.

Dustin would fight.

We will fight.

Because I'm not alone. I'm not the last of my kind.

And I'm saving us both from this monster.

"Was it you? Writing those notes all along?" I pinch my eyes shut, half of me not wanting to know, the other half already having accepted it. He doesn't answer, just huffs, a wounded child, finally told he can't have everything he ever wanted after a life of anything he could imagine.

Somehow, I understand that.

We're told we can grow up to be anything we want to be, but not everyone finds that pot of gold, some just find broken bits of rainbow, cling desperately to shards of color, and struggle to maintain hold of a single, jagged edge…and that's if they're lucky.

"And Thomas?" I ask, putting together the pieces. "That's how you knew about some of the details in your notes that only Dustin would, isn't it? Like the octopus or the stars."

He lifts his head as a strange sort of pride settles beside his anger. "You don't know, do you? Even after all these years, you still haven't seen the truth."

"What do you mean, *all these years*?"

"You didn't have one stalker, Shana Holiday." He smiles, brushing a sweaty strand of hair behind my ear. "You, my dear, are special enough for two." He winks. "*Eye see you.*"

"But…" My heart races, letters and words tumbling behind my eye lids even as I squeeze them shut to block it out. "…that one was from *middle school*. It's my oldest one."

Lawrence nods solemnly, and it's the same exact moment he does that all the water in my body rushes from my eyes and falls like waves down my cheeks. A shrill cry flies from my throat, nothing in its path to block it, my mouth wide as my eyes at the terror that spikes me with his admission.

"It was always me, Shana, your love letters. But of course, I knew you were too perfect for me. Too perfect for this world! I had to create a better one. A home," his lips curve, his eyes flashing with hope just as quickly as they do anger, "away from death. A place to dance your days away, free of pain or loss, a *habitat* all your own."

He tosses a handful of sugar packets at my feet and kneels beside me. "Like when we were kids." He frowns before he crushes a packet in his fingers. "No matter what I do, you still don't SEE me!"

My skin prickles, memories skittering as the sugar packets lay in a pile.

A roof.

A flash of Lawrence stacking the Stevia at Cowboy's Paradise, then another…

A boy with a hermit crab.

"It's you!" I gasp. "Lucy's brother!"

Larry.

His face twists with a demented sort of glee that chills me to my core. "That's right, darling. I've always loved you, but I knew I would never be good enough, so I waited. Unlike that imbecile you've attracted the attention of. *I* waited. Patiently. It was *my* turn. He had his, and he turned you down time after time! I WATCHED IT! He rejected my precious, perfect little dancer."

If heckles could rise any higher, mine would be in the sky. I pull at my bindings, but they're too tight at this angle. I've got to get myself turned.

"I always hoped you'd see me, even after my *pathetic* sister found my photographs and threatened to tell you. I burned them, and I burned her, too." He smiles, not a shred of remorse on his features. "Bye, bye, Lucile."

Tears break over my vision as I scan the room, Thomas is captured, I've been taken, *Lawrence killed his own sister.*

"But you only saw *him*, and I knew in my heart, if you could see what I see…you'd remember we've always been meant for one another. Remember our fun? Remember the notes I left you? None of this amateur *watcher* shit your criminal boyfriend plays at."

It occurs to me, the extent of Lawrence's delusions. Is he not a criminal now, too? At least Dustin did everything in the name of honor, saving those who needed him. Innocent girls being taken advantage of were brought to justice because of him, and it haunts him still every night.

Lawrence doesn't even see his faults.

He's proud of them.

He gets close again, lips brushing the shell of my ear. He must think I like it, because he rubs against me, a satisfied chuckle stumbling from his throat, and I try like hell not to vomit.

"I'm the real deal, baby. Watch you wake, sleep, even put you in a shiny cage of diamonds, so I can watch you sparkle anytime I please. Want to see?" He grins wildly. "I installed a ballet barre. And a pole, *of course.*" My breathing halts, chest seizing at the weight of his words.

"You sent me the music box after my mother died, didn't you? I always thought it was Dustin."

"I *loved* watching you dance. More than he could ever know!" His smile and his scowl are nearly identical, his eyes shifting from left to right so fast, I can't keep focus. "My sister could fly, but you could soar." He flicks open to an image on his phone, bars and lights and chains. "I've found a way to keep your wings clipped now."

"I didn't help him, Shana!" Thomas cries, working his chin up and down, loosening the gag around his mouth. When his eyes lock on mine, I fear him almost as much as the psychopath lording over me. But the boy who stole my trust is done playing possum now. He's a changed man, watching. Listening. Even without his hearing, he squints his eyes to read Lawrence's lips beneath the light.

It occurs to me as I watch his show of loyalty, that Thomas may always be my monster, but he's a fellow victim of a much bigger threat to me right now, and if he makes it out, so do I.

So does my baby.

Tears flow down his bloodied cheeks as he looks at the cage on screen and sees what I'm seeing. "I didn't do this! Tried to stop him, but he…he's been threatening my family! I'm different now, Shana, you have to believe me! I am not part of this!" His voice becomes a falsetto cry as Lawrence cracks a whip across his face. He snatches the hearing aid from his left ear, the only ear with hearing capabilities at all thanks to decisions he made long ago.

Not Dustin. *Him.*

"You would have raped me like you did the others," I say to Thomas, for the first time in my life.

Funny how it doesn't make me feel any better. Just honest. I know he can't hear me with his ears right now, but I find it worse for him that way. He sees it with his eyes, formed precisely by my lips. He feels it in his heart, tied up here with nowhere to go. Nothing to do but listen to the girl who got away.

He nods, tears and blood seeping over his swollen lips, still fresh from Lawrence's beatings, as the apology sails from inside him. My body energizes unevenly, hatred and disgust I crafted against the very man before me now warring with empathy, because *I'm me.* I'm Shana Holiday, even when I don't want to be.

And I feel his sincerity at my core.

"I'm sorry," he sobs.

Lawrence strokes his finger through the pooling blood on Thomas' face, bringing it to my lips as my childhood attacker hisses in pain. I cry out, shaking my head away, but I'm tied down, arms and legs bound, as he shoves the blood into my mouth and forces me to suck it, sounds of Thomas' protests echoing against my skull. I convulse, gagging uncontrollably when it hits the back of my throat.

"Taste how grateful you are. This is how grateful little dancers take their masters cocks after a long day of work." He shoves his finger back in, then scrunches his nose at me in disgust when I wretch, pulling away and wiping the spit across my cheek. "What's wrong, *baby*? You don't like it when I treat you like the nasty girl you are? But you like it when *he* does it, don't you?"

Smack! The sting across my face is instantaneous. Sharp and jarring. "Disgusting little slut, giving it up for him like a good-for-nothing cum dumpster when I would have *treasured* you. I watched you; you know…*waffle cone bull-shit.* I would have made you my QUEEN!"

I cough, the iron taste of someone else tinging my tongue, swirling with the sickening words he laces with my likeness, and acid rises from my gut as I projectile vomit across Lawrence's chest.

Vengeful, punishing hands shove me back, anger forcing his weight until my back hits the floor, and the chair cracks beneath it. *Good,* I think, because he hasn't noticed the break. If I can stall long enough, get untied…*I'll figure the rest.*

Placid beats go by, with nothing said nor done between us, and I use the stalemate to prod my fingernails into the edge of the ropes securing my wrists, as his chest heaves and sweat pours from his pinched brow. He stalks forward, wild as I've ever seen him.

Crazed.

"You think he's so good for you, but he's done nothing but half ass jobs of ending your tormentors. Can't you see? *I* have taken Thomas and brought him to you. *I* will kill him. *Slay him for you,* until his blood spills at your feet, and you can dance in the glory that is his ending, his suffering for you, my love. Law and Order. Justice!"

He straddles my body. It's still tied to the broken chair, but what he doesn't know is that it's only by one hand now.

I just need to keep him talking long enough to free the other.

My body shakes, but I thread my fingernails into the layers of rope, dismantling his plans strand by strand.

He can slay my monsters or dragons, whatever time may bring, and he can do those things all he wants, but as I've told Dustin and will tell any man who poses the same…

I'm the only one who can save me from myself.

It's taken me far too long to see that clearly, staring through the mirror. And while I used to think that made me a loner or an oddball, it really makes me a fighter. And you don't have to be alone to fight for yourself. You can do it surrounded by the ones you love.

"Thank you." I gasp, fluttering my lashes and feigning appreciation. I channel my inner Haans, acting as best I can and laying on the flirt, as I repose my hands behind my back, my entire body weight depending on my triceps not to give. My chest puffs, determination and grit seeding where they must, a reminder it's not just me I'm saving today.

It's *us.*

I drop my eyes to my tummy, a gift that means more than all the world, one I never even asked for but suddenly can't imagine living without. And I promise her in this silent moment; I won't go down without fighting for us.

My family.

Lawrence can't see my freed hands behind the chair, but he'll soon feel them. I do my best to fake a smile, beckoning him near.

It seems to be working. And it takes every bit of willpower not to drop the act, as he loosens his tie and sinks to a chair upright.

He doesn't set mine back up.

It feels like a punishment. A way to control me and the comfortability he may provide, and I thank God for this man's insanity, because he'd see my hands and it would all be over. I pray like Hell that won't be the case as my voice rises to a lustful octave.

"I mean it, Lawrence," I continue. "Thank you. It all makes so much sense now. It was always you, wasn't it?"

I tell him what he wants to hear. He needs me, this much I know from the immediate slack of his shoulders when I lick my lips and pretend to shudder. "Nobody has ever *killed* for me before." I flick my eyes to Thomas, now cowering and sobbing from his chair. "You would really do it for me?" His head tilts, pupils dilating at my new disposition.

"If you come closer, I'll show you what he taught me about kissing. I bet he did it all wrong. You could teach me better."

"I could." He palms his slacks, erection forming beneath them while I hold back the excess vomit threatening my digestive tract. Lawrence's breath is already enough to churn guts *without* the ick factor of his insanity.

And then it happens, he kisses me, tongue diving in and dragging along the edges of my own. I hate every nano second that passes. If there's something smaller than nano, I'd like to file for an individualized patent on hating his kiss *that* much too, but this is strategy.

I wonder what Dad would do? He'd relate it back to Shakespeare somehow, and Titus Andronicus did not spend all that time wining and dining Tamora just to throw it all away for simple revenge. No. He ended his enemies in style; her rapist sons baked in a pie she feasted upon before a dagger to her throat.

I can do this. I won't meander on the rest of the story where pretty much the entire cast dies regardless.

No. I'll kiss him, coffee breath and all.

He leans into me, and my muscles burn. I can press more than his pathetic excuse for a body, though, and I've never been more thankful for my training as I hold both of us up by two hands, my attacker unaware that we're resting in my palms. I suppose he imagines he's just crushing my bound wrists, chivalry and all.

Lawrence hums in appreciation of our tongue tie, and I try to imagine Dustin in his place, anything to distract from the man on top of me and what could become if I don't succeed.

Haans called me Licht during our date. I looked it up later, and it means light.

That's precisely what this is.

I've drawn this man to me, a beacon. A light. Not one stalker, but two. And isn't it shitty how all I was doing was being myself? Minding my own business? Wearing hoodies and leggings? It's standards like that I hate, too.

I want to vomit again, but I push it back.

I wasn't lying about binge-watching *Law and Order*. The more compliant I appear to this lunatic, the better this will be for me and the baby.

That's how I'll escape.

I want to cradle my stomach, even if it is too soon to know whether she survives this, to hold my hand against her tiny, forming heart and tell her it's okay.

I promise her that. Right here. Right now.

It will be okay, sweet girl.

I don't even ponder that I immediately know the sex. I just do. And she's mine to fight for. Mine to hold.

Mine to bring into this world, not his to take.

I am nobody's to take.

I am Shana Holiday, Not the Last of Her Kind.

Not a shy, pushover virgin.

I'm Business Elite's Finest, an Award-Winning Ballerina, World's Most Supportive Daughter, and a loud, proud *weirdo* with the best friends a girl could wish for.

Confidence pulsing, I let out a breathy whimper, baited specially for Lawrence, whose tongue is now wandering disgustingly down my neckline. Unfortunately, it's exactly where I need him to be, and I'll take whatever I must if it means we survive this.

I eyeball Thomas, getting his attention over Lawrence's hunched form. The lunatic is still licking trails over my skin that are so unappealing they might as well be from snails. I want to peel my skin from my body as I press back a sob and tears I dare not let him see, if he's to think I want this.

I motion to the door with my eyes. The keys hang from Lawrence's belt loop. I can't tell where we are, some sort of boiler room. Every so often there's a whooshing sound, like a toilet flushing by the back wall. Whatever it is, it's loud and requires a motor. There will be workers on this floor, *wherever we are,* and once I get free and grab the keys, I'll need Thomas to distract Lawrence long enough for me to escape and find one.

Somehow.

With Thomas' hands and legs still bound.

Shoot.

"Distraction," I mouth to him in total silence. I pray it's not too dim for lip-reading.

He nods immediately, and hope carries me forward.

"You taste just like I imagined you would. So sweet. Innocent." Lawrence winds his tongue around my earlobe, his breath hot and suffocating, but I lie all the same.

"You like that?" I purr, repositioning my hands while he's distracted. I arch my chest up. "If you lift my shirt, you can taste there, too. Just move your hand from my shoulder and put it where I *really* want it." I drop my eyes to my breasts, because if he frees my shoulder, I'm golden. I throw him my very best version of a flirty wink, and it sticks, *thank God,* because I wasn't even sure I did it right, chest still rising and falling so fast I fear he must sense my nerves.

A smile creeps across his face. It would be handsome if he wasn't a hostile stalker holding me captive. It would still be plastered to a money-hungry murderer, though. One who tried to steal my studio and force me to his will, coercing me to undress for him under the guise of another man.

One who killed his own sister.

Fuck you, I don't say, because I want to live.

Instead, I moan and wiggle, shoving my crotch into his knee for show. "I want it really bad. *Please, Larry.*"

His gaze drops to the hem of my borrowed T shirt, and his lip curls in disgust. "This his? This shirt?" He grips the fabric around my neck and twists, tugging until he's choking me, the tightness in my throat forced even smaller by constriction. My pulse sounds in my ears with each word he utters. "Is this filthy piece of scraps HIS?" He smells it, *like an animal.*

Obsessed.

His nostrils flare as he thrusts his pelvis into my still tied stomach. "Do you feel this? Pressing against my pants to find you? You do this to me, but then I see this filthy piece-of-trash shirt covering what's *mine*, and I want to burn it."

Panic rushes me, my breath staggering when he procures a lighter from his pocket. He strikes it with his thumb, the flame flickering across his gaze, luminating his empty eyes, and a smile that will forever haunt my nightmares. "Maybe I'll burn my name in your flesh, just above this used-up pussy. Everyone will know that you belong to *me.*"

My arms are searing in pain, my fingernails broken and bursting at the tips from splinters of rope shoved deep beneath them, but I will not let him win.

With the last piece of rope sawed free, and my bloodied fingers flexing for what's to come, I jerk my head toward Thomas as a signal.

I can't wait any longer.

Thomas grunts, growling and crying through his sopping gag, shaking his chair to come to my aid. The very boy who tried to take my dignity, my innocence, my *autonomy*…struggles at his ropes to save me from a monster I fear is far worse.

He's what Thomas sees himself as, and I can hear from his cries how he detests who that is. I wonder, through his cries, if purgatory is always after one's death. Perhaps this is judgement day. For more than just Thomas.

His arms pull at his sides, bound to the chair as he struggles to break loose, yanking at his restraints and rocking his chair to no avail.

I guess it's scarier that he can't even hear the asshole talk right now. All he sees is fire in this man's hands, and with his face toward me, Thomas has no way of reading his words. He stares ahead in horror as he watches Lawrence hovering above my exposed belly, flame so close the hairs on my skin tinge the air with a foul smell, and I wince.

"Leave her alone!" He roars, surprisingly loud through his gagged and swollen lips, and I'll be damned, but it works.

"What did you say to me, Ears? You wanna burn first?" Lawrence whirls around and snatches Thomas' hearing aid from the table between us and lights the thing on fire until it's sparking and smoking, dropped to the floor and crunched beneath his foot.

Yup. I might hate Thomas fucking Remington to the end of time, but Lawrence Lawson? *Fuck this man.* Shakespeare himself wouldn't bake him in a pie. He would taste so foul, you would have to vomit him back up.

And that's exactly what I do.

Vomit.

All over the back of him, because what he doesn't know, is I am standing now. And free, my feet untied from excessive rubbing and yanking at the broken joints of the chair when he was occupied with my face. And what rich little boardroom boy doesn't know is *I don't sit in meetings all day.*

I'm at the gym. And I'm twenty-eight years of pure, athletic, muscle.

"Hey Lawrence," I say, wiping the puke from my face as I sock him in the jaw. "That's for Lucy."

His hand darts to his cheek, embarrassment and true hurt snaking through. His brows pinch in as he clenches fists at his sides. "*You fucking liar!* I was going to propose to you here! For your mother, but you ruined it. Again!" He pulls a knife from his suit jacket and takes a step, eyes shining against the blade. "I'll have to kill you both now," he says dejectedly, face blank and resolved, like it's more of an inconvenience than anything.

When I think I have a shot, I shove him against the table and dash for the keys.

"Stop!" He screeches, scrambling to use the table and chairs for balance, but he slips on blood.

Thomas' blood.

And he falls back to the ground, right below Thomas' feet, and the two of us exchange a single glance, no sign language or lip reading needed for this message.

We kick him until he can't stand. "Stop! I will slice your toes off one by one when I get you in your cage, you horrible piece of trash! That's all you'll ever be with him, you know, smalltown white trash, ballerina, washed up in a water-damaged studio with no one! I know you, Shana! I've *watched* you! *I* can be there for you. *I can provide!* Just look at what I've built for you! You can dance your days away and never want or fear again! Just think!" His face lights up, obsession swirling through dark orbs he darts to mine. "No more people means no more loss. No more sadness. Just me and you, and all the time in the world to dance in your life-size music box. My pretty dancing doll, don't you see it?!"

He swipes at my legs, but I'm too fast, kicking and stomping on any piece of him I can land until he cries out, bloody and bruised, a crumpled paper like the ones he left me…waiting…watching…*defiling* my innocence and trust.

"You are wrong!" I scream at him, slamming the ball of my foot into his groin and sending him several inches across the floor with the force of my kick. "I am not alone. And I'll never be alone."

I snatch the knife from the ground and slice Thomas free of his chair and *God* does he sob, falling into my body and hugging my waist.

"I'm so sorry. I'm so sorry, Shana. I'm so sorry. What I did back then…"

"Stop it, Thomas." I crane my neck down to his. We don't have time to spare, so I'll only say it once. "It's past. I'm not saying what you did will ever be forgiven, because you don't deserve that from the girls who didn't get away like me. The ones who didn't have a Dustin fighting their battles for them when they were too weak or naïve to notice it was a battlefield at all. For Sarah and Tiffany and those who aren't here to tell it to your face, for them you are *not* forgiven Thomas, and you never will be." I pry his arms off me and slide them gently to his sides before I spin back around and snap my foot against a groaning and stumbling Lawrence, shoving him back to the floor with a crack of his teeth against the tile. *Woops.*

"Look," I tell a deflated Thomas, before I shove the keys in the lock. He reminds me of Dustin in this way. Of me, even, secrets and emotions bottled up for far too long, never moving on or breaking free.

No more.

I can choose to walk away from this nightmare, now and forever.

I can move on.

"It's been a long time since you made those choices," I say, carefully choosing my words. "Nobody can take back who that makes you or what you did. But you can write the rest of your story in whatever way you choose. And you have already started, by helping me get out of here."

Lawrence groans behind us, shoving to one elbow before Thomas knocks him out again and I wrangle the keys.

"Now, let's get the heck out of here before he wakes up and remembers a deaf dude and a one-hundred-and-ten-pound ballerina dismantled his grand stalker plans, yeah?"

We brace ourselves for what's to come, as I swing open the door, and the saltwater air kisses us in the face. *I know this floor.*

"The aviary!" Right above the aquarium. I turn to face Thomas. "That was the whooshing sound. The vibrations?" He nods at that. "The note said to come here, but that was when I thought it was from Dustin. I will my heart to slow as I think about what we need to do now. "We just need to hold him long enough for security."

I search Thomas' face, but he's already backing up into the room we just emerged from, eyes ahead and streaked with fear.

"Dustin!"

Chapter Thirty-two

DUSTIN

My fist smashes into Thomas Remington's face, knuckles vibrating with the impact, pins and needles surging through them as I clench tighter and swing harder for the second, then the third time, when my arm is yanked back. Before I can stop the motion, I'm pulling them forward, but they drag their feet, and I pull back the weight of my punch just as the sirens sound and blue and red light the field, reflecting in his blood.

"You don't have to do this," Shana shouts, shoving my body in place as it prepares to lurch forward. At Thomas fucking Remington. "It was Lawrence that brought me here. Thomas was…" Her eyes fall to her former attacker. One I thought I taught a final lesson to stay the fuck away from her over ten years ago. But he's back.

With my girl, bloodied and beaten.

"He helped abduct you!" I grind out. It's all I can do not to scream in rage and fury. The man I swore to kill is right here, and I could end it now. I could fucking end his life.

For all of them.

"It's not the same, Dustin. He was a kid."

"He knew not to fucking rape people, Shana, do not defend this piece of shit!" I snap at her, and she shuffles back. "Shay…I'm not going to hurt you," I say, horrified she'd even flinch at me. "I love you."

Her eyes find mine and hold me there, her captive. How ironic since she's the one with ropes cut at her wrists and feet.

"I love you too, Dustin. And you're here. But so is *he*. And I know what you want to do, and I get it. I know what he means to you. What he's done and how that's affected every one of us in this room. But *I* am choosing to move on from all of it."

Lawrence, lucid now and groaning on the floor, tries to push up.

Fuck! My eyes widen to the real predator. One I knew I could smell from a mile away, and I hate myself for not following my instincts then. I begin to panic, assessing the closest route around the table to restrain the fucker and keep Shay safe from Thomas at the same time, but she's there before me, already punching and kicking and sending him back down in a defeated whimper.

"You're going to so much jail, Lawrence. But don't worry, I bet there's plenty of sixty-nine in the state penitentiary." She clicks her tongue in triumph, and damn if that confidence isn't the sexiest thing I've ever seen.

Her fight.

That's what she's been saying all along, isn't it?

This is *her* fight.

"You don't want me to kill Thomas?" I ask, getting my answer with one look.

But it helps to hear it anyway.

"No more dragon slaying."

I nod, offering her my arm and throwing Thomas one of the discarded ropes at my feet to use on Lawrence's wrists.

"Tie him," I command, insinuating with altogether disdain, that I will skin him if he so much as looks at my girl, despite what she wants. He takes the rope and does as I suggest, securing Lawrence's wrists behind him and tying him to the table legs.

With all the restraint I can bear, I spare Lawrence Lawson a single glance before we leave, wishing I'd broken his other hand.

But Shana doesn't want that.

I don't want that.

Not if it costs me her.

I follow her out, cursing the one who scraped up her back, wrists, and God knows what else, but forcing my body to move forward.

Not behind.

I cover her shivering shoulders with my jacket, recognizing the torn fabric of her shirt as one of my own, and a warm sense of satisfaction settles in, knowing she chose to wrap herself in something close to me.

Even through the darkness, before she was taken, I'd been forgiven. And she didn't need me to save her, either. She may have wanted me close, but she didn't need me to lift her up at the gala. Not for her business, her honor, certainly not for her pride.

She saved herself with the strength of the moon, the power to move tempestuous oceans and light the darkest of skies.

"I really can't slay your dragons anymore?" I frown.

"No, but I do know something else you can slay for me."

"What's that?"

She smiles, bringing my hand to her womb, and shining so brightly, I can do nothing but beam right back.

"Fatherhood. Turns out the mini pill doesn't always work."

Chapter Thirty-three

DUSTIN

A ballerina dances in an open window, as the sun peeks over amber fields and coffee masks the air. Her nose crinkles.

"Ew, why do you brew the dark roast when I'm over? It smells like a skunk." She sinks to a butterfly stretch and breathes in with another coffee-induced nostril flare, returning to her yoga.

Who knew my whole world could fit so perfectly in the form of a beautiful woman sassing me before six a.m.?

Seems the whole town did. Word has started to filter around about the incident, despite a bulletproof NDA Lawrence's defense attorney must have been paid in gold to draft up.

We aren't supposed to tell anyone about the incident until the sentencing next month, but it's happening, and that's all that matters. Lawrence Lawson is going away for an exceedingly long time.

Most of me still wants to knock him out cold and feed him to the mountain lions, piece by piece, for what he did, but I suppose that wouldn't win me any points with Shana, now would it?

More importantly, a certain nimble someone might not let me give her cooking lessons if I act out again. My mouth curves, replaying the waffle cone session in my mind, at how completely she melted in my arms.

Cooking really isn't her thing, but she wants to learn for the baby, so *pancakes* are next week's lesson, and I pray like Hell it gets as messy as the last.

Today is for peace, though. For family.

Today, we tell my sister and Shay's father of the pregnancy. She wanted to wait until she had her second blood test, and yesterday we did, along with an ultrasound, to confirm the baby is doing well after the stress of…everything.

She is.

Strong and perfect, just like her mother.

Today is a good day, because it's also the day I tell *my* father our plans.

Peeling back these layers has been restorative for both of us. Sharing secrets has freed us from binds, physically and metaphorically. Even the ones we wrapped up ourselves.

I run my eyes over the woman I love, draped across my bed freely, glowing as the light surrounds her, and I pray that this never ends.

"Sorry about the coffee smell, but I can't miss my father before his trip. To give him my decision."

She grins, accepting the Gatorade I poured specially for her, my coffee-hating weirdo. "I'll accept your apology juice. Now, let's call Daddy Campbell."

"Don't call him that." I shiver. "It has creeper vibes."

"*You* have creeper vibes. You are aware you actually stalked me, right? You looked in my window to watch me undress and monitor the health of my houseplant."

"It doesn't count when you're amicable and attractive," I tease. "I'm like a friendly, vigilante spider-hybrid."

"No." She giggles, shaking her head at me hysterically. "That is nothing like what happened. And anyway, I never got an upside-down kiss, so if you *are* a spider-hybrid, you're a lousy one, and I'm one peeved-off Mary Jane."

"Peeved?" Now it's my turn to laugh hysterically. I love this girl more than anyone could ever comprehend. I tickle her to the bed and flip her around before she can protest, and I grin ear to ear when her laughter sings through the bedroom.

I lower my mouth over hers, upside-down as requested.

"Is this what you imagined?" I kiss her.

"Not quite," she says, eyeing my piercing. "See, in my fantasies, you spider manned me on my *other* lips." She winks, and fuck if my cock and my heart have ever felt more in sync than around this woman right here.

Dad's custom ringtone cuts through the moment and we both sputter, righting ourselves and accepting the video call.

"H-Hey, Dad."

"Son. Good to see you." He sounds sincere. "And Shana, I'm relieved to see you recovered. How is my grandson?" He beams with pride, as if he's the father himself. Strangely it doesn't bother me like it used to, and I sift it off like sand.

"Just the same as two weeks ago." Shana snorts, rolling her eyes. "You know *she's* only like seven weeks cooked, right? Most people don't even know they're pregnant this early. I don't want to…you know." She wiggles, voicing the concern she shared with me last night. "I don't want to count my chickens before they hatch and peep and, maybe even fly, ya know?"

I'm impressed she feels comfortable sharing it. She's come a long way from the girl who was scared to speak to others. My heart swells when my father meets her concerns like…like a *father.*

I'm grateful he cares, because we're trying now, he and I. And that brings me to why I asked him to call.

"Dad, I've decided to take the job with you. To be your apprentice." He doesn't respond, but Shana squeezes my hand in support of whatever I choose.

"No," he finally utters, desk drawer sliding open. "I will not have you work for me."

"But—"

"You will be too busy working for yourself. Between Sugar Stable and your new property on Mullins Road, you have a lot to tackle as you navigate fatherhood." He grins, crow's feet and all.

Shana elbows my side, but I don't understand.

"I have to earn Mullins, you said—"

"I know what I said." He frowns, leaning closer to the camera…and me. "I was wrong, Dustin. In so many ways,

I have been wrong in my life, but lately you and your sister have taught me, well, it's time I be *right*, not wrong. And if what's right is helping my son and his fiancée get two, no…*three* businesses up and running as they grow our family, then that's what I'll do."

"But the studio," Shana muses, "Pine Forest square. You said you'd let me and the others rent-to-own. Is that still on?"

"Of course," he assures her, "but not for you. For you, I have paid it off in full. The title is yours, Miss Holiday. Consider it an early wedding gift to my daughter in law…*I hope*." He winks at me.

"I can't accept this." Shana shakes her head at Dad through the screen.

"Well, you don't have to marry him. You can still keep the title…I know he's a lot."

Shana rolls her eyes and snorts, but he presses on.

"I can't let you. It's too much," she argues.

"No." He tilts his head to me. "It's not enough."

Shana looks on, but I just shrug, perfectly aware how deep his pockets run and not giving a fuck how much of that he gives to my girl. *Bout time he wasn't an ass*, I mouth, as she presses her lips together.

"Thank you, Mr. Campbell," she concedes.

"Don't thank me." Dad lights a cigar, waving it in the air. "I'm a selfish man, after all. Need to keep Business Elite's finest afloat if I want guest access to the twelfth-floor casinos, now, don't I?" He grins, taking a drag and nodding once before ending the call and all our fears in a matter of minutes.

Laughter cures all wounds, they say.

And by the time we're done, I think they might be right.

SHANA

TWO MONTHS LATER

The chill of winter bites at my exposed ankles. I knew I should have gone with the fluffy socks and boots combo. Grumbling, I yank my leggings down over my goosebumps and whine.

"Lemon just *had* to convince me to wear the ankle booties, didn't she?"

"You could have declined. Perhaps you like them more than you let on." Dad winks at me, a teasing gleam in his eyes.

"Old fart." I narrow mine in defense but drop it all with worry when he shivers. "Are you sure you want to stay for the whole thing? I'll go home with you if you're uncomfortable." I check my phone, noting there's still ten minutes before the talent show starts. Dad wanted to be here for it, the new program Dev and Hunter started up, after what turned out to be a life-changing past few months for them, too. And I thought *my* situation was crazy.

But that is a story all in its own.

"He's fine!" Lemon hushes me, scooting her butt in between us. "Pops over here has plenty of heat-warmers lining his jimmy-johns and so many prescription edibles that he has no idea how cold it is, do ya', Mr. Holiday?"

"Lemon! You gave him gummies?"

"What? No! Never. He had edible…arrangements. The fruit sensation, of course!"

Jeremy snorts, covering his face with his scarf, and I scoff at Lemon, but it's mostly for show. It's Dad's decision to be here. Whether I like it or not, he is done with all treatments and trials, unless it's for pain or sleep.

His time has come, after years of fight, and he wants to go down surrounded by the people he loves, not beeping monitors or wires holding him down.

I eye him warily and water surges my eye sockets, but I'm not alone. Lemon squeezes my hand. Jeremy's there with a smile. My baby kicks me from within.

I am not alone, and neither is Dad.

"It's okay, babe. He's happy," Lemon assures me. "He's involved. Let him have this."

"You're right." I wipe a single tear from my cheek and smile at my father, squinting into his binoculars and searching the stage for Ellie and the other children he adores to see. It's been a few years since he was out of bed long enough for events like this, and my heart tenses knowing it may be the last.

My hand cradles my belly. She won't ever know him, and that breaks my heart. But this is who he would have been for her. The grandfather who showed up. Who watched her dance.

"We're telling the others today. Dev and Hunter… all our friends," I tell Dad. "But I'm glad that you were one of the first to know. I'd have told you sooner if… well, you know." I sniffle, but his eyes still adorn me with praise. There's nothing like that look, the one your parents give you when you've made them proud. I'll treasure the memory of this very one.

Frame it in my heart.

And anytime I need it, there he'll be.

"What will you name the child?" he asks, setting the binoculars on his lap.

"Well, you'll be thrilled to know I convinced her to go with Randall for a boy," Lemon teases, knowing I'm one hundred percent convinced it's a girl. I just know. I roll my eyes at the continuous coup she and Dustin have to drive me nuts over that, and she giggles. "I'm getting popcorn, I'll leave you two to your rambles."

"We're naming her Rose," I say, trying not to cry. But he knows, wrapping me in a hug as he does it first, water spilling into my hair from his soul as he kisses my head and gives me his blessing.

"I don't reckon any other name would ever smell as sweet, would it?"

Tears flow down my cheeks, salty kisses from happy times. From kissed knees and first recitals. From driving lessons and college tours. For Shakespeare spoken in soft, subtle ramblings.

"I will miss you, Daddy."

"*If I must die*," he whispers, meeting my tear-streaked gaze, "*I will encounter darkness as a bride and hug it in mine arms.*"

"Measure for Measure," Dustin says, squeezing my shoulder in support. It feels good, safe, and I lean into it, easing off my father and settling into the arms of a different man.

I don't need him, no.

Because I've learned something about myself. I don't need anyone.

I *can* be alone.

But it's heartbreaking being the goddamned moon, isn't it? Sometimes you have to let the darkness surround you. But I know now.

I want to touch the stars.

And I love that choice.

Dad leans back, eyeing us with satisfaction as we remain wrapped as one. "I always liked you, Campbell, you know that? Knew it back when you decked that Remington fellow centuries ago."

"Centuries?" Dustin squints at me, smiling. "That's where you get your little isms, huh?"

"Well, it *ism* from her mother." Dad cackles, eyes crinkling and all.

"Why didn't you say anything?" Dustin grins.

Dad winks. "*My love is thine to teach.* I'm proud of what the two of you have become, my son. I'd tell you to take care of my daughter, but we both know she can do it herself."

"Unless it's cooking." Dustin claps hands with Dad as they both agree.

"Hey!" I interject. "That's not fair. I did really good with that second batch of pancakes, and you know good and well confectioners' sugar looks exactly like flour, anyone would have made that mistake!"

"Mhm," Dustin teases, flicking his lip ring, and I hate that I can't tackle him in more ways than one for his teasing in public like this, but my body heats with something more, too.

Something sweet and addictive.

The brooding barista, whittling his days and the tortured ballerina, dancing in the night. Because that's what we are, and life is sweeter when we're together.

Something like sugar.

Something like *us*.

THE END

Epilogue

SHANA

SIX MONTHS LATER

Is that a bow?" I whisper to Lemon from behind the most gawdy, hot pink ballet skirt imaginable, courtesy of my bestie, Devyn Lynn, of course.

"Yes, *it's a bow,* and it matches the tacky little pink boots, now thank her or we will all hear about it for days, you know she overthinks more than you."

"Fine," I grumble. "But I want a present opening break after this. The baby is hungry."

"The baby or you?" Lemon snorts when I give her the death glare. I'm eight months pregnant, hot, sweaty and *tired,* but my friends threw me this baby shower, and I love their thoughtfulness.

"Thanks, Dev," I smile, stuffing the skirt and bag into Lemon's overfilled arms. "And thanks for not hating us for keeping the secret so long."

"I'd never hate you, Shana. You're my best friend.

I couldn't have chosen a more perfect partner for my brother if I tried. Plus, we're finally going to be sisters like we always wished!"

"True!" I smile, grateful as ever for this. My family. "Maybe you and Ellie can teach her the rodeo thing one day. Where is Ellie, by the way?"

"On a date!" Devyn purses her worried lips. "I mean, it's just Jonathan, and Hunter's chaperoning, but can you believe that little sass-a-frass *had* to have the perfect boots to match her gun-holster." Jeremy, Lemon, and I exchange bewildered glances, and Dev just nods exasperated. "I'm tellin' ya! Y'all thought I was a cowgirl diva? I have met my match and middle school's barely begun!"

We all laugh at that, knowing better than most that anyone matched to Devyn is inevitably a force to be reckoned with.

It's crazy, seeing my best friend as a motherly figure and knowing I'll soon be joining her in that journey. A new chapter of my life, yet to be written.

But as my belly swells and as our businesses grow alongside it, I look back on the last few years of my life, moments of hiding and waiting for the light to shine.

I'm glad I'm no longer waiting, because sometimes life is just dark, and the only light around is the one you can't see until all the others have faded.

"There's one more gift," Lemon chirps, shoving a bag in my lap.

I groan, but she urges me on. "You want this one. I promise." A tear slides down her face. "Open it, Shay."

Memories spill free with the smell of the tissue paper.

Dad.

"By now, if you are reading this, I'm no longer in your sight. But remember, dear child, I am always in your heart. As I write this last goodbye, I smile from the depths of my soul. I did not lie to say I embrace this death like a bride. And I'll be full by your mother once more, just as full as I am to know that you spin for more than just a mirror. I'm forever with you, my Shaker, as you dance for your soul and the love it carries in its song."

The scent of his study lingers in the air that surrounds me, and I tug Lemon down for the biggest, most overdue hug of my life.

"Thank you for taking care of my father, Lem. You were like a daughter to him, and I can't ever repay you for that kind of love."

She shrugs, wiping her eyes. "I liked you better when you hid your feelings, you know?"

We laugh and hug and laugh even more when Dad's gift is revealed to be a parody book for babies, *To Pee or Not to Pee.* He would. I look to the sky and shake my head. "Old Fart."

"I know, right?" Lemon clicks her tongue, narrowing her eyes at an attractive older man whose daughters attend my dance classes.

Interesting.

"I was talking about my dad. Who were *you* talking about, Lemmy Cakes?" I quirk a brow, meandering to the snack table, closer to the man in question. She follows, of course. She has no idea what to do with Dad gone and has started nursing me through my pregnancy at this point like I'll go into labor at every turn, but that's when I catch her staring again.

"I know who that man is to me, but who is he to you?" I raise a suspicious brow.

Lemon scoffs. "Stupid Mr. Nashville. Big time music tour manager who works for my father. Has horrible tastes in anything and everything if you ask me."

"Seems like you can't stop staring at him. Horrible tastes and all," I tease. "He's an adorable father, you know. I teach his twins. All the moms at the studio gawk over him incessantly. There's a pool going on for which one he'll finally ask out." I press on, knowing she's fuming with jealousy. I can tell by the way she chews her lip. "My vote's on Maisy Trotweather."

"Oh my gosh, that gossip freak! He would never." Lemon shoves her tongue in her cheek when my eyes widen at her outburst. "Whatever. He's like forty or fifty or something."

"He is not fifty!" I laugh. "I'll give you forty-five, tops."

She rolls her eyes. "Well, he can take whoever he wants on a date, doesn't mean he can still get it up."

"Oh, come on, he's not that old!"

"Why are you pressing this, Shana? He's an elderly man with children to tend for. Leave him be."

"I'm not pressing anything." I giggle. "You keep staring at him and growling and drooling and…is that dark red lipstick?" I narrow my gaze. "You wore it for him!

You only wear red before a conquest."

"No, I most certainly did not, he likes the light pink kind better, thank you very much, and why the fuck do I know that? Damnit, Shana!"

"I'm waving him over. This is too good."

"Shana Holiday, don't you dare or I wi—"

"Mr. Nashville! Hey! Come here!" I shout as loud as possible, snickering when Lemon hunches down behind the cake.

"If you weren't with child, I would so punch you," she hisses.

"Good thing I'm with child, then."

"Ugh, seriously liked you better when you were shy."

"Miss Holiday." He nods. "Miss…Perkins?" He peers around the cake as Lemon shoots upright. They stare at one another for a tense thirty seconds of throat clearing until Lemon finally throws her hair over one shoulder and lifts a single brow.

"Nice khakis."

Okay.

His brow lifts back. "Nice clothes at all. Different from your usual style of none."

"Glad you noticed. Was worried you needed new bifocals or something."

"You know very well I've got 20/20 vision, Miss Perkins." He smirks. "Wouldn't give me so much to look at if you didn't."

Oh snap.

I fiddle with the snack table, sorting scones that don't even have differences as I hear Lemon snort incredulously.

"That's rich. If I wanted your attention, I would be a chair, then you could sit on me instead of facing your fears like a man…*Daddy*."

"Don't call me Daddy."

"Don't make me want to."

I clear my throat, stopping the thing I accidentally started before it gets worse. "Thanks for coming Mr. Nashville! Just wait till you see Kimmi and Cami's back walkovers, they are really coming along!"

I shove Lemon to the side, but before we can leave, he reaches for her hand.

She lets him.

"Your father tells me I'll be seeing you on next month's tour."

"Seeing and watching are two different things, *Nash*." Her violet eyes darken as a smile curves her lips, and she turns away, linking my arm and dragging me along with her.

"Walk super tall and confident!"

"Okay," I chortle, "you are so into that guy."

"What the fuck ever. Let's go have your baby now, I'm bored."

"Mhmm," I tease.

"I said whatever!" She swats my arm.

"You like him, you like him, you like that hot old dad," I sing through the field.

"You are such a weirdo, Shana Holiday. You're just… *you*, you know?"

"I know," I smile.

Because I love *me*.

Just the way I am.

If you want to read Lemon's story, don't miss the next book in the Pine Forest series:

Something Like Starlight
(Book 3–Coming This Year)

Also in this series:
Something Like Sunflowers
(Book 1–Devyn & Hunter's Story)

For updates, sneak peeks, or to follow my publishing journey, subscribe to my newsletter at *www.elsiebeabooks.com* or connect with me on social media. For professional inquiries, please email *elsiebea@elsiebeabooks.com*.

If you've gotten this far, please consider leaving a review on your chosen platform. Reviews spark growth for emerging authors like me.

Thanks for spending time with something close to my heart.

Something Like Sugar
XOXO,
Elsie

Please enjoy the following teaser chapter from *Something Like Starlight*.

Chapter One

LEMON

Listen up, bitches, this is my story, and I'll break the fourth wall whenever I want, thank you very much.

I'm Lemon. Yes, I'll allow time for that to sink in. *Lemon*.

Laugh it up. It's fine. I've heard it all: Lemonade, Lemon Cakes, Lemon Pie, Lemony Snicket.

But the worst one I ever heard was…

"Sour Patch!"

When said by my arch nemesis and brown-nosing, *Daddy Wannabe*, O.L. Nashville.

I snort. It doesn't even sound like a real name. It's more like a stage cover…a stripper name. And with that little nugget of brilliance sure to fire him up in all the ways I love, I saunter over to Mr. Mad-Eyes and cock my hip to the side, swinging my VIP pass around to fuck with him.

He likes things orderly, and I am the opposite of order.

"I'll pretend you didn't call me that little pet name again, since you're in control of the tour and obsessed with me and all, but don't think for one second I'm letting up on my quest to learn your full name and exploit it seven ways to Sunday, *Nash.*"

I call him by his nickname. The name only the men call him, my father and the other stupidly rich goons he lines his boardrooms with.

Most of the *women* at Perkins Global Records, usually assistants or interns unsurprisingly—if you know my father—offer a much simpler, sanctimonious title to Agent Tight-Ass, and that one's even worse. A breathy, lustful, submissive, *Mr. Nashville.*

Like he's important or something.

I roll my eyes as I hear it now, *yes, Mr. Nashville; right away, Mr. Nashville,* and the most gag-inducing of them all, *anything you say, Mr. Nashville,* through lash-fluttering eyes.

Well, fuck that.

I raise a brow in challenge when he doesn't respond, driving in the accusation of his inadequacy with one smirk, something men like him despise.

And damn, do I love being despised by men.

Like, *okay,* so you have balls and a ding-a-ling, whoop de do. Nobody cares. We could use your parts for reproduction and put you in cryo-sleep for the rest of the year, surviving just fine without you. We only *need* your sperm. *Men.*

I don't want Mr. Nashville's sperm, as it happens.

And I have a theory he's a bit salty by that fact, seeing as how I just swallowed throatfuls from the band he's managing on the bus, and he hasn't stopped scraping my body with his icy blue irises all week, licking those thick lips, permanently turned down in a scowl of disapproval.

I may or may not be sleeping with them. The band that is.

Yes, all of them. And don't judge, either. Ever heard of a why-choose romance? Women can have entire harems these days.

Anyway, I'm dumping them. It's day six, and that means what it always does for me.

It's in the past.

The record label will have brand-new talent to strut soon, and who knows? With my last job being caput and no prospects lined up to replace it, maybe I'll go on tour with them, too.

I don't do it just for the sex. My endless VIP passes to these tours are my escape. Always have been. Musicians, new cities, another chance to fall in love and feel the electricity that brings? I'm in every time.

I like it this way. Don't get me wrong, I more than anyone, *love* love.

My friends would say I'm a matchmaker of sorts. Find me a couple pining over lost time and missed connections, and I'm there for it. I will alter the elements themselves for a happily ever after. That's why I became an officiant, one of my three hundred and two jobs since I was seventeen, none of which I've stuck with, but that's beside the point.

I love *falling* in love, not necessarily staying in love. Much like my jobs, it's about the unknown…the chase, the catch and reward. The high you get when you willingly enter the storm.

But once it's all said and done, it's like everything else…over. And the high fades right along with it.

I don't need money.

We have lifetimes of it. So much so that my father doesn't even notice I give every scent I've earned since high school to those in need. It's sickening enough the thousands of dollars missing each month hardly moves the line graph his accountant keeps on my vault, but for me to simply hoard it away among piles of wealth when my neighbor's kid can't afford his epi pen?

I hate the rich, even if I am one.

I used to think my last job would be the one, a live-in care tech for a hospice patient, someone I knew on a personal level.

I was serving my community.

And unlike my other jobs, where I felt bumpered and boxed in by the oblivion of sameness, giving my attention to someone I grew to love like a second father, gave me purpose.

He died, as patients in hospice tend to do, and I grieved him right alongside his daughter.

Randall Holiday was his name. I can hardly say it aloud without breaking.

Regardless of whether I knew he was dying, preparing for it with the rest of his team and understanding the inherent biology behind his terminal illness, none of that mattered.

I was torn and broken by his absence in my life. I became part of his world, and then he was no longer in it.

Even if my own father is disappointed I didn't *stick with a job this time*, I can't do that to myself again.

I can't love and lose.

I need change like I need my next breath, something he will never understand being a self-made billionaire— structure and work ethic being his core values.

But when you grow up with unlimited money and zero boundaries like me, you learn what takes most people a lifetime to realize.

Life is moment to moment.

There is no up or down or right or wrong. It's just a bunch of beings, strung together by societal standards and reason; governed by self-inflicted constraints.

But *why?*

There's so much out there to experience. And being tied down by jobs or projects…or people, isn't worth it when you only get one chance to make your mark.

To truly live.

Jobs will replace you. People will leave you.

But adventures? You can keep them forever.

Besides, who wants one dick for the rest of their life if they can have a variety?

Does it make me a ho?

Some would say.

But *some* are patriarchal asshats, so I mean, meh.

I enjoy life, I love sex, and I live for my next thrill. And with more money in my trust fund than I can spend in three lifetimes, who the fuck cares if that's how I live?

Nash does apparently. He growls, a deep rumble that'd probably feel good on your clit if he didn't look so mad. With nostrils flared, he stares at me, as if he can read the dirty thoughts that strip him bare inside my mind, and he sets his jaw like he's gearing up for a fight.

With me.

On second thought, I think I like him mad.

But *ew, it's Nash*. I've known him half my life.

He's attractive.

Incredibly fit.

Okay, he's flat-out eye candy, but he's so *stiff*. And not in the pelvic kinda way, if that's what you're thinking.

He's closer to my father's age than mine.

He *is* a father.

I won't linger on why I'm suddenly hyperaware of that fact.

"Did you hear a word I said?" Nash snaps, irritated as always. Usually at me. "The band needs to get some writing in this stretch of the tour. From now until Centerville, they are on strict orders: *no groupies*."

His eyes flick down my body, assessing my slashed-up band tee and fishnets, shoved tightly into knee high, leather, zip-up stilettos because they're sexy as fuck and I do not apologize for that.

"Oh, Nash," I offer, earning an irritated groan, "You seem to have forgotten I'm not a groupie." I wave my VIP pass in the air, emblazoned with a bright blue stamp reading, *Quality Assurance*. "I was appointed to be here."

"Self-appointed," he grumbles. "I need them focused, Miss Perkins. Your father will—

I smile widely as I encroach on his big important man space and cut him off. "*My father* will be pleased to learn how smoothly you run his events when I tell him what an amazing time everyone had with absolutely zero hiccups, all thanks to his number one tour manager."

His eyes narrow as I reach my tip toes and whisper in his ear. "Don't worry, Daddy. When I'm done playing with my toys, I always put them back where they belong."

"Jesus, Sour Patch. If he knew the way you speak—"

"You gonna tell on me? I might be cursed to look young, but I'm twenty-eight you know."

"I'm aware."

I bristle with those words.

"Well, then you're *aware* I can speak to, and fuck, whomever I want. An entire band. Or two. Or three even. And despite what you might think, Nashy-Poo, it doesn't make a woman a slut for loving her body and enjoying life."

"I didn't say it did, I *said*—"

"You *implied* that I shouldn't talk sexy."

"No, I didn't."

"Yeah, you did Papa Bear. I said stuff about boy toys, you said don't talk like that, threw in some Daddy kink, and—"

"Daddy *what*?"

"Daddy kink." I blink at him. He can't be serious, right? "You know the routine: bad girl needs punished, sugar daddy gives her the spankin' she never got, and everyone gets a happily ever after."

His mouth hangs open like I've grown three heads.

"Have you seriously never watched porn?"

"What? Of course I haven't watched porn!"

"Bullshit."

"Excuse me?" Nash's voice drops low and menacing. "What did you say?"

Yeah, I definitely like him mad.

"I said *bullshit*. There is not a single man in this country who hasn't scrolled some tits or ass at least once. I mean, at the very least you've watched a few casting couches, right?"

"Casting...*couches*?" He seems truly stumped.

Maybe this man isn't lying.

Maybe he really is just a silver fox, single dude who enjoys work and *doesn't* want to fuck anything with legs.

Is it bad if that makes me want to play with him more?

Maybe that's why I plant my seed, crossing my arms over my chest so my boobs peek out the top of the cut-up band tee. His eyes immediately fall there, as predicted, and I let a smile steal my face as I clear my throat and they snap back to mine.

I like it when Nash stares.

He's done it this entire tour. And the last. And the one before that. Different bands then, of course, but each time, I wonder when he'll finally crack. At which point will he stop watching and join in?

Or would he take me all for himself, his salt-and-pepper beard brushing along my slick center, tasting me like I know he wants?

"I'll compromise with you," I say. "Let me ride the bus to Centerville. I have some friends I can visit.

"Do these friends have *couches* you'll be *cast* on?"

I don't miss the air of annoyance behind his inquiry. As if he has any right to judge what I do in my spare time.

"Maybe," I challenge. "Does that bother you?"

"That? No, that doesn't bother me, Sour Patch." His gaze scrapes down my body with a scowl that ignites my core. "It's everything else about you that does."

Acknowledgments

Wow! What a journey this book has been. What started as a cliffhanger at the end of my debut, turned into a high-stakes discovery unfolding beneath my fingertips.

Grief is a strange creature, which is why my first and forever thank you goes out to my mom. I wish you could be here to read these things I create, but I know I couldn't craft them had it not been for your love.

Thank you to my husband for clearing me when I'm clouded and loving me when I'm lost. For being the inspiration to every cocky smirk in this novel, the last novel, and all the rest to come. Book boyfriends are less magical because you're my example, and you outcharm them all combined.

To my children, hopefully this is the only page you ever read. Thank you for your patience and your fanatical support. You make me feel famous, but you are the true stars.

To my McCauley family (yes, Leslie and Grandma, this includes you too), thanks for cheering me on in everything I do. Book signings are more fun with my built-in entourage.

To Lesa, for keeping my kids on busy deadline days and giving them too much ice-cream…wait…no, *unthank you* for that. I appreciate you for more than just your paper-printing, even if you did let them use all the sprinkles.

To Cary, Allie, Lori, and Tiffany, thanks for being genuine friends. Every time I write a bestie, I think of one of you. And I'm not sorry for sending you inappropriate screen shots of my un-edited writing, either. Please expect it to keep happening.

To Kimberly, thank you for your knowledge of story structure and knack for seeing the voice in my dialogue. Shana and Dustin's intentions are stronger because of your insight.

To Ramona, for polishing this baby up until it shined like a diamond. Your professionalism and punctuality never fail me.

To Molly, for another stunning cover! You blow me away with your design. I can't wait to see what you have in store for Lemon. From the stage to the page. I couldn't do this without you.

To Erika, for legitimately everything. I never imagined a year ago when a random Bookstagram account signed up for my, very new and underwhelming, street team, I'd meet someone capable of such magic. From cataloguing my series references, to making graphics, to managing my arcs, street team, content pulls and timelines, I swear you're a wizard sometimes. I look forward to many more exciting collaborations to come.

To my street team, THE BEA HIVE for sharing and hyping my brand all year while I wrote this bad boy. To my alpha and beta readers, Maggie, Kelly L., Kelly M. and Elizabeth, I can't thank you enough for reading this at its messiest and sharing your ideas for growth.

To Meghan, my edge-painting goddess and world's most committed sensitivity reader, your insight on Dustin's dialogue and compassion was pivotal in transforming this into the swoony version it is today. Thank you immensely for your attention to the hearing-impaired representation within this plot.

Lasty, thank you, reader. You are the reason I breathe these stories to life. So many amazing stories exist in the world, and I'm eternally grateful you chose mine.

About the Author

Elsie Bea is a contemporary romance author from Richmond, Virginia. She lives 'out in the sticks' with her incorrigible husband, crazy kids, and a gaggle of dogs, chickens, and ducks. When she's not reading or writing, you can find her singing and dancing through her kitchen and spending time with family.